With a roar to rend the universe, the fabric of time warped and fractured.

In shock, they huddled together in the darkness. Trembling, Jessie whispered, "What's outside that door, Alex? Your world or mine? Or something else altogether? Something … *terrible?*"

He wrapped his arms around her, held her tightly, shook his head. "I don't know."

Jessie shivered, murmured against his chest, "I'm afraid. I'm so afraid."

"I know," he nodded. "I am, too."

TIMELAPSE

A Novel by

LORRIE FARRELLY

ISBN: 13-978-1469953502
TIMELAPSE

To Christian and Connor,
who light up the present and the future

PROLOGUE

The world ended in a blaze of light, shattering into fractured shards of impossible color.

Alex Morgan lay senseless, flat on his back on the floor, arms outflung, a steady trickle of blood seeping from a small, bruised gash behind his right ear. His last conscious thought had been: *Oh my God! An attack!*

But there'd been no terrorist attack, no bomb, no gas explosion. That day, the end of the world came only for him.

Had he had a few more seconds of consciousness before the floor plunged abruptly, flinging him backward against a huge metal filing cabinet, Alex might have thought: *The end of the world, and I'm going to pass out and miss it.*

Typical.

Ironically, it *was* typical. Alex had missed the end of the world once before.

Four years earlier – four years, one month, and twenty-one days, to be exact – a speeding, cherry-red Ford pickup, drunk driver lolling at the wheel, barreled through a red light just three blocks from Alex's and Casey's campus apartment.

As their car idled at the stoplight, Casey, barely twenty years old and hugely pregnant, could scarcely catch her breath.

"Gorgon Morgan!" she wheezed, wiping tears of laughter from her eyes. "That's it! The perfect name! I love it!"

"Good thing it's a boy then," Alex grinned. "A girl would've had to be Gorgonzola."

Casey loved that grin, the lopsided, quirky one that made him look even younger than she was, when he was actually four years older. With their tousled, sun-streaked, light brown hair, the two looked more like brother and sister than husband and wife, although his eyes were a dark blue and hers a deep sea green.

Casey's pixie cut was short as a boy's, sunny wisps feathering around her pretty, gamine features. As Alex's grad-student mop grew longer and shaggier, spilling over his collar, she teased that the hair that was clipped from her head magically appeared on his.

For perhaps the thousandth time, Alex thought Casey was a miracle. A bookish loner by nature, more sensitive and cerebral than his rangy build and strong, angular jaw suggested, he allowed few people close to him.

That Casey, sassy and carefree, had found her way into his heart continually amazed and humbled him.

As he leaned over to steal a quick kiss, she suddenly took a sharp breath and pressed her hands hard against her belly. Alex could actually see movement under her fitted tank top, a long, rippling roll.

"Oh wow, Alex!" she gasped. "Did you see that?"

His face paled. "Yeah. Yeah, I sure did. Jeez, Case, are you okay? Look, we're almost home. Do you want me to pull over? Maybe we should we go to the hospital. That was.... What's he *doing* in there?" He was beginning to babble.

Casey shook her head, her cheeks flushed warm and rosy. "He's fine. Just letting me know he's getting impatient. And I'm perfectly fine, too, honey. Okay, maybe a little tired. And starving! I just want go home, get something to eat, and take a nap. Oh, green light."

As a car horn blared impatiently behind them, Casey gave her flustered husband a fondly exasperated look. Alex shook his head, grinned again, and hit the gas.

"So," Casey began dreamily. "Seriously, I still like *Jackson* best, after your dad. What do you...?"

Her words were cut off in a horrific crash of crushed metal and shattered glass. The speeding pickup that slammed into the passenger's side of Alex's old Honda left Casey's young body mortally ravaged. Nevertheless, her tiny son – thanks to a brilliant University Hospital ER team – came wailing furiously into life.

Alex was unconscious from the moment of impact until two days later. Awakening dazed, disoriented, and in pain, he had to be given the news by his mother, Frannie, who wept with him as she struggled to tell him of the terrible end of his old world, and the fragile beginning of his new one.

CHAPTER 1

The four years that passed after the accident became a different, lonelier life for Alex, the life he secretly suspected he had always been intended to lead. His time with Casey, he now saw, had been a fluke, a great gift bestowed by accident, really meant for some other man.

Alex angrily wondered if his happiness and gratitude had drawn God's attention to Casey, causing Him to notice the cosmic blunder that had been made.

Fearful of drawing God's further attention, Alex quit talking to Him.

And so he steeled himself against feeling or wanting too much. Nevertheless, there was still one very large chink in the wall that surrounded his heart.

His son, Jack.

Alex would never hold Casey again, but every day Jack flung his small arms around his father's neck and hugged him tightly. His son rescued Alex from the darkest and most complete despair, allowing him to numb the portion of his heart that howled in grief for Casey, giving him a reason to go on living.

His bereavement had not prevented him from working – in fact, he welcomed the distraction. Alex moved in with his mother, who had herself been widowed several years before. She took in her grieving son and his baby with a secret relief that almost shamed her, given the tragedy of the circumstances.

Still, they were with her, and she was happy.

Stubbornly ignoring the daily reminders of Casey, Alex continued as a Teaching Assistant in American History at Capitol University in Georgetown, leading lively question-and-answer sessions with his students, lifting his spirits. Originally built as a technical college, Capitol's stately, classical brick and stone halls, formal yards, and gardens were now crowded by sleek, curving structures of glass and steel, angular sculptures, and water walls.

At night, after tucking Jack in and leaving his mother nodding off in front of her favorite battling-chefs TV shows, Alex worked on his doctoral dissertation long into the early hours. A year later, he'd earned his degree and was rehired at Capitol as an Assistant Professor.

He was a natural storyteller. Students not only listened to him, they often became so absorbed that they forgot to scribble notes as he brought the past to life.

However, Alex was only a lowly Assistant Professor. While Humanities Hall was being refurbished, he was given a tiny office in the Computer Sciences Building, a large, older building whose classic façade belied its state-of-the-art interior.

Vacated temporarily by a tech professor currently on sabbatical, the small office space, chock full as it was of computer equipment and random components, looked as though an IT geek had exploded in it.

Making Alex feel even less at home, the previous occupant's name was still prominently lettered on the office door – *Thaddeus Casterson, Ph.D.* – while his own name and field, *James A. Morgan, Ph.D., Am Hist*, was simply printed on an index card and thumbtacked to the adjacent bulletin board in the hallway.

Alex had met Casterson a couple of times and had not particularly liked him. Though they were close in age, he'd thought the pale, dark-eyed, intense man with the unkempt shock of curly hair, and with his eccentric ideas of computer-created utopias, was a little cracked.

He'd had the bulk of Casterson's equipment put into storage, but the office continued to cough up odd little gizmos and stray, unidentifiable components from time to time. He didn't mind, gave them a file drawer of their own, neatly labeled: *Area 51*.

CHAPTER 2

At five in the morning on a Wednesday in May, at the end of Alex's second term at the university, his cell rang, startling him out of an exhausted, restless sleep.

Little Jack had had a rough day, running a low-grade fever, fussing and fretting, and finally getting sick to his stomach. He'd woken several times that night, crying, wanting to sleep in Alex's bed, an all-too-frequent indulgence that Frannie *tsked* over with mild disapproval.

"Pleeeease, Daddy?" Jack whined, all big, adorable, teary blue eyes and quivering chin. "I'm scared when I'm all by myself."

"Come on, Jack," Alex said wearily, as patient as he could be in the middle of the night. "We talked about this. You're a big boy now, remember?"

"But I get bad dreams and it's *really* scary. And my tummy still hurts."

Alex doubted the upset tummy, as Jack hadn't been sick for several hours, but the little boy did seem to be going through some kind of monsters-in-the-closet and scary-dreams phase.

"Here, look," Alex said gently. "Let's turn your pillow over to the good dreams side."

"But you did that already," Jack protested.

"Well, I guess the dreams flipped over again," Alex improvised.

Even four-year-old Jack clearly recognized the lameness of this. "How do they do that?" he asked suspiciously.

"Magic!" Alex suddenly leaned down, playfully snuffling and growling as he nuzzled his son's neck. Jack giggled and squealed.

Alex gathered the child into his arms, holding him close for a long moment, then settled him back gently onto the pillow. "Get some sleep, son," he said softly. "I promise you've got the good dreams side now."

Jack yawned. "Will you tell me a story, Daddy? Please? Just a little one?"

I'm such a pushover, Alex thought, but he smiled in spite of his fatigue. "All right, then. Just a little one."

He took a slow breath. "Once upon a time there was a very brave and clever boy named Jack who was four years old. He fell sound asleep one night and dreamed he could fly. Now, just imagine how surprised he was when he woke up in the morning and discovered he was lying upside down on the ceiling. He had floated right up from his bed like a big, red, happy birthday balloon."

9

He spoke in a low, soothing tone, and soon Jack's eyes closed and his sturdy little body relaxed. Alex sat beside him a few minutes more, smoothing this son's unruly thatch of soft, sandy hair with a gentle hand. Finally he stood, stretching his back, groaning. As he turned to leave the room, he spotted the framed picture of his wife on the child's dresser.

"God, Casey," he muttered softly, "He's a great kid. It's just that most of the time, I've got no idea what I'm doing."

Sighing, he turned out Jack's light and padded back to bed.

Now, barely an hour later, Alex abruptly awoke, groggy and disoriented, fumbling for his cell, as its *American Pie* ringtone blared in the dark.

"H'lo?" he mumbled.

"Alex? This is George Sanderson. Sorry to wake you, but there's been some trouble at school. Your office has had a break-in. I'm afraid there's some damage."

Dimly Alex tried to make sense of this. "Dean Sanderson?" he repeated, finally placing his boss' name. "A break-in?"

"Yes. Night security thought at first there was a fire because they saw a bright flash in your office window, but when they got up there, they found just a lot of disarray. Shelves knocked down, books thrown around, drawers pulled out and dumped, wires pulled out of the wall, that sort of thing. They'd like you to come down and take a look, see if you can tell if anything's missing."

Aw, crap, Alex thought, but he said, "All right, thanks, Dr. Sanderson. I'll be there in a few minutes."

"Thank you, Alex. I'm sorry to have called so early, but I knew you'd want to deal with this before your classes started for the day."

When Sanderson hung up, Alex dragged himself, groaning, out of bed once again.

* * * * *

Sanderson had been quite right; the office was a mess. The desk, once against the wall, now stood angled in the middle of the cramped room, some of its drawers hanging open, others dumped unceremoniously on the floor.

Sighing, Alex stepped over debris and cleared some space on the desk, shoving scattered papers and torn, jumbled books aside so he could set down his laptop. He righted the desk chair and draped his jacket over its back.

He'd agreed to compile a detailed list of anything he found missing. The Security team had departed, and the Dean had promised to call over to the Physical Plant Department for a janitor and an electrician, who might or might not actually appear.

In the meantime, Alex was left to restore what order he could.

Tired and irritated, he pushed the desk back against the wall and began shoving in the drawers. When one jammed and refused to close completely, he swore and tried again, with the same result. Irritated, he realized something was in the way.

Pulling the drawer all the way out, checking that there was no obstruction in the drawer itself, he reached in the opening all the way to the back wall. His arm shoulder-deep inside the desk, he groped around until his fingers made contact with a small, smooth, hard object. He fumbled a bit to get a grip on it, then worked it free and pulled it out of the desk.

He found he was holding a cell phone, a small, sleek, state-of-the-art device.

Alex tried the power button, but the screen remained dark. A quick additional search turned up nothing in the way of an appropriate charger.

Well, he thought, *one more stupid thing for the Area 51 drawer*, and he tossed the cell down on the desk.

There was a sharp, electronic beep. Surprised, Alex picked it up again and looked at the screen, which promptly filled with an odd series of cryptic icons, none familiar to him. Now curious, he selected one at random, and abruptly the screen filled with the words *SYNC ON* next to a flashing date and time display, which were current and accurate.

"Okay," Alex murmured to himself. "So what the heck does *SYNC ON* do?"

He tried a few other commands, but the cell stayed stubbornly in the same mode. Deciding to fiddle more with it later, he slipped it absently in his pocket and resumed straightening his workspace.

Without warning, the cell suddenly emitted a shrill alarm. Alex jumped, fumbled for it in his pocket. And in the split second before darkness swallowed him, he saw the world explode.

CHAPTER 3

The position of the sun had changed, sparking in Alex some innate sense of the passage of time.

Jack! he thought with unfocused urgency. Then, as he tried to sit up, his head swam sickeningly, and he could scarcely think at all.

He shoved himself to a sitting position, his back propped against the wall. Uttering a heartfelt curse, he put his hand to the back of his head, wincing as his fingers made contact with the wound behind his ear.

He felt the unmistakable stickiness of blood. Gingerly, Alex explored the small gash and was relieved to find it messy, but minor. It hurt, though, and he muttered his opinion about it to himself.

Clumsily he reached for his jacket pocket, feeling for his cell phone.

No jacket. Vaguely he remembered draping it over the chair.

As he looked up, searching for his jacket, Alex was struck utterly dumb.

His desk and the shelves above it were packed with neat rows of books – not his own, but thick, dark, leatherbound volumes. He couldn't recognize any of them. More shelves ran floor-to-ceiling between the desk and the door, and these were neatly divided into dozens of slots for a staggering amount of paperwork.

No longer a mess – in fact, now severely tidy and organized – the office appeared to belong to an obsessive-compulsive IRS bureaucrat.

Utterly confused, Alex closed his eyes, shook his head, and took a few deep, steadying breaths. When he opened them again, the books and papers were still there. His vision wasn't blurred and he knew instinctively that he was awake and conscious.

But where the hell *was* he?

Alex stood, supporting himself with one hand against the wall. The room spun in a nauseating turn that forced him to close his eyes once more, but after a moment the wooziness passed and he was able to open his eyes and take a few unsteady steps to the desk.

He noticed at once that his laptop was missing, making him instantly furious. Angrily he picked up the books on the desk to check underneath. No laptop. Dropping the volumes again in frustration, Alex caught sight of their titles:

Revised Censorship Code of the United States, Volume 37

Statutes of Civil Order, A – L

Guidelines of Approved Information Dissemination: The Moral Imperative

Constitutional Deletions, Vol. 6

His heart began a tattoo in his chest. "Okay," he muttered, scarcely aware he was speaking aloud. "Gotta be some kind of idiotic practical joke. Damned crazy one, though. Okay, wait a minute, I've still got Casterson's phone."

He pulled the small device from his pocket, saw the screen had gone dead, and once again pressed the power button. Nothing. He tapped it, waited. Still nothing.

Alex muttered an oath and shoved the useless phone back in his pocket.

He looked about the room again, unsure whether he should admire the elaborate thoroughness of a practical joke or be alarmed that it might not be a joke at all. His gaze fell on the numerous small slots stacked along the wall that held neat piles of paper forms.

Curious, he reached for a handful and saw that some were simply numbered and blank, while a few seemed to be tax and licensing forms.

But there were others, odd and ominous:

Warrant of Accusation

Oath of Obedience

Property Seizure Authorization

Petition to Bear Child

Bewildered and apprehensive, he began to scan the section headings on the last form. At the top was space for the usual personal information – name, address, occupation, age, spouse's name. Oddly, there were no blanks for phone numbers or email.

Then Alex went cold as he read:

Requested date to discontinue Sterinol

Requested date of conception

Proposed sex of the child

Have applicants now or ever been accused of a Crime Against the State?

Designated Termination Center should the child not be the Desired Sex, or Otherwise Defective

With a grimace, tossing the papers on the desk, he reached for the telephone and snatched up the old-fashioned receiver. Puzzled that the phone had neither buttons nor dial, he stared at it a moment, then simply put the receiver to his ear and rattled the connector with his free hand.

"*Information Central,*" a toneless voice responded.

Hesitantly, Alex said, "Dean Sanderson's office, please."

"*That is not a valid option.*"

Frustrated, Alex decided repeating that request was useless. Instead, he asked for his home number.

"*That is not a valid option. This line is for authorized use only. State your current access code.*"

Confused, Alex hung up quickly, shoving the receiver back into its cradle. Unable to decide what to do next, he raised a trembling hand and shoved it through his hair.

"I don't freaking believe this!" Looking around a little wildly, feeling the beginnings of panic, he moved toward the window – large, paned, nearly opaque with layers of grime. He'd just take a look outside, figure out where he was, what the hell was going on.

The bullet that smashed through the glass, taking part of his shirtsleeve with it before embedding with a sharp *thwack* in the far wall, instantly changed his mind.

A startled cry tore from his throat. Dropping, he threw himself away from the window, but through the shattered pane, he could clearly hear shouts and gunshots outside. It sounded to him as though full-scale war had broken out.

Slowly, breathing hard, he edged along the wall toward the window until, without showing himself, he could just see the grounds below.

Screaming, trampling one another, a mob swarmed in panic and confusion across the grounds of the University Yard below. As Alex watched in stunned horror, a few of the most reckless turned to throw rocks and bottles at the riot-gear-clad troops sweeping like a relentless wave across the grounds, but most people ran for their lives.

Bodies littered the Yard, turning it to a bloodied battlefield. Some of the frantic protesters still gripped homemade picket signs as they bolted in blind terror, but most had dropped their signs and banners and were

17

retreating in a mad scramble for any cover or escape. Sirens and bullhorns blared as a caravan of police assault vehicles arrived, and troops continued to pour into the Yard.

Several squads of soldiers calmly turned the machine guns mounted on their vehicles toward the mass of the crowd and opened fire, while others began to storm the entrance to the Alex's building.

His shocked mind screamed: *Get out!*

Flinging open the office door, all but stumbling over his own feet, Alex barely had the presence of mind to check that the corridor outside was deserted. When it was, he began to run; already he could hear shouts and the quick pounding of booted feet coming closer.

He turned a corner and saw an elevator at the far end of the hall. He sprinted to it and slammed his palm hard against the call button, pumping it frantically. For several seconds he heard only his heartbeat pounding in his ears, his agonized breathing, and the rusty wheeze of the elevator slowly creaking toward him.

"Freeze! This building's off limits! Get down on the floor, hands behind your head – *now!*"

Alex started at the shouted command. Without looking back, he bolted for the nearby fire exit door, hauled it open and all but leapt through it. A heartbeat later the metal door exploded with the impact of a hail of gunfire. He barely escaped, flinging himself wildly down the concrete stairs, taking five and six steps at a time.

When he heard shouts and more gunshots coming from the stairwell below him, Alex instantly changed course and fled through a second-floor fire door. The acrid, stinging stench of gunpowder already filled this corridor.

Desperately, Alex tried the nearest office door, wrenching the doorknob in a frantic, sweaty grip. The door was securely bolted.

With a cry, a wild-eyed youth suddenly rounded a corner thirty yards to Alex's left, running hard. His shoes pounded and skidded on the tile floor, and Alex could hear his wheezing gasps clearly despite the clamor of the fight.

"Help me!" the kid screamed. "Oh God they're coming!"

The boy sprinted straight toward Alex, crazed panic in his young face. Behind him, three heavily armed men in riot gear stalked into the hallway. Seeing the boy, they stopped, calculated. Then, almost casually, one raised his weapon and fired. The kid's back exploded in a gush of blood and he flew into Alex's arms.

Alex staggered backward as the body slammed against him. Reflexively, he jacked his arms under the kid's shoulders to support the sagging weight of his body. For one long, terrible moment their eyes met, the young man's filled with anguish and bewilderment, Alex's with shock and horror.

Then the boy's eyes dimmed and Alex heard a rattling sigh. He went to his knees as the kid's dead weight pulled him down.

A raw sound of denial ripped from his throat. The kid's blood-soaked body slid from his grasp and slumped to the hard tile floor.

Shocked, horrified, furious, he stared at the troopers.

And for one reckless moment, rage drove out fear.

"What the *hell?*" Alex screamed.

The troopers stared at the distraught man, surprised that the fool not only held his ground, but was *challenging* them. When Alex snarled and lurched to his feet, they charged as one toward him.

He dodged to the side, ramming his shoulder hard against the bolted office door. He felt more than saw the troopers take aim.

Desperately, he rammed the door again, and with a sharp crack the frame gave way and the door burst in. Alex barely heard the shouts behind him, the explosion of fire splintering the wall and doorframe.

He barreled headlong into the office, diving hard for the floor, rolling.

Now there was only one means of escape. Scrambling to his feet, Alex seized a heavy desk chair and heaved it with all his strength through the window. A moment later he scrambled up and out onto the narrow ledge, nearly twenty feet above the ground.

As the troopers burst into the room, Alex Morgan jumped.

CHAPTER 4

Tangled in the shrubs and vines that broke his fall, Alex thrashed his legs free and scrambled to his feet. He didn't need the sudden hot pain of the bullet that ripped through his jeans just above the knee, grazing his leg, to encourage him to run. He had hit the ground running.

Abruptly he realized he was headed in the wrong direction, running straight toward ongoing skirmishes near the entrance of his building. He could barely see what was happening through clouds of dust and black smoke, but he could hear shouts and gunfire ahead.

Nevertheless, the bullets meant for him were at his back, so he drew in a huge gulp of sulfurous air and bolted straight ahead into the fray.

Military police vehicles filled the broad University Yard, barricading the entrance to the building. Streaked with blood, deafened by noise, heart slamming against his ribs, Alex sprinted through the smoke to a smaller group of heavy vehicles parked by themselves to one side of the Yard. He took cover in the narrow space between two of the massive, side-by-side military cargo vans.

A sudden burst of automatic weapons fire blew out second-floor windows just above the main entrance to the barricaded building. Alex's head jerked up. Thick gray smoke billowed from the burst windows.

And he now saw the words cut into stone above the doors:

FEDERAL BUREAU OF INQUISITION

Strewn about the Yard lay muddied, trampled picket signs and banners:

Restore the Bill of Rights!
Civil Rights for All!
Liberty Now!

Alex trembled with shock and exhaustion, unable to make sense of this waking nightmare. With great effort, he gave himself a hard mental shake.

For God's sake, think!

As his mind cleared, Alex realized that the tide of commotion in the Yard was shifting. Troopers who had swarmed into the building were now beginning to emerge, a few at a time.

A few dragged spent, wounded prisoners; more dragged lifeless bodies.

Some of the prisoners were being herded toward Alex.

Darting around the rear of one of the vans, he found the heavy cargo doors slightly ajar. He yanked at the handles and the doors swung open.

In the cargo hold were two long steel benches bolted to either side of the vehicle, leg irons cleated to the floor underneath at two-foot intervals. Haphazardly piled in the back were a couple of helmets, a riot shield, and a flak jacket.

Hastily Alex put on the jacket and one of the helmets. Dashing to the front of the van and pulling open the driver's door, he flung himself in behind the wheel.

A pair of armed, uniformed troopers dragging handcuffed, battered prisoners passed by him on the opposite side, moving between the vehicles. Glancing in the passenger-side mirror, Alex caught a brief glimpse of two captured youths, one limp, possibly unconscious, the other struggling bravely but futilely.

As the soldiers hauled their captives behind the van and out of sight, there was the heavy, dull thud of a blow, and all sounds of struggle ceased.

Alex felt the van sway. There was a scraping noise, a solid thump, the clank of metal, and then the cargo doors slammed shut, rocking the vehicle again. One of the troopers suddenly appeared at the closed driver's window.

Alex's hands shook as he clutched the steering wheel, his knuckles white. Feeling sweat stream down his face and back, he stared straight ahead, praying the helmet concealed his distress.

The trooper rapped hard on the window. Slowly Alex turned to face him, his throat bone dry. The scowling man signaled to him through the window, hooking a thumb to the rear.

Alex nodded, gave a jerky thumbs-up, and reached down for the ignition. Miraculously, his fingers closed over a key.

Thank you, he breathed.

Steadying his hand by sheer force of will, he turned the key, and the van's powerful engine roared to life. He stomped on the clutch, jammed the stick into reverse, and without so much as a glance in the mirror, hit the gas.

The van surged backward. A second trooper, still standing behind the cargo doors, yelped in alarm and leapt out of the way. Alex spun the van in a tight circle, then shifted again and floored the accelerator.

Avoiding the partially blocked access road, Alex jolted and rattled the van over debris, planters, low walls, and a stone pathway, finally hitting a curb and crash-landing recklessly on a perimeter road. From the front seat of a passing, canvas-covered transport, two troopers stared in amazement at his one-man demolition derby.

Sweat dripping in his eyes, Alex eased his foot off the accelerator and slowed the van to normal speed. He held his breath, feeling his lungs burn, and his stomach sank with dread as he watched the transport in the rearview mirror.

The other vehicle abruptly executed a hard one-eighty to pursue him.

Alex swore, thought: *All right then, here goes freaking nothing.*

He pulled the van to the side of the road and punched it to a stop. The helmet he wore felt stifling, as though it shut out all breathable air. Raggedly he jerked it off and wiped his streaming face with his sleeve.

The transport fell in closely behind him, rolling to a stop a few yards back. Alex kept his eyes glued to the side mirror as the trooper riding shotgun in the cab climbed out and paced toward him. The man gripped his automatic rifle casually, but Alex could see his fingers resting near the trigger.

He rolled down the window as the trooper appeared beside him.

"Yeah?" Alex growled, hoping to sound bored, gravelly, and irritated, praying his voice wouldn't crack and betray his raw nerves.

The trooper's pale, icy eyes scanned Alex's face, taking in the grime and sweat, the streaks of blood on his forehead and down the back of his neck.

He shifted the rifle and Alex tensed, reaching as casually as he could for his discarded helmet. It was all but useless as a weapon, but it was all he had.

Suddenly the soldier grinned, revealing uneven gaps of missing teeth. Those teeth he still had were dark and yellowed, and Alex could see similar stains on the blunt fingers poised over the trigger.

His eyes fell to the name stenciled on the soldier's shirt: *Humphreys*. The man's pocket bulged with a thick, battered pack of cigarettes.

"Dude, you headed back to the Compound?" Humphreys asked. There was a nasty glint in his eyes, but he kept right on grinning.

"Yeah," Alex grunted, praying it was the right answer. "Whaddaya want?"

The trooper jerked his head back toward the transport.

"We picked up some Freebie scum that was trying to get past the roadblocks. Figured we'd throw 'em in with your lot, long as you're headed back anyway. Looks like we're gonna be here a while, cleanin' up the mess. Chino over there'll ride along with you."

Alex glanced in the side mirror and saw a dozen bedraggled prisoners, men and women alike, with their shackled hands locked behind their heads. A squad of soldiers, including the casually indicated Chino, herded them roughly out onto the roadway from the back of the transport. Now Alex could see the captives' bloodied faces, their raw expressions revealing everything from fury and defiance to utter hopelessness.

Desperation, pity, and guilt tore at him, but taking on the stone-faced, heavily armed Chino was plain suicide.

"Nah, no can do. I'm full up," Alex said flatly. "They're scraping 'em up back there like garbage." He shrugged, praying he wasn't shaking. "There's another van coming along behind me might have some room."

His tone of voice carefully conveyed that he didn't give a damn whether it did or not.

Irritation crossed the trooper's face, then, surprisingly, he grinned once more. Grimly Alex recognized the expression in his eyes.

Glee. Simple, sadistic, vicious.

"Turkey shoot, huh? Shit, we're always missin' the fun."

Alex shrugged again. "Yeah," he grunted. "Well, you hurry, you might still get some action."

Humphreys glanced back to the transport. He shook his head at Chino, then looked back at Alex.

"Might at that," he said, reaching for the pack of cigarettes with his free hand. "More fun pickin 'em off when they're runnin', ya know?"

He leaned in the window. His voice dropped in confidence as Alex struggled not to flinch away from the man's fetid breath.

"Sarge wouldn't let us have at 'em much," he muttered in disgust, jerking his head to indicate the prisoners. "What difference would it've made to him? We coulda had some fun, and they're just gonna string 'em up anyway."

Alex's gaze shot back to the mirror. Desperately he tried to reassess the condition of the prisoners, but they were already being prodded back into the truck.

I'm sorry, he thought miserably. *Christ, I'm so sorry.*

To Humphreys, he simply shrugged with another noncommittal grunt.

The soldier held the grimy pack of cigarettes out to Alex, open end toward him. "Thanks,"

Alex muttered, taking one. He scarcely registered the unfamiliar logo on the package: *Long Gold*.

"So there's another van comin'?" the trooper mumbled, pulling a cigarette from the pack with his teeth.

Alex nodded. "Should be here any minute. They were loading it right behind me. Looked like they didn't have enough to fill it, though."

"Okay. We'll put em' on that one. Just as well," he added with a twisted smile. "It'll give us a few more minutes to play with 'em, Sarge or no friggin' Sarge."

Alex's stomach wrenched. "Wait!" he blurted. "Okay, hey, maybe I could squeeze 'em in the back, let you guys get on to the real fun."

The trooper started to answer, then his attention shifted away. A van identical to the one Alex drove pulled up behind the transport.

"Nah, never mind. Other one's here now." The guardsman slapped his hand once on the driver's door in dismissal and turned away.

Alex swore, tears of rage and desperation burning. He blinked, swiped a sleeve furiously across his eyes, and threw the van back into gear.

Hitting the gas, pulling into the street, he drove almost blindly. Once a safe distance from what used to be his school, and was God-knew-what now, he sped up and instinctively headed home.

CHAPTER 5

The Roosevelt Bridge was in sight as Alex turned onto 23rd Street, but save for police and various other military vehicles, the roads were deserted. He shook his head to clear his tear-blurred vision, but he couldn't clear away the nightmare.

It was still D.C., and in some ways remained unchanged. In other ways it was so changed as to be unrecognizable. Route 50 had disappeared. Alex was startled to realize he'd completely missed the turn for the Roosevelt Bridge. Abruptly the Tidal Basin stretched before him.

There were no expressway signs.

There were no expressways.

Veering right, he found himself at the entrance to the Arlington Bridge. He sighed in relief, feeling once again on familiar terrain. Then yet another shock hit him, sending cold sweat trickling down his spine.

He frantically double-checked the side mirrors, searching for familiar sights that should have defined the landscape, but were now eerily, terrifyingly absent.

The Washington Monument stood in the distance, but its counterpart at the west end of Potomac Park was ... *gone*. Where the Lincoln Memorial should have risen, a block of low, gray, industrial warehouses sprawled.

No flag flew to mark the slope of the Vietnam Veterans Memorial. There was no sign at all of the black marble Memorial itself, nor of its accompanying bronze sculptures.

It's the freaking Twilight Zone, Alex thought wildly.

Potomac Park and the Tidal Basin receded in the distance. As he passed the entrance to Arlington National Cemetery, he clenched his jaw at the sight of its fortified gate surrounded by a high fence topped with razor wire.

Alex turned south, away from the cemetery, onto a narrow, potholed, blacktopped lane. A few military vehicles and buses passed in the opposite direction, but there was very little other traffic.

As the road wound into a thickening forest of maple, birch, and oak, Alex caught sight of a faded wooden street sign: *George Washington Highway*.

* * * * *

No vehicle had passed for the last ten minutes. Alex's innate sense of direction told him he had to be near Alexandria, but the road remained as empty and densely forested as if he'd been deep in the Blue Ridge Wilderness.

Exhausted, unsure what lay ahead, he pulled off onto the narrow, graveled shoulder. Shoving the gearshift down into first and flooring the accelerator, he forced the van into a lurching ascent up the slope of the roadbed and into the shelter of the trees. The vehicle bucked and skidded and then came to rest, hidden from view from the road.

Alex killed the engine and sat slumped in his seat. He knew he was at the end of his rope, his reserves gone. Desperate for help, he decided to give the dead cell phone in his pocket another try. Prying it out of the snug front pocket of his jeans, he pressed the power button once more and willed the device to work.

With vast relief he heard the sharp electronic beep and saw the screen light up. *SYNC ON* flashed, along with the current date and time.

"Yeah, got that already," Alex muttered. "Give me some help here, will you? C'mon, c'mon."

He managed to display the icon screen again – how, he wasn't quite sure – but selecting them simply brought up an array of error messages interspersed with a few strange functions: DESYNC, AUTORET, TLSET. He fiddled with the keypad, but no matter how many times he tried, he could not succeed in placing a call. Despondently he conceded that whatever the little device was, it probably wasn't a phone.

That idea, at least, was easier to accept than admitting none of the numbers he'd tried to call actually existed anymore. With a deep sigh, he shoved the cell back in his pocket.

Sore, shaking, cold sweat drying on his face and back, he folded his arms over the steering wheel and dropped his head to rest on them.

His head throbbed. Closing his eyes, he fought a sick wave of nausea.

Suddenly a solid metallic *thump* shook the van. Alex's head jerked up. *Oh God, the prisoners!* He'd completely forgotten them.

Removing the key from the ignition, silently praying it would open the cargo doors as well, Alex climbed stiffly from the van, favoring his bullet-grazed right leg. Leaning heavily against the side of the vehicle for support, he pulled off the flak jacket and let it fall in a heap to the ground. His shirt was plastered to his skin with sweat and dark smears of blood.

Limping to the rear of the van, he fumbled for a few moments with the key. His fingers wouldn't cooperate, and he had to concentrate with great effort on inserting the key into the lock.

"C'mon," he hissed. "C'mon, for the love of...."

Suddenly, the key turned and the lock released. He jerked the handle down hard and the cargo doors swung open.

The windowless hold was dark and stifling, the air stale. Alex blinked. He squinted into the dim interior, made darker by the thick shade of the trees, and he heard someone take a long, shuddering breath.

Two people were shackled to the steel benches, facing one another. On one side lay a young man, slumped over at an odd angle on the bench, his eyes closed, his feet splayed in their chains, his still hands manacled together in his lap.

Alex thought he'd passed out.

He reached in and gently shook the man's leg. "Hey," he said. "Hey, come on, buddy, wake up. It's all right. You're safe now."

"He's dead."

The flat pronouncement startled him. He looked in confusion to the other youth, who glared back at him with fierce, shuttered eyes. Alex swallowed, uncertain, at a loss for words.

"He was dead five minutes after they threw us in here."

Alex stared into the boy's furious gaze. This kid's just a baby, he thought, wondering dully why that should surprise him, after all he'd seen that day. Fifteen, maybe sixteen years old.

"I'm sorry, kid," he said flatly, all emotion finally wrung out of him.

A look of momentary confusion flickered in the boy's eyes, then quickly disappeared, leaving Alex uncertain whether he'd seen it at all. The kid straightened up in his filthy, bloodstained clothes and pressed his back hard against the wall of the van.

A slouched cap fell down over his forehead and ears, and Alex thought that he looked like something out of *Grapes of Wrath*: a mini-Tom Joad. Even with the cap obscuring most of the kid's face, Alex could clearly see dark, swelling bruises and scrapes.

"So."

The boy tried to snarl, but his light, slightly husky voice cracked, betraying his youth and fear. Alex could see him catch himself angrily.

"So go ahead," the kid tried again. "You might as well get it over with, you bastard. I'm not gonna beg."

Alex was taken aback; then, abruptly, he understood. "Jeez, kid, you think I'm going to hurt you?"

Muttering an oath, he hauled himself stiffly up onto the floor of the van. The boy shrank back farther, although he was already nearly flattened against the side wall. His eyes narrowed and he drew in a shaky breath.

"Look," Alex said evenly, "I'm not going to do anything to hurt you. All I'm going to do here is try to find a way to get you free."

Lifting the chain of the leg irons, he heard the boy wince. The kid gripped his manacled hands together close against his belly as though a spasm of pain had hit him.

"Where are you hurt?" Alex asked as he carefully examined the locks.

At first there was no answer. Alex looked up and noted with some surprise that the kid's eyes weren't brown, but a deep gray ringed in black. The pupils were so dilated he could barely see the irises. The boy's eyes glittered with a suspicious brightness, and Alex knew he was trying to hold back tears.

The skin beneath the kid's eyes was bruised, his lower lip cut. It no longer bled, but the swelling was noticeable.

He watched Alex's every move with suspicion, his shoulders trembling in spite of his sullen glare.

Alex met that gaze steadily. "I know you don't trust me, but I'm not a soldier or a cop. I stole this van. I'll try to help you if you'll let me."

The boy said nothing and his expression didn't change. Alex finally gave up trying to talk to him and turned his attention instead to the shackles, working the van key into the lock, where it definitely did not want to go.

He was surprised to suddenly hear the kid's shaky voice, all at once devoid of most of its belligerence.

"They hit me some, but mostly they didn't bother much with me. I'm okay, but...." He drew in a sharp breath. "The cuffs are really cutting into my ankles."

Alex immediately checked the boy's pant legs. He felt sticky, sodden cloth and his fingers were suddenly slippery with blood.

"God," he muttered. He seemed to be talking to Him a lot today.

The irons had rubbed the kid's ankles raw and made a painful mess, but Alex thought the abrasions weren't too deep. If he could get the cuffs off and find some water to get the wounds cleaned up, the scrapes should heal quickly.

The ignition key was hopeless. Alex slipped it into his front pants pocket and reached around to his back pocket, fishing for his Swiss Army knife. He snagged it, pulled it out, opened a blade, and began fiddling with the lock.

"Will that work?" the kid asked almost grudgingly, and Alex heard the first note of painful hope in his young voice. It tugged at his heart.

In spite of the boy's bravado – or maybe because of it – he seemed small, hurt, and vulnerable. A surge of protectiveness rose in Alex's chest, and his heart squeezed hard with the thought of Jack. This battered, rebellious boy was someone's child, too.

He shoved away thoughts of his son and concentrated on the lock.

"I hope it'll work," he replied. "Always does on those old *MacGyver* reruns."

"Huh?" the kid said, confused.

"I said it always works ... on TV," Alex repeated, his words hitching as something gave inside the lock. He shifted position awkwardly and renewed his effort.

"Yeah, whatever," the boy sighed wearily, then he gasped as one of the shackles slipped against a lacerated ankle. He groaned against his will.

"Sorry," Alex said, pausing a minute to lay his hand soothingly on the boy's leg. He could feel the tense muscles beneath the rough denim. "I think I've almost got it. Can you stand a little more?"

The boy grunted through clenched teeth. "Just get 'em off. I'm okay."

"Okay." Alex patted the leg encouragingly and went back to work.

"Who are you?" the boy asked suddenly, his voice strained.

"Name's Alex Morgan. I teach at Capitol. I was up in my office today when the whole world went.... God, I don't know what it went. Totally stark raving loco." He shook his head. "I've got to get home."

"Where's that?"

Alex sighed. "Falls Church. If there even is such a place in this freaking insane nightmare."

There was a sudden click, and then a clank of metal, and the shackles fell away from the boy's left ankle. He groaned in relief. Alex jammed the knife blade into the second restraint, and with a now-expert twist, released it as well.

"There you go," he said in grim satisfaction. "At least now you'll be able to...."

The boy sprang to his feet. With all his strength he swept his manacled hands, clenched together into one locked fist, hard up under Alex's jaw, slamming his head back and sending him sprawling against the opposite bench. Only the dead man's legs cushioned the impact of Alex's neck and back against the edge of the bench.

The boy vaulted over him and leapt from the van. He sprinted into the woods and was gone.

Alex groaned a heartfelt curse and hauled himself up. Damned freaking ungrateful brat!

Hurting, livid, he jumped to the ground and took off in hot pursuit, knowing his longer legs and greater strength would give him an advantage.

The boy ran with astonishing speed and agility, considering his ankles were raw and his hands were chained in front of him, hindering his balance.

He nearly got away.

He leapt recklessly into a wide, shallow creek and plowed across it like a bounding deer, feeling an exultant burst of freedom. His cap flew off, his shaggy, dark mop of hair damp and tangled with sweat. Then the weight of Alex's body hit him squarely in the back and they fell, sprawling, splashing, into the water.

The boy crawled to his feet and slopped through the water, clawing at exposed roots on the creek bank as he began to scramble up the muddy slope. Alex tackled the kid again, grabbed his shirt, and dragged him the rest of the way to the top. The boy rolled to his back and swung another clenched-fists haymaker, which Alex barely dodged.

Fed up, Alex all but body-slammed the kid. He grabbed the small, chained hands with one fist and shoved them down to the ground above the boy's head, his other hand locking around the kid's throat. He pinned the struggling body to the ground with his own.

And felt soft, unmistakably feminine curves.

"Oh, shit," he sighed, dropping his head in exhausted dismay against the soaking wet shoulder of the girl squirming furiously beneath him.

CHAPTER 6

Jessie's mind raced desperately. The moment Morgan threw his long body down on hers, she'd known it was all over. Exhausted, terrified, frantic, she struggled with all her strength, but he was too heavy. She could scarcely breathe, much less escape.

Alex's weight pressed her down, his hand still clamped on her throat. Her arms, shackled together and stretched over her head, strained her bruised ribs painfully and squeezed her lungs. Her pulse roaring in her ears, Jessie made one last attempt to free herself, bucking violently beneath her captor.

"Don't ... do that," Morgan ground out in a low, warning tone.

With a shock, Jessie felt him tense and harden against her, and she froze in terror.

She was new to the Freedom Brigade. She'd only been in the Resistance a few months, but even after that short a time, she knew to expect the worst should she be captured.

Her body stiffened and she closed her eyes, trying to empty her mind and retreat into an unfeeling void. But Jessie had a dramatic imagination, and it tormented her now. Morgan would rape her and kill her and leave her martyred body out here in the woods for the wild animals.

Tears stung as she squeezed her eyes tightly shut. Jessie thought wildly that there might be wolves and bears. Paul and Alana would never even know what had happened to her.

Suddenly the weight of Alex's body shifted. Jessie released a great exhalation of air, then drew in a long, gasping breath. Her aching ribs protested, but the air was so sweet that she felt a sudden resurgence of hope.

A firm grip on her wrists hauled her up to a sitting position. Clutching her wrists, Alex half-knelt atop her, one knee pressed across her hips, pinning her. He pulled her upper body forward so that her hands were held out in front of him. She shoved against him but could not pull herself free.

"Cut it out," he ordered gruffly. "Sit still and give me your hands." His voice was rough, exasperated. Jessie stared at him, momentarily frozen as she tried to decide what to do.

He had the knife out again and was digging at the lock on the wrist manacles.

"You hit me again," he said coldly, "and I'll toss you back in that van and leave you there 'til next Christmas. Is that clear?"

Alex hoped he sounded dangerous enough to be convincing. In truth, he'd never threatened a girl in his life. In pure frustration he gave the lock an angry wrench. It finally dawned on Jessie that he really was trying to help her. After a pause, overcome with relief that he wasn't going to rape and kill her, she jerked her head in a small nod.

Concentrating on the lock, Alex didn't notice her acquiescence. He gave her shoulder a small, rough shake.

"Is it?" he demanded.

"Yes," she whispered. She didn't trust her voice, and in fact, even that one small word quavered.

He worked in glowering silence for a moment, then finally seemed to relax. Though she would never admit it, Jessie was relieved when he gentled his grip.

Alex dug at the lock, unable to ignore the delicacy of the hands he held in his. Jessie's wrists were scraped raw, and he winced at the sight of them. He felt a fulminating anger at those who had done this to her.

Those sons of bitches.

He shifted position slightly, keenly and uncomfortably aware of her hips under his leg. He felt the color rise along his cheekbones. She was frightened, dangerous, dirty, bruised and bloody, and she'd decked him but good.

He shouldn't have felt anything for her but anger, yet beneath the wild cropped hair, the stubborn defiance, the grime and bruises and boy's clothing, he saw a confoundingly, enormously appealing girl.

He clenched his jaw against a sudden, traitorous, unwanted desire, and a taut muscle ticked in his cheek.

"What's your name?" he demanded, more harshly than he'd intended.

Jessie swallowed, her throat dry.

"Jessie," she mumbled, trying to sound surly. She was chagrined to hear how small her voice sounded.

He paused and looked her in the eye. She was startled to see a glint of what might have been grudging amusement.

"James?" Alex asked dryly.

She did not smile. "O'Neil."

He fiddled relentlessly with the lock. Her wrists were painfully abraded, and when she winced and drew in a sharp breath, he tried with surprising gentleness to distract her.

"Okay. So how old are you, Jessie? Fifteen? Sixteen?"

Jessie frowned, and her chin came up with injured dignity.

"Twenty-two," she retorted.

Alex laughed, a snort of disbelief. "Yeah, right, and look, there goes a pig flying by."

"I am!" she insisted. "Well, I will be, anyway. Next March."

He studied her again for a moment, then shook his head and went back to work.

"I thought you were a boy," he admitted, the ghost of a smile quirking one corner of his mouth as he wryly considered the enormity of his mistake.

If possible, her chin lifted even higher. "That was the idea. Political activism's a capital offense for a woman." She said this with no little pride.

Watching Alex's reaction carefully, she saw with satisfaction that his face paled and every hint of smile disappeared.

He cleared his throat.

"Who was the other guy in the van?"

Jessie shook her head. "I don't know. I never saw him before today."

"Somebody must care about him." Alex's voice was grim. "They've got a right to know what happened."

Jessie sighed, thinking of Paul and Alana and how they would feel if she disappeared. Seeing her pained expression, Alex eased up a little.

"The guards back there were calling you guys 'Freebies'. What does that mean?"

Now it was Jessie's turn to snort in disbelief.

"You're telling me you've never heard of the Freedom Brigade? Where've you been, under a rock? Everybody knows the Brigade." Her voice strengthened as she felt on firm footing. "There are hundreds of us now, and some day there will be thousands more!"

Alex's brows knit. Jessie winced a bit as he continued to work the lock.

Now that she could breathe easily, the pressure of his leg across her lap and his sheer closeness were making it difficult for her to think clearly. She kept losing her train of thought.

Her wrists, raw and scraped as they were, were soothed by his touch. The weight of his leg was intimate and possessive, strangely comforting and exciting all at once. With a rush of heat Jessie remembered the sensation of Alex's whole body covering hers.

Embarrassed, flushing with color, she looked down and was startled to see the bloody rent in the leg of his jeans.

"Hey, your leg's bleeding," she said in surprise. Then, contritely, "I didn't do that, did I?"

He met her eyes, unsure what to make of her conciliatory tone. She'd actually sounded concerned, but he didn't completely trust her not to haul off and whack him again.

"No, it happened earlier today, at the univer– ... at the riot."

Alex gave the knife another twist. All at once the cuff popped free from her right wrist. Jessie breathed a sigh of relief as Alex went to work on the other wrist.

"Where do you live? I'll take you home. Your folks are probably worried about you." He looked at her. "With damned good reason, I'd say."

Stung, she said, "I'm on my own. I've been going to school." At his skeptical look, she simply shrugged.

He nodded and concentrated again on the handcuff.

"I moved around a lot this summer, staying with friends, you know?" Her inflection rose as though it were a question. "Getting involved."

Alex snorted. "Yeah, I'd say you got involved all right. What the hell was going on back there, anyway?"

Jessie heated at once to the subject, her shoulders squaring and her eyes flashing. She nearly inflated with zeal.

"The demonstration was supposed to be peaceable. We were going to march all the way to the White House. But then the Guard showed up, and the whole thing went...." Her words trailed off and she shuddered in spite of herself.

Alex was stunned. "Wait a minute. The Guard? The *National Guard?*"

He wasn't naive. He'd read about Kent State. But he knew that tragedy had involved raw, panicky troops. The troopers he'd seen in action today had been vicious, professional killers. They'd relished every opportunity for brutality.

Jessie nodded, staring strangely at him. "Of course they were the National Guard. Who else would they be?"

Alex shook his head. Then he asked, "What were you protesting?"

"We were demanding our civil rights. Freedom from tyranny. We want the Constitution and the Bill of Rights restored." At his look of dismay, she added, "I learned in the Brigade that there was a time when America wasn't under martial law, but it's been so long now, most people don't know it or have forgotten. We won't, though. We'll never forget and we'll never give up. *Never.*"

After a pause, she sighed and sounded suddenly wistful.

"To tell you the truth, though, sometimes it's hard to imagine what it would be like to be free. Can you even picture it?"

Alex wouldn't have thought anything else could surprise him today, but all at once Jessie was looking at him with what actually might have been trust.

"Can you?" she repeated.

Alex nodded. "Yes," he said simply, but deep in his chest he felt the greatest despair he'd known since Casey's death.

Suddenly, the last lock snapped open and released Jessie's wrist. She blew out a breath and rubbed her arm.

As she pushed at Alex's leg and began to wriggle free, he glowered at her. "Don't even think about running off, Miss O'Neil," he warned, taking hold of her elbow. "We're sticking together. I've got an awful lot of questions, and right now, you're the only one with answers."

CHAPTER 7

"Where are we going?" Jessie asked a little sullenly, looking out the passenger window of the cargo van. She cared more about the answer than she was willing to admit.

"Home," Alex grunted, the muscles tensing in his jaw. "I've got to find my family. And then I've got to find his."

Briefly he patted his shirt pocket, where he'd placed the dead youth's identification card.

Alex had freed the young man's legs from the floor shackles and dragged him from the back of the van to a secluded spot in deep shade.

A quick search of the young man's pockets had produced a wallet with identification and a wad of bills. Alex studied the ID card.

He didn't recognize the format, but the necessary information was there: a black-and-white photo, name, ID number, and address.

John Patterson Phillips was number 5002-389-0056. He'd lived in Silver Spring. Alex had carefully placed the card in his shirt pocket and bent to replace Phillips' wallet. Jessie had plucked it from his hand.

"You might as well take the money, too. He doesn't need it anymore, and we might." Her words were callous, but her downcast eyes and guilt-ridden expression told a different story.

Alex scowled. "I've got money. I don't need a dead man's."

Her cheeks reddening, Jessie pulled the bills from the wallet. She dropped the billfold beside the body, then looked up defiantly at Alex.

"Well, I do," she retorted. Turning on her heel, she strode back to the van.

Alex watched her go, then leaned down to compose Phillips' body as best as he could. He spoke a few brief, gruff words and turned away.

* * * * *

Alex and Jessie drove on poorly paved roads through gray towns that looked as though they belonged in a struggling, barely developed nation. Bicycles and motor scooters, often with three or four riders on the same bike, and several dilapidated buses belching exhaust passed by, but few cars.

People walking on the streets, oddly similar in appearance regardless of whatever ethnic type they might be, seemed at once overdressed and worse for wear in the warm weather.

It was not that the clothing was particularly unusual, Alex thought, but just that it was uniformly dowdy and old-fashioned. The colors were somber and dull, the fabrics rough: unbleached cotton and heavy wool. Very few of the women wore slacks; few people wore jeans. Those who did were in denim overalls or heavy, shapeless work dungarees.

No designer jeans. No designer anything, as far as he could see. Dresses were long, drab, shapeless, and heavy.

Time warp. It wasn't the first time Alex had thought it. This had to be some ghastly nightmare of a future, the result of ... what? Invasion? Plague? Nuclear or biological attack? Some terrible natural disaster that brought about economic collapse?

But when? And – Good God Almighty – *how?*

When he got home – if, please God, he still had a home to get to – he would make Jessie tell all if he had to wring her sweet little neck to do it.

"You're married, huh?" she asked suddenly, breaking into his silent brooding, startling him.

"What?"

"I said, you're married, aren't you? You look like a guy who'd be married."

Alex glanced at her.

Why should she care? he wondered, but supposed she was just trying to make conversation.

"I'm not married," he said tersely.

Jessie frowned. Alex was obviously still angry at her. Well, so what? She'd just asked a simple question, the getting-to-know-you kind. He was way too touchy, and despite being sort of good-looking, he was, Jessie thought, *really* strange.

Alex took a turn that looked vaguely familiar, discovering to his vast relief that they were now on Arlington Boulevard. His sense of direction kept them headed north as they passed through a few more small towns and outlying neighborhoods.

Alex recognized the lay of the land despite so much that was alien. No malls, no supermarkets, no big discount stores, no electronics stores, nor any fast-food restaurants. And always there was a drab, down-at-the-heels look, as though the future was actually the past: a replay of the Great Depression of the 1930s or the old Soviet Union of the fifties and sixties.

As he drove, Alex half-listened to the scratchy transmissions of the van's police-channel radio. As far as he could tell, there'd been no mention of the vehicle he'd stolen. Squawky dispatches directed mop-up of the riot and other military deployment in a staticky, coded shorthand he couldn't always decipher.

One thing was clear, however: there was no distinction between military and civil police. Martial law was clearly in force.

He prayed one cargo van more or less wasn't worthy of anyone's attention.

Jessie interrupted Alex's worry. "Kids?" she asked.

"Huh? What kids?" He looked along the road in confusion until he realized she was asking if *he* had kids.

"Oh. Yeah," he said hoarsely, an enormous lump in his throat.

She waited, watching him expectantly. He shifted uncomfortably in his seat, knowing she had no idea that her question stabbed him through the heart.

He sighed raggedly. "I have a little boy, Jack. He's four. He's with his grandmother. His mother – my wife – died a few years ago."

Jessie digested that information but offered no comment. Alex fixed his attention on the road ahead. All at once a small lane cut across Arlington, and he caught a glimpse of the faded street sign: *Annandale*. Abruptly he turned hard to the right.

Jessie braced herself, slapping her palms against the dashboard.

"Hey, take it easy!"

Righting herself, she studied the neighborhood. It was semirural, rundown, nothing to look at.

"You know this place?" she asked. "There's not much out here."

Alex shook his head in frustration and doubt. "Maybe, I don't know. The land looks familiar, but I can't ... I just don't *know*."

He slowed the van to a crawl and studied the small, clapboard and brick houses spaced far apart on either side of the bumpy road. He sucked in a breath.

"I think we should be coming up on Hillwood Lane pretty soon. See if you can spot it."

Jessie watched intently for a few minutes, then pointed at a warped wooden street sign ahead. "There," she said.

They turned onto Hillwood, a rutted dirt road. Clouds of dust and clumps of gravel kicked up, pelting the underside of the vehicle. After a mile or two, Alex stopped the van in the middle of the lane. He sighed, and his whole body seemed to slump in defeat.

"It's gone," he said miserably. "It might as well be the dark side of the moon. Everything's gone. Everything."

Jessie was surprised by the depth of sympathy she felt for Alex. She laid a comforting hand on his arm, wanting to make things right for him. Feeling him tense, she quickly withdrew her hand.

She cleared her throat to cover her embarrassment.

"Look, Alex, maybe ... maybe you're just lost," she suggested. "Are you sure this is the way?"

He shook his head and dropped his forehead against his arm on the steering wheel. He was in complete despair, worn out, unable to think clearly anymore. How had he ended up in this endless, insane nightmare?

Yet he'd been aware that, for a moment there when Jessie'd placed her hand on his arm, he'd felt a small wave of warmth and hope. She'd pulled back almost immediately, but he'd felt it.

"Alex, I've got an idea," she said. "Maybe your family moved. We could go look up their records in a Registry Office. Everybody's supposed to be registered, although, um, not always with their real names."

Alex looked up instantly, grasping at Jessie's suggestion like a drowning man.

"Registry Office? What's that, and where do we find it?"

Her surprise was evident. "Boy, you really are out of touch, aren't you?" At his warning scowl, she went on patiently. "Ok, Alex, look, every fair-sized town's got one. If we backtrack to the center of Falls Church and hunt around a little, we should be in business."

She narrowed her eyes and scrutinized him again. "You *sure* you're from around here?"

With a scrape of tires and a spray of gravel and dust, Alex wheeled the van around and headed back to Annandale, trusting that it would, as it once had, lead up to Broad Street and the center of town, whatever that might now be.

As they drove, he took a deep breath and prepared to ask Jessie the question he most needed answered, the same one he most dreaded. How far into the future was he that his home had become this bleak, hopeless place?

"Jessie," he said, jaw tight, "Tell me the date."

She gave him a *you can't be serious* look, but then sighed and answered gamely. "May twenty-seventh."

"No. I mean the year."

Now Jessie rolled her eyes. "Oh, come *on*," she snorted.

"I mean it, Jessie. Tell me the year," Alex repeated grimly, and Jessie's flip response died on her lips. *How crazy was he?*

She gave him the same date Casterson's cell phone had – the same one it had been when he'd gone to work that morning. And Jessie saw immediately from Alex's stunned, incredulous expression that it was the wrong answer.

CHAPTER 8

Jessie was almost certain Alex was deranged. He seemed completely disoriented, and she was worried that his strange behavior would endanger them both.

A few hours earlier, she would certainly have tried again to escape from him, had she had the chance. But now, something had changed. She didn't like it, but she seemed unable to break the growing bond she felt with him.

It wasn't his grim conviction that he was out of place and time, nor his bizarre questions. It was the depth of his emotion that touched her. Jessie was beginning to feel such a completely irrational attachment to him that she wondered half-seriously if insanity were catching.

But she realized no one had ever really needed her before, certainly not as desperately as Alex did.

"Help me out here, Jessie. Is this the right way?"

His words interrupted her confused thoughts. Shaking herself, she quickly surveyed the area.

"I think so," she nodded. "It looks like we're getting closer to town. Wait," she said suddenly. "Turn down this road here."

Puzzled, Alex nevertheless obliged, pulling the van onto a gravel side lane. The houses alongside were very small, and while attempts had been made to keep them up, there was a pervasive bleak, neglected look to the neighborhood. Between some of the houses were rubbish-strewn vacant lots surrounded by rickety board fences.

The fences were plastered with frayed and peeling political posters. Noticing they were all of the same person, Alex thought the sharp-featured, heavyset man looked as though he'd been forced at gunpoint to smile. While the fellow had obviously intended to look benevolent, the tight grimace on his face was off-putting and did nothing to warm the coldness in his dark eyes.

Though faded, some of the posters still bore legible printing beneath the portrait:

FORWARD INTO THE FUTURE.

Well, with an unbeatable slogan like that, whoever he is, he's got my vote, Alex thought wryly. But the face was oddly familiar, and it nagged at the back of his mind, troubling him.

Jessie tapped his arm. "Pull over there by that vacant lot."

Alex did as she said, but he looked around in some puzzlement. Why did she want to stop here? The whole area was a dump.

He asked, "What's here?"

Without answering his question, she simply said, "Keep the engine running."

"Wait. Where are you going?"

Alex reached for her, but Jessie flung open the passenger door and hopped from the van before he could stop her. Quick as the agile boy he'd first thought her to be, she scaled the nearest fence and darted across the vacant lot. She hopped another fence at the far side and dropped down out of sight into a small, enclosed back yard. Above the fence Alex could make out the tops of a rusted swing set, a corrugated steel storage shed, and a bent, old-fashioned, revolving clothes tree full of drying laundry.

One piece at a time, the laundry disappeared.

Moments later Jessie jumped back in the van beside him, breathing hard, clutching a wad of clothing.

"Okay," she nodded, yanking the door shut. "Go go go. Get us out of here."

As Alex pulled away from the curb, it was all he could do not to floor the accelerator in panic.

"Dammit, Jessie, are you out of your mind?" he croaked. "You took a hell of a risk back there. What if somebody'd seen you?"

"It would be a lot more dangerous to walk into a Registry office the way we look right now," she said, catching her breath. Then she added, with a disapproving primness that struck him as ludicrous, "And Alex, would you *please* stop swearing? It's blasphemous."

He stared at her incredulously, taking his eyes off the road a second too long. The van hit a pothole and swerved. Alex hissed a fervent oath, wrenching the wheel to correct the swerve. Beside him, Jessie hissed and held on.

Alex shook his head. She was some piece of work.

"Okay, let me get this straight," he said with deceptive calm. "Today you and your radical buddies instigated a riot, then you picked a dead man's pockets, and now you've just swiped what's likely some poor family's entire wardrobe. But you object to my *language*?"

Jessie sighed. He just didn't get it at all.

"No," she said, "you don't understand. If you keep cussing, people will notice and you'll draw attention. You could even get arrested for disorderly conduct or public indecency or disturbing the peace."

Alex paled. After a moment he nodded.

"Okay. Okay. I get it. And I apologize. So it's not the old Soviet Union around here, is it? It's freaking – sorry – Afghanistan."

Jessie gave him another pinched look, then turned away. Once again she had no idea what he was talking about, but for the most part, she was satisfied. He'd try to be more careful with what he said. For now, it was enough.

After a half-hour's search, they found a government-run service station in an industrial area filled with warehouses. Nervously Alex pulled up to a diesel pump as Jessie rummaged in the glove compartment. She murmured a small sound of satisfaction and pulled out a handful of stamped paper vouchers. As Alex killed the engine, she stuffed the papers into his hand.

"Give the guy a couple of these," she said. "Tell him to fill it up." She lowered her voice urgently. "And for heaven's sake, Alex, don't say anything else. Not *anything*. I'll just be a minute."

She sorted through the stolen clothes, made her choices, then climbed out of the van. She strode nonchalantly to a door painted with fading letters: *Lavatory.*

Alex started at a heavy rap on the driver's-side window. Unrolling the window, he handed out the vouchers without a glance at the attendant, ordering, "Fill it," in his most bored, officious tone.

The attendant took the papers and nodded. As the man moved away from the window, Alex sighed and closed his eyes.

He was suddenly aware of Casterson's device pressing against him in his front pocket. Opening his eyes, he squirmed slightly and fished it out. Amazingly, even after the fracas in the creek, it appeared unharmed.

The screen still displayed the time and date, confirming Jessie's assertion that it was the same date he'd awakened to that morning. But that this was not in any way the same world was horribly clear.

Either Alex had completely lost his mind – a distinct possibility, he thought – or else....

"No. No freaking way." He snorted at the insane idea taking insidious form in his mind.

The device was probably just a malfunctioning cell phone. Okay, he supposed it could be one of the new generation iPorts – he hadn't seen any of those yet. Not very damn user-friendly, though, unless....

Alex was no longer sure he hadn't hallucinated everything that had happened since he'd hit his head in his office. This little device – if you could get it to work – probably did nothing more than let you tweet what you had for lunch, buy tickets for ball games, tell you when you had a dentist appointment, or take pictures of your cat, although he hadn't seen anything on it remotely resembling a lens opening. To suspect it might have altered the fabric of time itself was worse than idiocy.

It was madness.

Alex had to get home. He absolutely *had* to find his family – that was all that mattered now. After that he could take time to rest, to think, to study the device, to talk to Jessie at length.

And as though his thoughts had conjured her, Jessie appeared at the passenger door, opening it and climbing up beside him.

With an almost comical double take, Alex stared at her and felt his heart stumble in his chest.

How could he have missed how lovely she was? He hoped his tongue wasn't hanging out, she was that beautiful. He'd have hauled her into his lap then and there if he hadn't been certain she have punched his lights out.

Jeez, he must be even further gone than he'd thought.

In spite of scrapes and bruises, her skin was now clean, fresh, and glowing, with high pink color in her cheeks and freckles dusting her nose. Her deep gray eyes were tired but clear under long, thick lashes. Her hair – a chocolate-colored pixie mop that just brushed her nape – made him hungry to slide his fingers through it.

The plain, blue-gingham shirtwaist dress she'd put on was too big, but she'd cinched in the waist with a belt. Alex thought that his two hands would just about span that waist, and his body tightened at the thought.

Embarrassed by his reaction, which he *really* did not need, he awkwardly cleared this throat.

"It looks ... you look...." He laughed – a humorless bark – at his own inane stammering. "Well, I sure wouldn't mistake you for a boy now."

Flustered, Jessie shoved a wad of clothes into his hands. "Your turn," she said, her self-consciousness making her tone brusque. "Hurry up. We can't stay here long."

"Yes, ma'am," Alex replied, a ghost of a smile tugging at his mouth.

Jessie met his eyes and could not help a small smile as well.

He said, "Lock the doors while I'm gone. I'll be quick."

Jessie watched him stride away, the spare clothes bunched under his arm. She realized her heart was thumping.

When Alex had almost smiled, she'd been unable to catch her breath. She'd had the craziest urge to throw herself into his arms.

Jessie caught herself. *Whoa, girl, don't even go there.* She sighed, shifted restlessly on the seat, and waited impatiently for Alex to come back.

* * * * *

In the dingy washroom, Alex stripped and inspected the damage. The worst of it was the nasty gash, just above his right knee, from the trooper's bullet. The wound was raw and crusted with dried blood, but he saw with relief that it was not deep, and it was no longer bleeding.

Now that the graze had his attention, it hurt like blazes. He washed it as thoroughly as he could, the cold water bringing some relief.

After tending his leg, Alex pressed cold, wet paper towels to the cut at the back of his head. Other than a dull ache, it wasn't giving him much trouble. It had been messy, but again, not serious.

He pitched the towels into a corroded metal trashcan in the corner and bent down, thrusting his head completely under the water faucet. His headache eased in the blessed coolness. Desperately dry-mouthed, Alex turned his face to the water and drank deeply. He didn't care whether or not it was safe to drink; that was the least of his worries.

When he'd washed off most of the grime, sweat, and dried blood, Alex was relieved to find that, other than the cuts on his leg and behind his ear, and the angry, purpling bruise under his jaw where Jessie'd slugged him, he was more or less whole.

Reflected in the cracked, grimy mirror above the rusted sink were his bloodshot eyes and his face drawn with stress and exhaustion. He'd have to rest soon or he'd be unable to function at all.

He shrugged on the clothes Jessie had stolen and was pleased to find they fit well enough. The coarse fabric was rough, but since it was not new, it had softened enough to be fairly comfortable. The mirror now revealed a tall, shaggy-haired, weary, scuffed man in a faded blue shirt and baggy workpants. He was also wearing – in spite of the warm weather – a nondescript, shapeless, brown wool jacket.

Alex thoroughly searched the pockets of his discarded jeans and shirt, removing Casterson's cell phone, his own wallet, the dead man's ID card, the Swiss Army knife, and his spare change. He placed the articles carefully into the pockets of his new clothes, one of which already contained a crumpled cotton handkerchief, then wadded up his ruined, bloodstained clothing and stuffed the whole mess into the trash.

He checked his appearance one last time in the mirror, running his fingers through his grimy hair. It simply tumbled back over his forehead in damp, tangled disarray. Apparently he'd be working the hobo look.

Alex shrugged. It would have to do.

I can do better once I get home, he thought. *If I get home.*

His stomach pitched in a spasm of grief and fear.

Oh God, please, he whispered. *Please let me find my boy.*

CHAPTER 9

Downtown Falls Church looked like it slumped in the belly of the Great Depression. A hardscrabble air of desperation hung over the town, as though it might simply crumble and blow away at any moment.

Cruising through the center of town as slowly as possible without attracting undue attention, Alex's fingers clenched on the steering wheel when another military van passed by in the opposite direction.

Cold sweat trickled between his shoulder blades, plastering his shirt to his back, but to his vast relief, the troopers paid his vehicle no mind. He was acutely grateful for the grimy windshield, which made scrutiny of the cab's interior difficult – if not impossible – from the outside.

So intensely was he watching the passing vehicle, squinting in the sideview mirror long after it had passed from sight, that he was startled when Jessie tapped his shoulder.

"Alex?" she asked, her voice tinged with impatience. "Did you hear me?"

"Huh?" He shifted his attention to Jessie, then back to the road ahead.

A lone traffic signal swung above an intersection two blocks ahead – a relatively busy intersection by local standards. Alex counted one rattletrap bus, one troop transport, two motorcycles, an old black sedan he half-expected to disgorge Al Capone, and three heavy-frame, wide-tire, single-gear bikes, all of them sporting dented wire baskets on the handlebars.

The bike riders – two weary-looking men and one haggard, middle-aged woman – all had their baskets precariously loaded with bags of groceries and a few lumpy, string-tied parcels.

"I said, pull over here, will you? Come on, Alex, it's okay. The soldiers are gone."

Alex glanced again at Jessie and realized she was eying him anxiously. He rolled the van to a stop at the curb and looked up and down the street. He frowned, eyes narrowing as he scanned the tired storefronts.

The only identifiable businesses on the block were marginal, Ma-and-Pa operations: a corner grocery, a hole-in-the-wall pharmacy, a secondhand store, a rundown five-and-dime with faded placards in the front window.

Brillo pads never rust! boasted one ad, its cardboard corners curling, red letters sun-bleached to pale pink, and *Yes! We have hula hoops! (Limited supply)*.

"Is one of these the Registry office?" he asked uncertainly. Nothing he saw gave him any hope of finding his way home.

Jessie shook her head. "No, of course not. I only asked you to stop because I need to go in the drugstore for a minute."

"Oh."

Alex's cheeks reddened slightly. Even marriage had not cured him of the average man's don't-even-go-there aversion to all matters of feminine hygiene. Despite his embarrassment he studied the smudged, tinted glass window of the pharmacy with caution.

"It doesn't look safe," he said. "I'm going in with you."

Jessie shook her head. "No, I'll just be a minute. You need to stay here and keep the motor running. I'll be right back, I promise."

"Wait. Jessie, wait a minute."

As she reached for the door handle, Alex caught her arm. She looked at him, her eyebrows raised, her head cocked. He held her firmly, pulling her a little too close, narrowing his eyes suspiciously at her.

"You're not going to swipe anything in there, are you?"

Jessie's eyes widened in surprise, then she gave him a wicked smile.

"I might."

"Jessie, for Pete's sake! You can't just...."

"Don't worry," she said, touching her finger to his lips, effectively shutting him up. "I'm not going to get in any more trouble." Leaning forward as though to confide a secret, she said, "I hate being told what to do."

Jessie slipped her arm free of Alex's grasp and got out of the van. As he scowled after her, she turned back to face him.

"Be right back," she said easily, and shut the door.

* * * * *

Alex had worried himself into a tangle of nerves by the time Jessie returned. She settled in and opened a small, brown paper bag, fished inside it, and surprised him by retrieving a round, pressed-powder compact and a bottle of foundation.

"Okay. Go," she said, and as he eased the van away from the curb, Jessie frowned into the cheap, warped metal mirror of the compact.

She mugged, turning her face this way and that, inspecting the damage. Alex's jaw tightened as she gingerly dabbed and patted, covering scrapes and bruises on her cheek, forehead, and chin. Once again he felt the desire to murder the bastards who'd hurt her.

Jessie snapped the compact closed and turned to Alex for inspection.

"There. How's that?" she asked.

Alex glanced at her. With the concealing makeup there was little sign of her bruises, at least on a casual once-over.

But he would remember every one.

* * * * *

"Okay, that's it. Over there, see? Down in the next block?"

Alex could hardly miss the hulking concrete building that covered most of the block. As he parked at the curb directly across the street, he could see the engraving above the front entrance:

BUREAU OF RECORDS AND PUBLIC REGISTRY.

He shut off the engine and studied the entrance. A constant flow of people trudged in and out; the crowd worried him.

He said uneasily, "There're a lot of people here, Jessie. Maybe we should try again later."

She shook her head. "It's always like this. They close at five, so we don't have much time. If you want to find your family today, we'll have to risk it."

She studied the entrance, worrying her bottom lip, then added, "It'll be all right, I think. Just let me do the talking, and don't look so ... intense, okay?"

Alex winced. He knew what she really meant was, *Don't look so crazy.*

He took a deep breath. "I'll do my best. But we're not going to run smack into a Wanted poster in there with your mugshot on it, are we?"

"No, don't worry," she said, knowing he wasn't joking. "This was the first time I ever got caught."

He sighed. "Look, Jessie, you don't have to do this. I don't want to put you in any more danger. I can make out okay from here on."

Darn him for making me care. "Are you ditching me?" she asked, trying to sound affronted.

Gravely Alex shook his head. "No. God knows I'm grateful for your help, but I won't hold you. You've done so much for me already, and I know the risk you're taking."

Jessie considered this, not quite willing to admit this unpredictable man was definitely, dangerously growing on her. Why was leaving him so hard?

Knowing it was probably a huge mistake, she said, "Okay, tell you what. Suppose I stay around, you know, just until you find your family. Besides, the way you are, if I left you by yourself now, you'd likely be in trouble inside of five minutes, and then I'd be stuck feeling all responsible."

Alex didn't seem to know quite how to take her answer. He hesitated; then, before he completely realized he was going to do it, he leaned over and kissed her. His mouth slanted over hers with a hunger and yearning that, even in her innocence, Jessie couldn't mistake for mere gratitude. Her lashes fluttered closed and she heard her own small, startled intake of breath.

Almost of their own accord, her arms wrapped around his neck as a small moan of pleasure escaped her lips.

With a muffled groan, Alex broke the kiss. As he gently untangled their embrace, he found

Jessie gazing at him with stormy gray eyes that revealed as much surprise, confusion, and longing as he felt.

Where had the jackhammer in his chest come from?

Couldn't be my heart. That's buried with Casey.

The insanity of the day had overcome him, that was it. How else to explain this crazy hunger for his own, personal little Bolshevik?

"Sorry, Jessie," he muttered gruffly. "That was out of line. It won't happen again."

Jessie's temper flared. He didn't want to kiss her again? *Ever?* Well, *fine.*

She turned stiffly away from Alex and pushed open the passenger door, but not before he'd seen the wounded pride in her eyes and felt a stab of shame. Well, she'd be rid of him soon enough, he'd see to it.

He climbed out of the van, walked around to the passenger side, and tried to take her arm. She shrugged him off. "Come on," she said flatly. "Let's get this over with."

As they started toward the Registry office, Alex scanned the street warily. Protectiveness overcame awkwardness, and he slipped his arm around Jessie to shelter her as they walked. She recoiled and shoved away from him.

"Don't!" she hissed.

Affronted, Alex yanked back his arm. "Take it easy," he said angrily. "I wasn't exactly planning to throw you down and have my way with you right here in the street."

"You moron!" Jessie whirled on him. Darting a quick look to be sure no one was paying them any attention, she hissed, "Use that scrambled brain of yours to think for just *one* minute, will you? Public displays of affection are forbidden. You could get us picked up again!"

Alex's jaw dropped in dismay. He blew out a breath and raked his hand through his hair. There were land mines everywhere. Finally, he simply nodded. There was nothing to say.

CHAPTER 10

The gloomy Registry building was cavernous, yet Alex immediately felt closed-in and claustrophobic. The interior was oppressive, dimly lit, and blighted with terrible acoustics. Sound was both muffled and distorted, creating a painful din of diffuse noise that made conversation nearly impossible.

The poorly circulated air was musty and stale. If defeated resignation had an odor, Alex thought, this was it: stale sweat and discouragement, layers of dust, old paint, ancient carbon ink, and moldering paper.

Long queues of listless, dispirited people snaked in every direction. Surly clerks leaned on scarred wooden counters behind grimy glass windows. If absolutely compelled to work, they did so at a snail's pace, reluctantly dispensing and even more reluctantly accepting one official form after another.

Alex tried to look on the bright side. As numbing and disheartening as it was, the pervasive inertia of the place did have one advantage. No one seemed even remotely interested in his and Jessie's business.

Jessie scanned the signs over the windows: *Information, Directory, Travel Permits, Interstate Visas, Identification Documents, Vital Records.*

"Come on," she all but shouted above the noise. "Let's try the Directory."

Dutifully they got in line; after forty-five minutes they finally reached the bored clerk at the window. He ignored them.

"We need an address, please," Jessie said loudly, but politely, swallowing the resentful anger she always felt at these slug-like bureaucrats.

"Name?" the clerk grunted. His job consisted only of looking things up, and it was the one thing that most aggravated him.

Jessie looked expectantly at Alex.

He cleared his throat, spoke up.

"Frances Morgan."

The clerk sighed heavily, but he picked up a thin, dog-eared book and thumbed through it. Eventually he paused and ran an ink-stained finger down a page. Then he snapped the book shut and shook his head.

"Nope," he said, summing things up.

"What do you mean, 'nope'?" Alex demanded.

"Just what I said. No Frances Morgan in the book."

"Look again," Alex said with dangerous calm.

The clerk's face darkened. Alex felt Jessie stiffen in alarm beside him.

"Now, wait," she said to the clerk. "Maybe Mrs. Morgan lives out of the area. Is there anywhere we could find that out? I just *know* you must understand all about these important things."

She pouted prettily and met the clerk's bleary gaze with wide, ingenuous eyes. He seemed to wake up a bit.

Alex's shoulders stiffened. He watched in disbelief as Jessie flirted outrageously with the clerk, actually batting her eyelashes at him. Alex ground his back teeth.

The clerk stared at Jessie. His gaze traveled from her inviting pout to the curve of her breasts beneath the shapeless dress. A leer formed slowly on his doughy face.

He said, "Well, yeah. Yeah, sure. I guess, uh ... I guess you could try Vital Records. They got birth and death and residency records, stuff like that. They might find an old address you could start with."

She rewarded him with a huge smile. "Thank you, Mr....." She glanced down at the bent, grubby name plaque propped on the counter in front of him. "...Drier."

Drier swallowed. With a megawatt smile and another flutter of eyelashes, Jessie turned away, a clamped-jaw Alex in tow. They wove through the shuffling crowd into yet another barely-moving line.

She said something inaudible, her expression dark as a thunderstorm. Alex bent his head so she could repeat it close to his ear.

"I hate those creeps!" she whispered angrily.

Alex nodded. "My sentiments exactly."

Jessie huffed out a breath, folded her arms, and lapsed into silence. They settled in to wait, inch forward, and wait some more.

* * * * *

"James Jackson Morgan. Frances Alexander Morgan. James Alexander Morgan."

Alex loudly, carefully repeated his parents' names and his own to an even more disinterested clerk than Drier. As a hopeful afterthought, he added Jack's name: "Jackson Kelly Morgan."

The clerk laboriously wrote down the names on a grimy pad, repeatedly scratching letters out and starting over, until Alex thought he would leap over the counter, screaming like a madman, and wring her pudgy neck. Finally, completely oblivious to his distress, she turned and lumbered off toward the endless ranks of metal file cabinets that stretched as far as he could see into the vast storage space of the building.

Scowling, Alex muttered bitterly, "Computers down today, huh?"

Jessie frowned at him in bewilderment.

"What's down? Down where?"

He snorted and shook his head. "Never mind. I have to keep reminding myself it's about half-past 1930 around here."

"Well, keep your comments to yourself and just be nice to the old toad – I mean lady – will you? Make her mad and we'll have waited ten years for nothing."

Her small, pokerfaced wisecrack managed to relieve some of Alex's ill temper, but not much of his anxiety or impatience. "You think she'll actually find something?" he asked.

Jessie considered, then shrugged. "I think there's a pretty good chance. If your family lived around here once, they probably still do. It's not very easy to relocate. Anybody wants to move more than about fifty miles away gets buried in permits and visas and who knows what else. Most folks stay put."

"Then what the hel – heck – happened to my house?" Alex all but hissed the question.

Jessie shrugged again, but looked troubled. With no way to be certain of anything, they simply had to wait. Alex sighed and shoved his hands in his pockets. Time all but stopped.

Finally, fifteen minutes later, the clerk returned at an ambling pace. She carried three yellowed sheets of paper smudged with fading, purple carbon ink.

"There's no records on James Alexander Morgan or Jackson Kelly Morgan."

She made this pronouncement with smug satisfaction, pleased to be able to say *No*. Unhelpfulness was her hallmark of a job well done. However, she couldn't deny the documents in her hand, so she slapped them down unhappily on the counter in front of Alex.

"We got Birth and Death Certificates on James Jackson Morgan and a record here of a Frances Alexander, but there wasn't no Frances Alexander Morgan. Here's the copies."

"Nothing on the others?" Alex asked, his voice strained. Jessie saw that the print on the documents was so faint and smudged as to barely be legible. Alex was staring blindly at them, a muscle ticking in his jaw.

"That's what I said, wasn't it," the clerk snapped, clearly done with him. "You want these, it'll be nine dollars."

Jessie reached into the skirt pocket of her dress and pulled out some bills. She handed them to the clerk, who all but snatched the money, acknowledging the payment with a grunt. Jessie turned, nudged Alex's arm.

"Come on, let's get out of here."

"But what if...." Alex began.

"Next," the clerk called, looking pointedly past him.

"No, wait, please, wait." he said urgently, leaning toward her on the counter. "I need you to look for one more name. Please? Just one."

He knew it was crazy, but he had to try. The world was insane, upside down. What if there was a chance his wife was alive? Even a tiny, one-in-a-million chance? If he didn't ask, he'd never forgive himself.

He felt Jessie at his side, her tension palpable. He knew his behavior was making them conspicuous once again, but he didn't care.

He forced himself to smile at the clerk.

After a long moment, she finally heaved a put-upon sigh and grumbled, "Gimme the name."

Alex nearly leapt across the counter to hug her. He took a deep breath around the lump in his throat and said carefully, "Casey Shannon Kelly."

The woman wrote it down – Alex all but mouthing each painstaking letter as she traced the name in clumsy capitals – then lumbered off again toward the vast ranks of files. Puzzled, Jessie cocked her head, looked at him.

"Who's Casey Kelly?" she asked.

"My wife."

For a time Jessie said nothing, seemed not to react at all. Then she slowly nodded, her expression unreadable.

"Jessie," Alex said, bending to her, his words quiet, strained. "I'm sorry, but I have to know. If there's any possibility at all, I have to know."

"You told me you weren't married," she said slowly.

"I told you the truth," Alex explained. "There was ... an accident. A drunk driver. The doctors were able to save our baby, but Casey, she ... she was too badly hurt. She only lived a few hours after Jack was born."

Jessie paled. "Oh, Alex, I'm so sorry."

He nodded, looked away.

Jessie frowned, bewildered. She waved a hand in the direction in which the clerk had trudged off and asked, "But then, why did you ask that clerk...?"

Alex cut her off. "I know it doesn't make sense. But nothing that has happened today has made any sense, either. I thought, maybe since everything's so different, Casey might be...." He stopped, realizing – again – how crazy he sounded. "Well, anyway, I just need to be sure, that's all."

Jessie shrugged. She thought, *if you're dead, you're dead*, but she stood patiently again beside him.

More long minutes passed. People in line behind them grumbled and shuffled, but most seemed resigned to the wait. And though Alex still held his parents' records, he seemed almost to have forgotten about them. Jessie nudged him and said, "Can I look at those?"

"What? Oh, yeah, sure. Here," he said, handing them over.

"Did you read them?" she asked.

Alex shrugged. "Don't need to. I've got copies of both of their birth certificates and Dad's death certificate at home. He was born in March of 1953, died of cancer six years ago. Mom was born in Springfield in 1956."

He sighed impatiently, well aware of the mutters, shifting of bodies, and shuffling of feet behind him. "What's taking the dam ... *darn* clerk so long?" he grumbled.

Jessie shrugged, absorbed in reading the papers. A few minutes later, she looked up, tapping the top document with her fingertip.

"You're right, Alex. Your dad was born in Alexandria on March 16, 1953, just like you said. But you're wrong about his death."

He turned to her, puzzled.

"What?"

Jessie double-checked the document silently, then began to read aloud in a strained whisper.

"James Jackson Morgan was executed by Federal Order in the District of Columbia on June 13, 1970, for acts of sabotage and treason against the State."

She looked up, her expression stricken. Alex simply stared at her in stunned disbelief.

"On ... on the day he was h-hanged," Jessie stammered, "James Morgan was only seventeen years old."

CHAPTER 11

Alex was struck dumb. He understood the each word Jessie said, but he couldn't grasp the meaning of them altogether. It was a terrible mistake, surely. How could there be any truth in such an atrocity?

The execution of a seventeen-year-old boy? By the federal government? In this day and age? It simply could *not* have happened, and certainly not to his own father! The man had been an elementary school principal, for crissake!

Feeling sick, Alex blew out a shaky breath and tried to think clearly. He told himself, *I'm here, standing here, obviously alive.* Had his dad died for any reason in 1970 – and Alex could not bear to consider that it might have been by execution – he himself would never have been born. Nor would have his adored son, Jack.

Alex swallowed a churning nausea. *No, that's not possible!* There was nothing more important to him than Jack. His son *was* alive, and he *would* find him.

But he had to deal with this. Somewhere in this relentless nightmare was the way home, the way back to his boy.

He gave himself a hard mental shake, realized Jessie was watching him anxiously. He made an impatient, dismissive motion with his hand.

"Okay, forget about that one. It can't be right. What about my mother's birth certificate? Is it correct?"

Jessie shifted the papers in her hands. She read silently a moment or two, felt her heart sink.

"It's not a birth certificate, Alex," she sighed. "It's another death certificate."

Seeing him stiffen in shock, Jessie fell silent. As unhappy as she was, she couldn't imagine the agony he must feel.

"Read it," he said stonily.

"Alex...."

"Read it."

Jessie studied his face. His expression was steely, but his eyes were desperate, wild. She nodded, swallowed, and read the document to him.

"'Frances Elizabeth Alexander, born in Springfield, Virginia, on April 4, 1956, to Frank and Elizabeth Alexander of 251 Willow Street, died of complications of scarlet fever on February 7th, 1965, aged 8 years and 10 months.'"

She looked up, her eyes stricken. "Oh, Alex, that poor little girl."

Alex exploded. "That's insane! Why wasn't she treated?"

"Treated? With what?"

"What do you mean, *with what?* With that ... that *pink* stuff." He could picture the little bottle of pepto-bismol-colored antibiotic that he'd occasionally given Jack, and the name came to him. "You know, amoxicillin."

Jessie shook her head. No, she didn't know, and at this point, she didn't care. She'd noticed that people were losing patience with the wait, and especially with the agitated man clearly holding up the line. Uneasily she leaned closer to Alex, lowered her voice so only he could hear.

"Alex, please, I know you're upset, but this poor little girl obviously can't have been your mother. We'll get everything straightened out somehow. Just ... you have to stay calm. And if that stupid woman doesn't come back in about two minutes, we're leaving. You're − we're − attracting too much attention."

Alex scrubbed a hand across his face. He gave a brief nod, hoped he could keep it together.

"Got a couple records for Casey Kelly," the clerk announced, startling them both. Neither had noticed her shuffle back to the window.

Muddled, Alex said, "What?"

Jessie reacted instantly.

"We'll take them," she said quickly. "How much?"

When the clerk answered, Jessie extracted another six dollars from her pocket and tossed the bills on the counter. Quickly scooping up the papers and grasping Alex's arm, she tugged him away from the counter. As soon as he started to move, she dropped her hand. With some difficulty, he followed through the shuffling lines of people, occasionally losing sight of her, until finally he saw her waiting for him at the exit. She shouldered the door open and all but shoved him out.

She urged him quickly across the street and into the shelter of the van, its filthy windows shielding them from any suspicious eyes.

Alex sprawled in the driver's seat and dropped his head back against the headrest, closing his eyes.

Jessie touched his arm. He shook her off.

"Just ... give me a minute."

"Wait, Alex, look. Look at this. There's a marriage certificate here, and unless there are two Casey Shannon Kellys, I think your wife.... I think she might still be alive. Just like you hoped."

He didn't respond, didn't seem to have heard her.

"Alex, *listen!* There's no death certificate here! Casey's not dead!"

"*What?*"

His head jerked up. "Give me those!" He snatched the papers from Jessie's hand.

Alex scrutinized the marriage certificate like a man obsessed. Rifling rapidly through the other papers, he saw Jessie was absolutely right.

There was no death certificate for Casey Kelly.

Oh God, could it really be? Could she – could she still be alive?

Hope speared through him, his fatigue gone in a heartbeat.

Alex flipped back to the marriage certificate and read it yet again, his fingers gripping the document so tightly that his knuckles went white and the paper crumpled in his hands. Then his breath caught.

In the first thrill of hope he hadn't noticed the space marked *Spouse*, but he certainly saw it now. He all but choked on a groan of denial.

Unless his name had suddenly become *Patrick Brendan Malloy*, Casey – *his* Casey, *his* wife – was married to another man.

He laughed. The bitter, hollow sound of it chilled Jessie far more than if he'd shouted or screamed or cursed.

"Well," he rasped, tears in his eyes, "of course she's married to someone else. Who the hell would marry a man who was never born?"

He balled the paper in his fist, tossed it aside.

Jessie picked it up, smoothed it, and turned to him. "Alex, don't. Don't do this to yourself." When he ignored her, she said, "Didn't you see? She has an address in D.C. We ... you want to go see if we can find her?"

Alex looked away, his eyes blurring with tears. He scrubbed a trembling hand over his face.

God, what should he do? What did he even feel?

Confused? Insanely. *Angry?* Furious. *Grateful?* Beyond words. But mostly he was ... *afraid*. He was scared right down to the bone.

If he found Casey in this madness, who would she be? According to the certificate, she was not his wife. Would she still know him? Love him? Or was this woman not his sweet, lost Casey at all?

If she was not, he'd have to face losing her all over again, and he'd had all the loss he could stand for one day.

Finally he closed his eyes and shook his head. "No," he said. "Not today. Not right now."

He rubbed his eyes with both hands to ease an ache so deep he couldn't begin to reach it. Jessie waited, watching him anxiously. The urge to hold him and give comfort was so strong that she caught herself actually reaching for him.

With an enormous effort of will she clasped her hands in her lap on top of the documents and did not touch him.

Alex sighed, his body shivering despite the stuffy heat of the closed van.

He muttered, "I've got to think." She was alarmed at the stark emptiness in his voice.

Finally he turned his head and saw the distress in her eyes. He attempted a smile, managed a crooked grimace.

"I guess I'm pretty lousy company, huh?"

Jessie shook her head. "You're tired, Alex. We both are. We should try to find a place to rest. Get something to eat."

He closed his eyes again. "Whatever you want. It doesn't matter. I don't know what to do anymore."

He looked so lost. Jessie felt tears sting her eyes. "I'm really sorry, Alex. I don't know what else to do to help you, either."

The catch in her voice got through to him, shook him out of his exhausted self-pity. He opened his eyes and turned to her. He took the papers from her and stuck them in his jacket pocket, then he reached out and took her hands in his own.

"Aw, come on, Jess. Don't do that," he said wearily. "If it weren't for you, I'd probably be howling in the middle of the street until they came and took me away."

He fished in a pocket and pulled out the threadbare handkerchief he'd found crumpled in it. "Here, take this," he offered, and pressed it into her hands.

"Thanks." Jessie sniffed and wiped her eyes. What was wrong with her? She knew she was wrung out, but freedom fighters were supposed to be tough and practical and stout and intrepid and ... well, all those things she was determined to prove herself to be. She couldn't – wouldn't – sit here sniveling.

Jessie sighed, blew her nose, and cleared her throat.

"We'd, um, we'd better see about getting some food and supplies and finding a safe place to park the van. We can probably camp in it tonight, but we'll have to ditch it somewhere in the morning. We don't dare keep it much longer."

Alex straightened up, took a deep breath, and started the engine. "Okay," he said. "Okay. Tell me where we should go.

"East, I think. Maybe toward Arlington." As they pulled into the street, Jessie said hesitantly,

"Um, Alex? Uh, just one thing I was wondering."

"Yeah? What?"

"You're not *really* crazy, are you?"

CHAPTER 12

W hile Alex, grumbling about the lack of GPS, negotiated wrong turns and dead ends, Jessie resolutely turned a deaf ear and urged him on. In Arlington they finally found a small, busy commercial hub with a military surplus store. Inside, people doggedly picked through racks of rough, heavy outerwear, bins of shoes, and shelves stacked with an odd assortment of appliances, fixtures, furnishings, and hardware.

With a bit of scrounging, Jessie and Alex found some camping provisions and two marginally clean, secondhand sleeping bags. A shabby market was in the same block, its unappealing stock heavy on uninspired canned goods. When they'd filled a handbasket and tried to check out, Alex discovered that Jessie had been wise to take the money she'd found in the dead man's pocket.

True to the *just-one-damn-thing-after-another* pattern of his new life, Alex's own money was useless.

When he'd placed some bills and change on the checkout counter, the cashier peered at the money, frowned, then shoved it back at him.

"We don't take no foreign money," he said flatly.

For a moment Alex was completely flummoxed. As he fumbled to retrieve the money, some of the coins scattered. Jessie snatched them up, then handed the clerk a wad of bills from her own pocket.

"Sorry," she said to the cashier, smiling prettily in apology. She turned to Alex.

"Never mind, Pierre," she said. "I'll pay this time. We'll change your money at the bank tomorrow."

Alex's eyebrows rose in surprise, but he quickly caught on, nodded, and mumbled, "Merci, chérie."

A foreigner. Jessie had taken a risk with the charade, and the cashier eyed them suspiciously. Before he could decide to challenge them for proper passport and visa, Alex scooped up the two paper grocery bags. He and Jessie left the store as hastily they could without making a run for it.

Breathing a sigh of relief as they reached the busy street outside, Alex glanced down at Jessie, who was turning over several coins in her hand, examining them curiously.

"*Pierre?*" he asked dryly, one eyebrow arched.

"Canadians are still occasionally allowed into the country," she explained absently, studying the coins as she walked. "*Pedro* would have made him *really* suspicious. Mexicans have hardly been allowed in the States for years."

Alex scowled, tried to think of a reply. Before he could, she looked up at him and held out his half-dollar coin in her open palm.

"It says *United States of America*, but who's this guy on it?"

Alex stared at the coin. His heart sank.

"John F. Kennedy," he said.

She frowned, fingered the coin. The name meant nothing to her.

She selected another, a dime, showed him. "And this one?"

Teeth gritted, he said tersely, "Roosevelt."

Jessie snorted, scoffed, "No way. Roosevelt had this fat moustache and funny little eyeglasses. Spectacles. I've seen pictures."

Alex shook his head. "Not Teddy. Franklin."

"*Benjamin Franklin?* Are you kidding? He didn't look *anything* like this."

Alex sighed, shook his head, no longer sure why he was even bothering to argue. Jessie looked at him in exasperation, but she closed her fingers over the coins and said nothing more.

They reached the van, where Jessie quickly opened the cargo doors. The sight of the floor shackles, which had made Jessie shudder and Alex's stomach pitch when he'd loaded the supplies from the surplus store earlier, no longer fazed them. He set the groceries inside beside the camping equipment and closed the doors. He turned to Jessie, gently took her hand and unfolded her fingers. He picked the dime from her palm and turned it over a couple of times, fiddling slowly with it as he studied it.

"His name was Franklin Delano Roosevelt," Alex said carefully, as though explaining to himself as much as to Jessie. "He was Teddy's cousin, and he was the thirty-second President of the United States, during the nineteen thirties and forties."

A wry smile quirked Jessie's lips. Abruptly she tossed the rest of the coins into the gutter.

"Yeah, right," she said dryly. "Bet you got 'em in a curiosity shop." Turning on her heel, she headed for the passenger door of the van.

Without expression Alex watched her go. He bent down and retrieved two of the coins from the street. For a moment he juggled the Kennedy half-dollar and the FDR dime together in his palm, then he pocketed both coins and moved around to the driver's door.

* * * * *

They drove in silence through town. Jessie closed her eyes and rested her head against the side window. Alex glanced at her with a surge of emotion that surprised him. She was young, beautiful, courageous. And everything was insane.

Her reaction to the dime had told him one vital thing – whatever cataclysm had caused this bleak, nightmare world must have happened in the very early twentieth century.

Jessie'd known about Theodore Roosevelt, but she'd never heard of Franklin. It was unlikely Teddy would have become famous much before his stint with the Rough Riders in the Spanish-American War, even though he'd held office before then. Who would ever remember an Assistant Secretary of the Navy? No, whatever happened had to have occurred after the turn of the twentieth century.

It gave Alex his first real glimmer of hope. He knew that era; he'd practically lived it during the long months of writing his doctoral dissertation. Tomorrow he'd find a public library. If he could read the history of Jessie's twentieth century, he could find out what disaster – or maybe multiple disasters – had robbed him of his family and the world he knew.

Knowing what had happened might not change things back, but it would be a start. And it might help him keep a grip on his sanity.

In the darkening twilight, bright lights on a building ahead caught his eye. Alex pulled the van to the curb. Jessie opened her eyes, looked around in confusion.

"Why are we stopping? Where are we?"

"Movie Theater. Look."

TRIBUNAL CINEMA. Alex studied the squat little building with the flickering marquee. *What*, he thought, *Majestic and Bijou were already taken?* Beneath the marquee were a dimly lit ticket booth and even darker theater entrance.

Puzzled, Jessie studied the marquee. *The Guard Strikes Back.* Under that, in smaller letters, some of them missing: *Br d Pit* and *Angelin olie*.

She shrugged, seeing nothing of interest. *The Guard Strikes Back* was so old she'd seen it five years ago.

"So what?" she asked, but scarcely had the words left her mouth when the light dawned. She groaned, "Oh, come on, Alex, a *movie? Now?* I'm starving!"

He ignored her, thought a little maniacally: *Jim, it seems we've beamed down to a world where Brad and Angie are known, but JFK and FDR are not. Fascinating.*

He chuckled dryly, a cracked, unhinged sound.

Jessie slanted him a worried look. "What? What is it?"

He snapped out of it, met her eyes.

"Nothing. Nothing's the matter. We can eat later. Right now, we're going to the show."

She began to protest, but he'd already gotten out of the van. As he crossed to the passenger side to open her door, he looked back up to the marquee. Beneath the stars' names were even smaller words:

Movietone News.

CHAPTER 13

Alex sat in shocked silence as the flickering newsreel played out on the screen. The announcer's booming voice, familiar from archival films Alex had studied in college, crackled from the speaker.

Seattle, Washington! Elite troops of the National Guard continue to clean out dangerous pockets of resistance from so-called Freedom Brigade insurgents. Ever vigilant in their Assault on Terrorism, the Guard stands strong against the heresy and lawlessness of these radicals, valiantly protecting the citizens of the Sovereign United States!

The announcer ranted on as Alex stared at the flickering images on the screen, transfixed by the horror of captured, handcuffed protestors, many of them terrified teenagers, being brutally shot down where they stood. He couldn't bear to watch. He couldn't look away.

Blindly, he reached for Jessie's hand.

When she felt his fingers wrap hers in a desperate grip, Jessie stiffened, but a moment later she sighed and closed both hands around Alex's.

She watched his face instead of the events onscreen. The Guard's atrocities were nothing new to her. They occurred on a regular basis, and her fury at them was one of the reasons she'd joined the Brigade. Did Alex feel that outrage as deeply as she did?

He began cursing savagely under his breath. This time Jessie was not shocked at the words, but deeply moved. She could see tears streak his cheeks. Her throat constricted, and tears of her own stung her eyes. Hot emotion ached in her chest, and in that moment, holding his hand tightly in her own, Jessica O'Neil began to fall in love with Alexander Morgan.

The newsreel scene changed. *President Speaks to Multitudes* appeared on the screen above the Seal of the President of the United States. Strains of the *Hallelujah Chorus* swelled on the soundtrack. Footage, choppy and grainy, of an enormous, bonfire-lit rally began.

A large crowd of people, surrounded by countless ranks of heavily armed soldiers, half-heartedly waved flags and cheered on cue.

Standing on a raised platform before a huge portrait of himself, dressed in preacher's vestments, the President of the United States – the same man Alex had seen on posters – ranted furiously into a microphone, chopping the air and thrusting a fist to heaven as though calling down the Wrath of God.

The announcer's voice-over blared:

Dateline: Washington, D.C. The True-President-for-Life of the United States addressed a cheering crowd of twenty thousand devout citizens on historic Capitol Mall. To thunderous applause the President revealed his anxiously awaited new Edicts. In his own words: "These righteous new laws will eradicate, once and for all, the Constitution's corrupt influence on the justice system of the United States of America!"

Alex hissed an oath, a single rasp of anguish and rage. Jessie clutched his hand, signaling him desperately to be silent.

The President's flushed, feverish face filled the screen in extreme close-up, his dark eyes blazing with the cunning and fire of the true fanatic, his waves of black hair swept up into a lacquered pompadour. A shock of recognition hit Alex with the force of a physical blow. He'd known he'd seen that face before, but he hadn't been able to place it. Now, he knew.

Even before the Announcer wrapped up the news spot, Alex knew.

And so a grateful nation cheers our leader, the Moral Savior of America, President Isaac Sedley Casterson!

The newsreel abruptly shut off, its theme music wobbling to a scratchy finish. The projector stuttered as *Coming Attractions* flickered on the screen. Alex stood up, pulling Jessie with him.

"I have to get out of here."

He ground out the words in a harsh whisper. Dragging Jessie with him, afraid he would be sick before he got outside, he all but sprinted up the aisle.

She couldn't keep up with him. Once outside the theater he began to run. Her hand was pulled from his grip.

She raced after him, stumbling as her ankle wrenched sharply. Jessie hopped painfully to a stop, wincing as she bent to rub her foot.

When Alex reached the van, he slammed a fist repeatedly against the hood, then leaned over, bracing his hands against the vehicle, pulling for air, fighting nausea. His stomach heaved and he swallowed hard against the choking bile that rose in his throat. *Casterson.*

Thad Casterson, you crazy son of a bitch, I knew it! he groaned, heartsick, furious. *What did you do to us with your little toy from hell? What in God's name did you do?*

CHAPTER 14

Leery of risking the light of a campfire, Alex and Jessie huddled on sleeping bags in a small clearing, darkness held at bay only by a small, shuttered camp lantern. A few yards away a broad, shallow stream wandered through a dense wood that Alex was fairly certain had once been an upscale Arlington neighborhood.

They'd spent some time deciding on a safe place to camp. The van was well obscured by trees and they were a good mile from any road. Alex had brought the vehicle in by driving up the rocky creek bed, praying grimly all the while they wouldn't break an axle or mire in mud. When the creek narrowed dangerously, he'd stopped. Jessie had cautiously surveyed the site and pronounced it acceptable.

They'd been too famished to do much talking. Jessie devoured two canned ham sandwiches with scarcely a breath in between, washing them down with a quart of reconstituted milk. Alex put away twice as much.

Sighing, Jessie lay back on her sleeping bag, contentedly rubbing her stomach.

Alex couldn't stop watching the small circles her hand made over her belly.

"Are you okay?" he asked, a little gruffly.

"Uh huh," she sighed, her lashes fluttering closed. "Stuffed. You'll have to roll me out of here tomorrow."

I'd rather roll with you here tonight. The abrupt, blunt lust that gripped Alex took him by surprise. Embarrassment burned in high color along his cheekbones, and he was grateful for the darkness.

He cleared his throat and shifted uncomfortably, but he couldn't stop watching Jessie. He remembered how it had felt to have her small, lithe body wriggling furiously under his. At the time she'd been struggling to get away from him, but now …

Okay, not such a good idea to imagine her wriggling now.

He muttered an oath under his breath. Jessie's eyes popped open and she sat up. Her lips pursed charmingly as she tried to look stern.

"You're swearing again, Alex," she scolded, not unkindly. "It's a bad habit."

"I know," he said, raking a hand through his hair. "Sorry. Sometimes I just can't think of a civil way to say what I'm thinking."

"Well, all right, I guess I can try not to be too scandalized, just this once."

Alex gave her a bleak smile. Touched, Jessie scooted closer to him and tucked her legs under her, leaning lightly against him. It was a companionable gesture, and it eased, just a little, his awful loneliness.

"Tell me about your little boy."

Jessie's voice was gentle, but Alex stiffened at her words, and she felt a tremor pass through him. A long, silent moment passed, and just as she'd decided he couldn't answer, he said, "I've got a picture of him."

Slowly Alex fished out his billfold and thumbed through it, his fingers trembling slightly. He retrieved a small photograph and handed it carefully to Jessie. He held on to it a moment too long before letting her take it, reluctant to let go.

Taken the previous spring at his nursery school, the wallet-size photo showed a sunny, grinning Jack. His clear, bright blue eyes sparkled with happiness and no little mischief. With a deep pang, Alex remembered how much his son loved the ratty superhero t-shirt he was wearing, how he'd insisted on putting it on that day no matter how much Alex tried to dissuade him. He blinked hard.

Jessie gazed at the picture, fascinated, and just like that, felt a deep yearning tug at her heart.

"Oh. Oh, he's so cute. He looks just like you. And look at his goofy smile, like the sun just came out." She sighed. "He looks so happy, so real. Like he's right here. It's a wonderful picture, Alex, and worth every penny you paid for it."

Puzzled, Alex repeated blankly, "Every penny I paid for it?"

She nodded. "This isn't just one of those photos somebody tinted. It's a real color print, and I know how expensive they are. But I'm so glad you got it. Now I'll always know exactly what Jack looks like."

With a wistful, lingering look at the child's face, Jessie handed the photograph back.

Alex took it and stared at it a few moments, his thumb running lightly over the child's face in a painfully tender caress. Jessie watched a dark shadow of pain cross his face, and she reached out wordlessly and touched his hand.

At her touch he seemed to snap back. He nodded, but he said nothing as he slipped the photo back into his wallet with great care.

For a while, neither of them spoke. Finally, Jessie shifted a little, sitting up straighter. She cleared her throat, fixed Alex with a serious, okay-now-we-have-to-talk expression.

"Alex, there're some things you need to tell me," she said. "I want to know about those weird coins you have. I want to know why you think Teddy Roosevelt's cousin was this President ... Franklin. And you told me you were a teacher. What exactly do you teach, anyway?"

Alex shrugged. "History. American history."

Jessie stared at him, then burst out laughing, a peal of disbelief.

"No way! Come on, Alex, you can't be serious! You didn't even know who the President was!"

He rubbed a hand over his jaw and, in spite of himself, felt his mouth quirk at the ironic truth of her accusation. He knew a great deal about history, except what he knew was now mostly wrong.

"Guess I'll have to re-grade all the tests, huh?" he said.

"Yeah, I'll say." She was smiling – until she saw him absently pat his pocket. "And about that little device you carry around – yes, I've seen it. What is it?"

He gave a short, humorless laugh and shrugged. "Sure as hell wish I knew."

When Jessie frowned, opened her mouth to speak, Alex said abruptly, "I know Casterson."

She jerked back, gasped, "The President?"

Alex shook his head. "No, but there's got to be a connection. The coincidence of the name and family resemblance are too great."

"So," Jessie swallowed so hard it was an audible gulp. "So which Casterson do you know? And *how* do you know him?"

Taking a deep breath, Alex took her hand and laced his fingers with hers. She stiffened slightly, then relaxed as his thumb gently stroked her hand. For a long time he seemed to be lost in thought, then slowly, he began to speak again.

"Okay, let me try to start this whole thing back at the beginning. That would have been, um, I guess now that would have been ... "Alex's voice faltered. Raggedly he cleared his throat. "Um, it was last night, early morning, really. I got a call that my office at the university had been vandalized...."

CHAPTER 15

"So," Jessie said solemnly, studying Casterson's cell phone. "You think your colleague Casterson tossed his own office, and this is what he was looking for?"

Alex nodded slowly. "Yeah. Yeah, that's what I think."

"But if he ripped the room apart and couldn't find it, how did you?"

He shifted beside her. "I was trying to set the room back in order. The phone was jammed in the back of the desk. I found it when a drawer wouldn't close.

"I didn't think much of it; it didn't even seem to work at first. When the display screen finally came on, I didn't recognize any of the icons. I'm still not sure what that SYNC ON function does, but I'm pretty damn sure – sorry, darn sure – it's nothing good."

Jessie turned the device in her hands, fascinated by it. *Date. Time.* That strange phrase: *SYNC ON.* How did the little screen light up like that? It was too thin to have a light bulb in it, and no battery she'd ever seen would have fit inside. It was a marvel, but at the same time, it was disturbingly alien to her. Even without Alex's suspicions as to its purpose, it gave her the willies.

"Okay," he continued, "Look, don't say it, I know this is going to sound nuts."

Jessie slanted him an eloquent look that said *So what else is new?* and he shrugged. "Yeah, like everything else I've said, right? But for what it's worth, here's what I think: somehow, using this device...." He indicated the cell phone. "...Thad Casterson screwed something up a long time ago, and I just caught up with the whole damn mess this morning."

Jessie's brow furrowed. "Run that by me again. How is that even possible?"

"I don't know, but I'm guessing the only reason I'm still alive, and am the only person who seems, um, *surprised* to be here, is because I had the device. If I hadn't had it...." Alex paused, his face pale and drawn. "If I hadn't had it on me today, I think ... I think I would've just ... disappeared."

Sick with pain, he closed his eyes, struggling with his grief. If he let the horrifying thought that he might never see his son again overwhelm him, he would go mad on the spot. With effort, he turned his mind away from it.

"So you really think this little machine let – what was his name? Thad? – go back in time? To change history? Or rather, to change what you say is *your* history? Alex, that's pretty far-fetched, even for you."

Alex's head ached. He rubbed his eyes wearily.

"Yeah, I'd have to agree with you there. But here I am, Jessie, in the right time but the wrong world. I know I'm awake, and you're going to have to take it on faith that I'm sane. So, as unbelievable as it is, that leaves the device, or rather, the devices."

Jessie stared at him. "More than one? There's more than one of these things out there? Doing God knows what?"

Alex said, "There has to be at least one more. You have to synchronize *to* something, and Thad Casterson would never have stopped searching for this one if he hadn't had another. I have to assume that he still has the other device. Maybe after he used it to change whatever the hell it was he changed, he never used it again. Or, not yet, anyway."

"Not yet?" Jessie asked anxiously. "So what happens if he does?"

"I don't know. Maybe things will get better. Or much, much worse."

Jessie was silent, worrying her lower lip. Finally she asked, "Do you know how to work this one?"

His expression grim, Alex shook his head.

"Not a clue. I've tried a few times to figure it out, but I can't even get a function menu to work. Tomorrow, when it's light, I'll work on it some more."

At her bewildered frown, he said quietly. "It's something I can do that might help you, Jessie."

Jessie blew out a breath. "Okay, well, even supposing you figure that thing out, I've got to tell you, Alex, I can't help you any in the cataclysm department. Believe me, I'd welcome a change from the way things are, so I'm pretty sure I'd've noticed if something world-changing had happened."

"Look, Jessie," Alex said. "The point is, I damn well *did* notice. And I've got to find out what Casterson did that screwed up everything I ever knew. There's got to be some moment – maybe around a hundred years ago – where the events of my world suddenly morphed into yours. And since all the browsers seem permanently down around here, I'm going to need a library."

Jessie frowned. "A what?"

"Oh, for crissake!" With an infuriated growl Alex lurched to his feet and strode angrily from the clearing. Then, realizing even in his angry haze the futility of bolting blindly into the dark woods, he stopped abruptly and slammed his fist against the trunk of a tree.

When his rage had finally vented in scraped knuckles and an inspired stream of curses, he turned and, breathing raggedly, slumped against the tree in defeat.

Jessie followed him, as upset as he was.

"Darn it, Alex! You have to stop doing that! I can't help it if I don't know what you're ever talking about!"

He gave a harsh, bitter laugh. "Sorry. Again. Sometimes I just...." He took a breath, calmed himself, looked at her. "There's no such thing as libraries, right?"

She shook her head. "I don't know. Maybe there is and we just call them something different. Tell me what a ... a...."

"Library," Alex supplied flatly.

"Yeah, what a ... library ... is." She shrugged. "Maybe I'll recognize it."

Alex shoved his hands in his pockets, his tone grudging, almost unwilling.

"Okay, okay." He sighed. "A library is a place where you can read and borrow books. They've also got magazines, newspapers, historical documents, CDs, DVDs, stuff like that. You can look up anything you need to know."

Though she didn't recognize some of the objects he mentioned, Jessie brightened instantly. "Oh, I see! You mean the ODI! Or a place something like it, anyway."

Alex straightened and took a step toward her. "What's the ODI?" he asked cautiously, his eyes narrowed.

"Office of Dissemination of Information. The main office is in D.C., of course, but some of the larger towns have branches. There's probably one in Arlington or Alexandria." She was so happy to tell him something she thought would impress him that she was nearly babbling.

Alex nodded, but he did not smile. Who knew what kind of "information" got disseminated in this world?

"All right," he said slowly. "We'll try that tomorrow. We also need to find a post office."

He paused, then asked sarcastically, "You know, where they *disseminate* the mail?"

Jessie was offended and a little hurt by his tone. She'd really thought to please him.

"I *know* what a post office is," she retorted huffily.

"Good." Alex rubbed his eyes again. They were watering with fatigue. "I want to send Phillips' ID card to his home address. Let them know what happened to him, where to find his body."

Jessie sucked in a breath, shaking her head.

"Alex, that's not a good idea."

He glared down at her.

"Oh? Why not?"

She swallowed a sigh of discouragement. He just never seemed to get it. She was getting awfully tired of walking on eggshells and spelling everything out for him.

She took a deep breath and summoned all her thin, remaining patience.

"First of all, the mail is censored. Heavily. If you just drop the card and a note in an envelope, it'll be discovered for sure. The police will threaten Phillip's family. Plus, it'll give them more chance to pick up our trail."

She was right, of course. It was all too much. Alex felt drowned by frustration and hopelessness. More alarmed by his despair than by his previous anger, Jessie changed tack and tried to be as encouraging as she could.

"But wait, now that I think about it, maybe we could hide the ID card somehow. We could, I don't know, wrap it up in a postal itemization form or something. Those are pretty tedious; maybe they wouldn't check too carefully."

He nodded absently, but his cornered expression didn't change. Doggedly Jessie pressed on.

"The ODI's another matter entirely, Alex. You have to apply, justify your request, and get special clearance."

Without a word, he turned, stalked abruptly away from her, and strode back to the clearing. He dropped down flat on his back on his sleeping bag and flung an arm across his eyes. His head pounded dismally.

"No, Alex, wait!" Jessie called after him. "There might be a way after all."

He uncovered his eyes and looked up at her skeptically.

Jessie hesitated, then realized that, despite his unpredictability, she really did trust him.

"See, I know a Brigade section leader," she said softly, but Alex heard a note of fierce pride in her voice. "His name is Paul Rudin. I know he'd help us get the papers we need to get into the ODI. They'd be fakes, of course, but they'd be good ones. He could do it, Alex."

Alex sat up, his expression unreadable. "You're sure about this guy?"

Jessie nodded. "Paul works at the main Registry Office in D.C. He clerks there." She almost smiled then. "And believe me, he can be more useless than the best of them." She paused briefly. "I trust him, Alex."

He didn't smile at her small joke, but immediately considered the idea. Could they risk a foray back into downtown D.C.? The place was crawling with troops.

His brain seemed mired in mud; it was impossible to concentrate. God, but he was tired. He drew his knees up to his chest and buried his head wearily in his arms.

A wave of tenderness and sympathy washed over Jessie. The urge to hold and comfort him was so strong that she moved toward him almost against her will.

Her sudden shriek brought Alex leaping to his feet with a shout of alarm.

"What? What is it?" He was beside her in one step, hauling her protectively against him, wrapping his arm tightly around her.

"There!"

Shuddering against him, Jessie pointed to the ground with a trembling finger. "Oh Lord, something c ... crawled over me!"

"Okay, I'll get the light. Just stay still and don't move." He eyed her sternly, as though he expected her to disobey. "You hear me?"

Jessie had no intention of moving. She nodded, shivering, her eyes wide with alarm.

Alex released her and grabbed the lantern. He shone it on the ground, shielding the light carefully with his hand to limit its range.

Almost at once he picked out a slithering movement in the carpet of leaves and moss. Alex's blood froze as he made out the sinuous chestnut and cream bands, the spade-shaped viper's head.

"Copperhead," he whispered hoarsely.

Jessie gasped. "It crawled right over my foot! Oh God, I just can't ... I can't stand snakes!"

"That's okay," he said gently, giving her a reassuring squeeze. "Neither could Indiana Jones."

"What?" She looked at him a little wildly.

He said, "Here, why don't we move your sleeping bag into the van. Would that be better?"

Jessie looked up to the van, and swallowed hard. She'd been chained in that cargo hold with Phillips as he'd died. It was one thing to toss some supplies in there and shut the door on them, but to *sleep* in there.... Still, there were *snakes*. Finally, reluctantly, she nodded.

"All ... all right. Yes, I think that would be better." Then, after a pause, she said, "Thanks, Alex."

Impulsively she rose on tiptoe and kissed his cheek.

He stopped still, a tremor of confused emotion going through him. Touching Jessie as often as he had in the last hour had tightened his body against his will, leaving him hard and wanting. Now her innocent kiss, a gesture of affectionate gratitude, had rattled his control far more than it should have.

Edgy, embarrassed, Alex set Jessie away from him a little too abruptly. As she frowned at him, bewildered, he snatched up her sleeping bag, turned it inside out and gave it a furious snap. He asked her to inspect it, then he climbed stiffly into the back of the van and spread the bag out on the floor between the side benches, covering the leg irons with the edges of the sleeping bag so she wouldn't have to see them.

When he was finished, he reached down a hand to help her up. Even as she stood in the van, well above the ground, she was trembling visibly. Instinctively, against all better judgment, Alex pulled her close and wrapped his arms around her. As her warmth flooded him, his heart kicked in his chest.

"It's okay, sweetheart," he murmured gruffly. "There're no snakes in here."

In spite of the warmth of the night and the still, stagnant air trapped in the van, Jessie shivered against him.

"No," she whispered, her voice breaking slightly. "Only ghosts."

Jessie closed her eyes. She didn't want Alex to see her so frightened, so raw and vulnerable. She'd tried so hard to be a fighter, to live up to her own lofty ideals, and she'd wanted so much for Alex to admire her, to believe in her, to like her, to need her.

"Jessie." Her name was rough and tender on his lips. Slowly she opened her eyes, looked up at him.

He lifted her chin gently, his gaze locking with hers. Alex couldn't believe what he was about to ask. He'd known her less than twenty-four hours. It seemed like forever.

"Jessie, sweetheart, do you want me to stay in here with you?"

The gentleness of his tone could scarcely mask the tightness in his voice, the tension in his body. He searched her eyes in the pale lantern light, saw fear change to hesitancy, hesitancy become yearning, yearning become desire.

"Yes," she whispered. "Yes. I want you to."

He framed her face in his hands and bent his head to her. His lips brushed hers lightly, once,

113

twice, then hunger claimed him and he groaned as he deepened the kiss.

Alex pressed one palm against the small of Jessie's back and drew her to him, cupping the back of her head with his other hand. Her arms wrapped around him and she splayed her palms against his back. She returned his kiss hungrily, surprising herself with the depth of her need.

Jessie pressed herself into Alex's embrace, her fingers digging into his back, his strength and urgency thrilling her. The two of them had nearly lost their lives that day, now she wanted every bit of life she could get. Despite the terror and insanity of the day, and despite all her doubts and unanswered questions, Jessie knew that, right now, Alex Morgan was the man she wanted, the man she needed.

And she couldn't wait any longer.

Her head arched back as Alex trailed kisses along her throat, pausing only when he reached the top buttons of the faded shirtwaist dress. Need gripped him, stronger than any he'd felt since Casey. With trembling fingers he worked Jessie's buttons free and slipped his hands inside the soft, worn fabric, sliding it from her shoulders. He cupped her breasts, brushing them with his thumbs, drawing a soft moan of desire from her. He took her mouth again.

"You taste so good, baby," he murmured against her lips as he tugged at the belt that held her dress at her waist. "So good."

The oversized dress fell to her feet. Jessie kicked off her shoes and stepped out of it. She had no thought of modesty, wanted only to be closer to Alex, to feel his skin against hers. The need to touch him was as urgent as her need to breathe.

In her innocence, Jessie was at first startled, then thrilled, to feel Alex aroused against her. He held her closer yet, fitting his hips to hers, letting her adjust to his body. She gasped slightly, then squirmed hungrily against him, ripping his already fraying self-control to shreds.

He kissed her again with a passion that left them both gasping. Jessie hummed with wordless pleasure.

"Jessie, sweetheart," Alex whispered hoarsely against her parted lips. "Tell me what you want."

"You." Her own forwardness surprised Jessie, but she didn't care. She was long past propriety, carried away with emotion and lust. "I want you, Alex."

Their kisses became wild. All but frantic now, she pulled at his shirt; he grabbed at it and pulled it off over his head. In moments, most of their clothing lay scattered at their feet.

Jessie all but leapt into his arms, her legs wrapping around his hips. Alex went to his knees, his mouth still devouring hers. He laid her back on the sleeping bag. She pulled him down to her, twining her arms around his neck.

"Jessie, God, you're so beautiful."

His whisper was hoarse against her mouth. Breathing hard, Alex pulled back a little, raising himself on his elbows. He gazed down into her smoky gray eyes.

"Alex," she gasped. "Show me how to love you. I want you so much. I've never loved anyone before. I've never...."

Her words trailed away as she saw his eyes widen in shock, felt his whole body go still. To her dismay, he pulled back, his expression stricken. His jaw hardened to granite and he sat back on his knees. He seemed to shudder, then looked away from her.

"What? Alex, what is it?" she whispered, tears stinging her eyes. She felt the blood drain from her face, felt suddenly cold as ice. "What happened? What's wrong?"

The raw pain in her voice reached him as though from far away, and slowly he looked back at her. For one terrible moment his eyes were blank, as though he did not recognize the young woman who lay vulnerable and exposed beneath him on the floor of the cargo hold.

With a stab of guilt and shame that twisted his heart, Alex thought, What am I doing? I must be losing my mind. Casey could be alive!

But it wasn't Casey's shivering body he had pinned to the floor. Alex blinked, seemed to wake up. And realized Jessie was weeping.

He reached down and laid unsteady fingertips tenderly on her cheek, then touched her lips. Slowly he bent down and kissed her with infinite regret, tasting her tears.

Jessie did not close her eyes. Trembling, she watched him, wary now, her breath hitching.

Alex sighed, ended the kiss, let his head drop until it rested against her shoulder. "Christ, Jessie, I'm sorry. I'm so sorry, baby."

Eyes dark with hurt, she shook her head slightly, but otherwise did not move.

"I'm sorry." He said it again, a bleak whisper. He lurched to his feet, turned away, and jumped down from the van. He strode off into the dark.

Trying to calm her breathing, Jessie lay on her back, staring at the ceiling of the vehicle. A few tears trailed down her cheeks, hurt and disappointment ached in her throat. What just happened? Alex had been so excited, so tender, and she'd wanted him with a passion she could scarcely believe. And then, all of a sudden, he just ... left. Left her alone and cold.

Jessie sat up, swiping furiously with the heel of her palm at the tears scalding her cheeks. She groped for Alex's shirt and struggled into it. Barefoot and barelegged, heedless now of any snakes but the two-legged, male variety, she jumped down from the van and stormed after him.

CHAPTER 16

Jessie found Alex knee-deep in the creek, clad only in the baggy workpants, sluicing cold water over his face. He shook his head hard, and droplets flew in every direction from his wet hair. He turned to look at her as she approached, but he couldn't stand the look of hurt and betrayal in her eyes. He turned his gaze away and wiped water from his face with his forearm.

"I'm really sorry, Jessie," he said quietly, before she could say a word. "I don't know what else to say. I don't know what happened. I just couldn't...." He stopped, shook his head again.

"Don't you lie to me, Alex Morgan," she spat at him with the heat of her shame, "and say you couldn't. You certainly could have. I might not have much experience, but I know that much."

She took a long, steadying breath, bewilderment overtaking her anger. "What happened, Alex? Why did you run? Did I do something wrong? Or is it because I'm not her?"

Alex swallowed, a muscle ticking in his clenched jaw. Jessie was right to be hurt and angry. And she wasn't alone. Despite the cold creek water, he was still so achingly hard that it was going to be a long and miserable night. Worse, he felt like a heel for leaving Jessie wanting, for making her think she'd disappointed him somehow.

Is it because I'm not her?

God, how had he made such a mess of things? Casey was his wife, and now by some miracle it seemed he might find her again. He should be overjoyed, full of hope.

And he was hopeful about Casey. He was. So why were all his urgent, passionate, confused, tender feelings for Jessie?

Somehow his loyalties had gotten mixed up. When he was making love to Jessie, when he'd suddenly realized it was her first time, he'd been overwhelmed with regret and remorse. He'd feared hurting her. He'd feared he was cheating on Casey.

And he couldn't seem to say anything other than that he was sorry.

Jessie persisted. "I don't want you to be sorry. I want you to tell me why you stopped, why you left me."

Alex winced. "It wasn't because of Casey, or at least, not just because of her." He shook his head. "I don't know how to deal with the possibility that she's alive. But I ... I wanted you, Jessie. I still do. I guess I just lost my head. I'm sorry." He grimaced at his lame repetition of the apology. "I should never have touched you. I sure never meant to hurt you."

"Oh, well, thanks a lot for your concern," she retorted, angry tears stinging her eyes once more. "But don't you give it another thought. I'm just fine, Alex. And I agree. Letting you touch me was a big mistake." Turning her back on him abruptly, she walked blindly a few strides, then broke into a run back to camp.

Miserably Alex watched her go. With a bitter curse, he yanked Casterson's device from his pants pocket, tossed it up onto the dry bank of the stream, and threw himself down full length into the cold, shallow water. Maybe, he thought, if he was lucky, copperheads could swim.

* * * * *

Alex awoke to the first rays of dappled sunlight slanting through the trees. He lay sprawled on his back on a damp sleeping bag, the cell phone once again snug in a pocket of his damp trousers. They were uncomfortably clammy against his legs; the humid night air had done little to dry them.

He groaned as he remembered the previous night. He had to figure out how to make up with Jessie. They still had a lot to do, and he needed her. He'd begun to hope she might need him as well.

He turned over and immediately groaned as his body protested. He could clearly feel every laceration, bruise and wrenched muscle. His head ached dully and his jaw and leg were stiff and sore. Yet he'd managed to sleep – sheer exhaustion worked wonders – and now he actually felt a small spark of optimism.

"Jessie?" he called out. "Hey, Jessie! Honey, are you awake?"

When there was no response, he rolled to his feet. Absently rubbing the rough stubble of beard on his jaw, he limped across the soft, leaf-littered forest floor to the van.

"Jessie? We gotta get going. Come on, honey, it's daylight. You need to get up and...."

He stopped short at the open rear doors of the van.

Jessie's sleeping bag lay spread on the floor, just as he'd left it. Atop it was a wad of money and a note. Numbly, Alex picked up the note and read it, his heart sinking to the pit of his stomach.

Pain hit him, sharp and hard.

Alex, you'll need this money. Yours is no good. Please don't try to find me. If you need help, remember Paul Rudin at the D.C. Registry. He's a good man. Good luck, and I hope you find your wife.

There was no signature.

"Goddammit!" Alex nearly doubled over in despair. He leaned against the van, covered his eyes with his hand. His hunched shoulders began to shake with grief. Staggered by the depth of his loss – his son, his mother, his job, his world, and Oh God, now Jessie – Alexander Morgan hung his head and wept.

* * * * *

His first stop that day was a busy post office in Arlington. It hadn't been hard to find, but by the time he did, his nerves were stretched almost to the snapping point. Keeping the van much longer would be a serious mistake. The radio was finally broadcasting the license number in staticky spurts.

He'd spent an hour searching the area around the campsite for any sign of Jessie. He'd followed the creek bed back to the road. There'd been no other tracks, and he knew she must have gone that way.

Finally, hoarse from calling her name, he gave up searching on foot and began looking for her as he drove. By mid-morning he knew it was useless. She must've hitchhiked or caught a bus, and there was no telling now where she might be. He didn't even know where she lived.

Then he'd heard the APB transmissions giving the van's plate number. Knowing it would do neither Jessie nor him any good if he were captured, he reluctantly gave up his search, at least temporarily.

At the post office, keeping his face averted from other patrons, avoiding eye contact with anyone, Alex purchased a first-class stamped envelope from a vending machine in the lobby, then selected one of the forms, thick with triplicate copies, from the large rack on the wall.

It seemed to be a standard government employment application. Using a pen he found chained to the lobby counter, he filled out just enough of it with fictitious information to make it appear legitimate. Alex took Phillips' ID card from his pocket, copied the dead man's address onto the envelope, then turned the card over. On the back he wrote a brief note.

Deeply regret to tell you John Phillips died from wounds received at the Civil Rights demonstration at the Fed Bur of Inquis.

Alex sighed and fiddled with the pen. After a moment's thought he scribbled succinct directions to where Phillips' body could be found, then:

He died for freedom.

He set the pen back down on the counter, tucked the card in between the copies of the form, then folded the form and stuffed it into the envelope. He dropped it into the *Outgoing Mail – Approval Pending* slot and quickly left the building.

It didn't take him much longer to find the police station, a fortified military post in the center of town. It stood two blocks from the post office, and he quickly spotted the large, securely fenced parking area filled with official vehicles.

Into the belly of the beast, Alex thought. *Hope hiding in plain sight really works.*

Heart pounding, he swung the van into the entrance of the lot. With scarcely a glance, the disinterested sentry waved him through the high, woven-steel security gate. Alex breathed a sigh of relief, infinitely grateful for the van's grimy windows and the reliable boredom of the ordinary grunt soldier.

He drove slowly to the farthest corner of the lot, where several heavy-duty, police motorcycles were parked. They were sturdy street patrol vehicles, well maintained and powerful. Alex parked the van parallel to the row of cycles, angling between them and the guard booth. Several of the motorcycles were now obscured by the van.

Reaching into the glove compartment, he removed the last of the gasoline vouchers, stuffing them into his pants pocket. He also pocketed the van's ignition key. Might as well make moving the vehicle as inconvenient as possible. He climbed down from the van and moved swiftly to the cycles, extracting the Swiss Army knife from his back pocket as he did so.

He chose a bike that looked nearly new. Squatting on his heels, he began digging out the ignition.

"Hey, you! What're you doing?"

The challenge came from behind him. Alex froze. Then, calming the furious hammering of his heart by sheer force of will, he rose to his feet and turned around to face the trooper who confronted him. He read the name stitched on the trooper's sharply creased uniform shirt: *Brewster*. The man's service revolver was drawn and leveled at Alex's belly.

Alex shrugged ingratiatingly, at the same time palming the knife so the trooper couldn't spot it.

"Hey, Trooper ... uh, Brewster," Alex said cheerfully. "Whoa! Take it easy, man. Everything's cool. Ray couldn't get out here this morning to take a look at the bikes, so Maintenance Pool sent me over instead."

Slowly, lazily, he angled his body slightly away from Brewster, jerking a thumb toward the newest bike with a rueful grin. "Sucker ain't six months old, and it's already misfiring. Wouldn't ya know? Like they say, musta been built on a Monday, huh? Here, take a look, why dontcha. I got the work order right here."

Mindful of Brewster watching his every move, Alex reached slowly into his jacket pocket and extracted the vital records certificates from the Registry Office. After a long, silent moment, in which Alex's shirt plastered itself to his back with cold sweat, the trooper moved closer. Warily his eyes shifted from the papers in Alex's outstretched hand to the motorcycle. Finally he shrugged and lowered the pistol, let it hang by his leg, barrel pointed down.

"Yeah, I can see that. And I know what you're saying, man," he agreed. "We've had nothin' but trouble with these pieces of crap, mine included. Keeps stalling out on me." He pointed disgustedly to another bike in the row. "So can you fix'em up today? How long you think it's gonna take? We could sure use...."

Without warning Alex brought his knee up with all his strength into the trooper's groin.

With an explosive expulsion of breath Brewster dropped his gun and collapsed to the ground, doubling over and clutching himself in agony, choking and retching. Without hesitation, too wired to feel the slightest regret, Alex grabbed the weapon and slammed it into the downed trooper's skull. There was a low grunt, and the man was quiet.

Alex opened the rear doors of the van and hefted the trooper's limp body onto the floor of the cargo hold. He stepped inside with him and pulled the doors closed. A short time later, Trooper Brewster, who now bore a remarkable resemblance to Professor Alex Morgan, exited the van in full uniform.

Alex closed and locked the cargo doors and returned to the row of bikes, Brewster's keys and a small kit of supplies in hand. He found the cycle the trooper had indicated, stowed the kit in its saddle compartment, and mounted, praying that the bike wouldn't stall out on him.

The engine cranked to life. Alex breathed thanks, and a minute later he passed the guard booth, giving a casual farewell salute to the sentry. Dragging his booted foot in the driveway for balance, he turned the bike back out onto the main road and roared away.

He knew where he was going. He'd memorized every word of Casey's marriage certificate. The address for Patrick and Casey Malloy was an apartment near Woodley Park. The certificate was six years old, but there was a good chance they were still there. Alex backtracked to the Arlington Bridge, his sense of direction surer now.

Just before leaving Arlington, he stopped at a barbershop for a shave and a regulation haircut. He'd winced as the clippers trimmed around the cut behind his ear, but the barber, after a moment of shocked silence and a nervous glance at the service revolver at Alex's belt, said nothing and made a noticeable effort to be more careful.

Afterward, as he stared into the mirror while the barber hurried to get his change, Alex scarcely recognized himself. Shorter hair drove all traces of the kindly academic from his features and left him looking harder, older, and far less individual. The line of his jaw – strong, still bruised under the chin – was accented. His eyes, once quiet and contemplative, glinted back at him now, sharp, cold and blue as ice.

Holy shit, he thought, unsure whether to laugh or shudder. *I'd scare myself.*

He took his change without a word and strode from the barbershop. Outside, he pulled on Brewster's helmet and kicked the cycle into life. If Casey was alive, he would find her.

CHAPTER 17

Alex couldn't resist a tour of Washington. The half-familiar, half-alien sights were staggering to him, a nightmare where he couldn't wake up, a fascinating wreck he couldn't take his eyes from. He got lost time and again, failing to recognize everyday places because he constantly searched for landmarks that no longer existed.

The worst loss was that of the Lincoln Memorial and the adjacent Vietnam Veterans Memorial. Their absence, he realized, must have left a gaping hole at the emotional center of the nation. Almost as distressing was the disappearance of the Jefferson Memorial. No graceful, columned dome with towering bronze sculpture stood above the clear, windswept water. The Tidal Basin was little more now than a shabby dockyard, a scummy backwater slick with oil and garbage.

The White House and Capitol Building, however, stood as they always had. So did the Washington Monument, but no line of eager tourists, cell phone cameras clicking from every possible angle, crowded its base. No ring of American flags whipped in the wind above Potomac Park, circling the majestic obelisk.

Many of the Smithsonian Buildings appeared unchanged until Alex studied the signs. What had once been the Hirshhorn Museum was now a Federal Detention Compound. Alex didn't want to imagine what might be going on in the Sculpture Garden.

The Air and Space Museum was still just that, although it had been pressed into further duty as an all-purpose military museum. A banner hanging from the entrance trumpeted the latest special exhibit: *Control and Contain: The Triumph of Isolationism in The Twenty-First Century*.

The face of the city was drastically altered. It was dirty and grim, its streets in poor repair. This was clearly a city under military occupation. Jeeps, motorcycles, and transport trucks passed Alex so regularly that he was becoming eerily at ease with them. No one spared him so much as a glance.

Despite the oppressive atmosphere that pervaded Washington, the streets were busy. People walked with their heads down. Virtually shrouded, they moved at a steady pace, even in the summer heat. No one paused to admire city views.

Alex turned west and then north from the Capitol Building. He skirted the Federal Court

House and Judiciary Square. Head constantly turning to try to take in everything, he suddenly braked so hard that the bike's wheels skidded and the acrid smell of scorched rubber filled the air. Alex never noticed.

He stared in gut-wrenching horror at Judiciary Square, unable to believe what he saw, his breath jammed in his throat. He gulped audibly.

This was a place of public execution. Two bodies hung from a scaffold at one end of the square, swaying obscenely in the heavy, humid air. Alex forced himself to look only long enough to read the large placards dangling in front of their chests.

Traitor.

Saboteur.

Alex's gorge rose violently in his throat and he tore off his helmet, choking for air, fighting nausea. He could hear the pitiful cries for water and mercy from prisoners chained to pillories positioned in long ranks about the square. Sentries taunted them, sneering and laughing. Here or there one beat a prisoner into silence.

A lone, hulking, armed sentry, seeing Alex choke and retch, stalked toward the motorcycle, peering suspiciously as Alex hunched miserably over the still-rumbling cycle. The big man scowled at the sight of a federal trooper reacting with obvious revulsion to the well-deserved fate of a bunch of worthless perps and Freebies. He held his rifle at the ready.

Alex lifted his head, pulling hard for air, just in time to see the guard striding toward him, not twenty yards away. He swallowed convulsively as he fumbled with the helmet, yanking it back on as fast as he could. Hands shaking, he slammed the bike into gear and sped away into traffic. The sentry raised his rifle, aiming at the dead center of Alex's back.

"Hey, Voles, whaddaya think yer doing?" a voice barked behind him. The guard turned to see another sentry standing behind him with an annoyed, belligerent look.

Voles spat. "I was just gonna have some target practice. What's it to you, Braxton?"

Braxton snorted. "Are you crazy? That was a freakin' trooper, dude. Don't you get enough practice right here? You screw with another trooper and there'll be hell to pay for all of us."

Voles spat again. "I like moving targets, ya know?"

He turned suddenly, raised the rifle, and picked off one of the prisoners chained to a pillory. The bound woman jerked, then slumped lifelessly in her chains. The other prisoners froze in terror.

Braxton clapped Voles on the back, comradeship restored.

"Aw, yeah, dude, I know," he said sympathetically. "But you're just gonna have to suck it up."

* * * * *

Alex rode in blind fury until his shocked senses recovered enough to warn him he was circling the same blocks again and again. He knew he had to clear his head and get a grip on his raw emotions. God help him if he accidentally circled back to Judiciary Square. He pulled over to the curb near Union Station, wrenched his helmet off again, and raggedly wiped the sweat and tears from his face.

He hadn't thought things could get any worse, but he saw now that *worse* was just getting started. A ragged sound of anguish, almost more animal than human, escaped his throat.

Casey's death at so young an age had taught him that life was fragile and uncertain and, more often than not, bitterly unfair. He thought he knew all there was to know about grief. Still, he had always taken his freedom for granted. He'd lived with pain, but he had never feared for his right to life and liberty.

Until now.

In that hour Alex's priorities shifted. Given the chance, he would try to find Casey, and he *would* find Jessie no matter what stood in his way. But first of all, before he did anything else, he was going to find out what the hell had happened to his country.

CHAPTER 18

Jessie flung herself into Paul's arms, burying her face in his bony shoulder. For a long moment, she clung to him as though for dear life.

He didn't mind. In fact, holding Jessie had been one of the few recurring pleasures of his life. Still, he knew her very well, and the trembling of her body against his spoke volumes.

Bone-deep relief flooded him. He'd been worried about her damn near to death.

"Well, hey there, Jess," he murmured affectionately, trying without much success to disguise the anxiety in his voice. He stroked her back with a soothing hand. "Wondered when you'd show up. You gonna tell me what happened?"

She sighed against his chest deeply enough to ruffle his shirt, then she looked up into his warm, worried brown eyes. As kind as he was perceptive, Paul searched her face with concern.

"Hi, Paul," Jessie answered, smiling tremulously. She kissed his cheek, then released him with the reluctance of a shaky ice skater letting go of the safety rail.

Paul Rudin was not a handsome man. He was spare to the point of gauntness, his features angular and irregular. But he had an irresistible smile, and Jessie loved the kindness and strength evident in his face.

It was here with Paul that she was most at home. He was family, and she had always felt closer to him than she had even to her parents. Now he and Lani were all she had.

He worked to compose a stern frown on his face. He always had to work at being mad at her.

"Where've you been? I've been going nuts looking for you since you and your idiot friends got your school shut down."

Jessie folded her arms across her chest and tipped her chin defiantly. Just because she and Paul loved each other didn't give him the right to treat her like a stupid child.

"The people have a right to the arts, Paul. They have a right to the free exchange of ideas. I know for a fact that once upon a time in this country there was such a thing as the right to free speech."

He looked at her with a hard, humorless smile, his fond indulgence turning rapidly to harsh impatience. God, but she was such an innocent, such a babe in the woods.

"Yeah?" he scoffed. "Who told you that load of hogwash?"

She stared him straight in the eye. "You did."

"Oh." Paul coughed, hiding a real smile. "Well, I guess it must be true then, huh?"

"Must be," Jessie retorted levelly.

Turning away from her, he moved into the kitchen of his apartment, where he crouched to open the door of a tiny refrigerator.

"But for God's sake, Jessie, you have to be more careful. *The people* aren't going to go to jail for you. They aren't going to step between you and a bullet when some trooper decides to waste you." He paused and looked at her over his shoulder. "You want a beer?"

"No, thanks."

Paul got one for himself and shut the refrigerator door. He turned back to Jessie and regarded her levelly.

"I mean it, Jess. It's not playtime anymore. What you kids did was incredibly stupid. Stupid and dangerous."

Then, almost to himself, as though he still couldn't believe what she'd done, he muttered, "*David Mamet*, for Pete's sake. What were you doing, a Festival of Condemned Subversive Playwrights?"

Jessie walked across the small room to him. He leaned back against the counter that separated the tiny kitchen of the ground floor apartment from the only marginally larger living room. She placed her hand on his arm with an urgency that surprised him.

"I need to be part of things. I'm not a little girl anymore, and I'm not afraid."

"No," he acknowledged. "I can see that. But," he added dryly, "I *am* afraid."

She gripped his arm tightly, until she saw with some satisfaction that she had his complete attention.

"You've got to understand, Paul. I want to work with your section. I can help you. I know I can. I'll do anything you tell me, and I'll do it well, I swear."

His face hardened.

"Not a chance, Jessie," he retorted, shaking his head emphatically. "Out of the question. Absolutely no way am I going to send you out to get killed."

"You're still alive," she said reasonably.

He gave a harsh, derisive laugh, a sharp expulsion of breath.

"Oh yeah, I'm alive," he replied, "But you really want to be like this?"

Abruptly Paul unbuttoned his shirt and wrenched it open, revealing the great jagged scar that ran from the hollow of his throat diagonally across his chest to his rib cage. His chest was badly disfigured, the entire left side sunken into a concave depression where three ribs and half his left lung were missing.

He stared down into Jessie's eyes, his anger deep and stark.

She met his gaze steadily, then gently traced the line of the scar. It had never frightened her; it was simply part of Paul. She heard him draw a ragged breath as he reached down and stayed her hand.

"Don't," he said, a dark edge of warning in his voice. "I won't let them hurt you, Jessie. Not ever."

"Please, Paul, listen to me. You know I love you. Things will be better one day because of what you do, because of the sacrifices you've made. But I'm an adult now. You have to let me help you. If you ever loved me at all, you owe me that much. Please give me a chance."

He shook his head. "I'm not going to win this one, am I? If I say no, you'll just find somebody who'll say yes, won't you?"

Jessie stretched up to kiss his cheek, gently closing his shirt with her fingers.

"I'm going to do my part, Paul. I don't have any choice."

When he didn't reply, she turned away and moved back into the living room. She opened a small cabinet and took out a blanket and pillow.

He sighed. "You want the cot? I can fix it up in a minute."

"No. The couch is fine. And I'll help with the rent, okay?"

"Jessie." His voice held its low warning note again.

She plumped a couch pillow. "Hmmm?"

"You still haven't told me what happened. Where you've been."

She turned slowly to face him, her delicate features drawn with weariness and, he thought in a fresh surge of protectiveness, with hurt.

How can I, Paul? How can I tell you about everything that's happened to me? How can I tell you about Alex?

Jessie swallowed hard, tears starting to burn behind her eyes. She managed a bright, shaky smile and said lightly, "I will, Paul, I promise. But not right now, okay? I'm kind of tired."

He nodded, his dark eyes narrowing as he studied her.

"All right," he said. "We'll let it go for now. But there can't be secrets between us, Jess, ever. It's too dangerous. And it's not going to be that way in our family. Do you understand?"

She nodded and dropped down gratefully on the couch.

Paul set his beer down on the counter. "Get some rest. I'll fix us up something to eat."

She was relieved to escape his scrutiny. Paul Rudin's sharp brown eyes missed very little.

"Where's Lani?" Jessie asked, yawning. His wife was usually home by now.

"She's out at a meeting, trying to organize an operation to undo some of the damage your little thespian troop did, not to mention the full-blown riot at the FBI. Half the town's been shut down tighter than a drum."

He didn't sound angry anymore. Oddly, Jessie thought she heard a touch of pride in his voice.

"Sorry," she said. When he raised a skeptical eyebrow, she added contritely, "Really, Paul, I am."

He nodded and busied himself in the kitchen for a few minutes. He set some water to boil for spaghetti, one of the few things he could cook reliably and therefore one of the few things he ate when Lani was gone.

When he turned back to say something to Jessie, she was curled up on the couch, sound asleep. He walked over and covered her tenderly with a blanket, then leaned down to kiss her cheek.

"Bane of my life," he whispered to her fondly.

CHAPTER 19

After several dangerous and frustrating dead ends, Alex located the main branch of the ODI. He'd actually ridden past it twice, but each time his untrained eyes had seen only the Library of Congress building. Finally he'd actually read the sign over the entrance:

*UNITED STATES OFFICE OF
DISSEMINATION OF INFORMATION.*

He parked the motorcycle and took the steps of the entrance three at a time.

The vast, circular main reading room was nearly deserted. One lone clerk sat slumped in his seat at a huge desk in the center of the room, an enormous pile of documents before him. Methodically he fed them into a shredder, yawning as he worked.

As Alex walked straight up to him, the clerk, a plump, balding man with the eyes of a weasel, looked up in startled surprise. Not many troopers cared about reading anything, and even fewer bothered to get permission to do so. The clerk figured this one must be here on some errand for a superior.

He hoped the soldier wasn't bringing him more stuff to shred. He was way behind as it was. Wouldn't be long before his gutless, butt-licking boss would be on his case again.

"You need something?" the clerk asked in the bored tone Alex had come to expect.

"I want to see the books and documents you have covering the first three decades of the twentieth century."

The clerk snorted incredulously. "You're kidding."

Alex shook his head grimly. "No, I'm not. I need to see them now." Alex had nearly added *please* before catching himself.

The clerk's smile faded in confusion and he shrugged.

"You know the rules, soldier. You gotta have authorization. You got any?"

At Alex's blank look, the clerk sneered. "Nah, I thought not," he muttered, reaching down to shove another paper into the shredder.

All at once he was jerked to his feet by the front of his shirt. With a squeal of terror he felt the cold steel muzzle of Alex's service revolver jammed beneath his chin. In his abject fright he could scarcely breathe, and he was suddenly in great danger of losing control of his bladder. His eyes bulged wildly in their sockets.

"Will this authorization do?" Alex asked calmly.

* * * * *

After the cowed clerk led him to the materials he needed, Alex took the man's keys and locked him in a storage closet deep in the bowels of the building. Alex returned to the stacks, pulled an armload of books, and settled down to read.

It didn't take him long to realize there wasn't as much information here as he needed. The books were not histories, they were works of propaganda, and he had to struggle to separate fact from fancy, truth from invention.

The books did agree that Theodore Roosevelt's Presidency had been ended by an assassin in 1902. There was little elaboration and few details, other than that he had been struck down while making a Fourth of July speech on the Capitol lawn. Alex's head swam. Roosevelt should have lived nearly twenty years longer.

Following Roosevelt's assassination, Thomas Sedley, an ultra-conservative Senator from Maryland lauded by the books as a "Savior" and a "Visionary," assumed the Presidency. As Roosevelt had himself been a Vice-President stepping in for a murdered President, there was, in 1902, no Vice-President to step in for him. Adding to the power vacuum, the Speaker of the House was suddenly taken ill and died only a few hours later.

Alex suspected the poor man had been helped along.

Sedley apparently had engineered a vote of confidence from both Houses of Congress. A year and a half later, in 1904, he was elected to retain the Presidency by a landslide. How this was accomplished, when it was obvious to Alex that such a man would never have been acceptable to the majority of the American public, remained unexplained. However, he suspected the ballot-counting system Sedley had used was the same coercive one found to be so effective in many another totalitarian country.

Alex found the first mention of Thad Casterson in an obviously whitewashed chronicle of Sedley's career, and it nearly brought him bolt upright in shock.

Thaddeus Isaac Casterson was Thomas Sedley's son-in-law.

Following Sedley's usurpation of the Presidency in 1902, his line of descendants had become a virtual dynasty, occupying the White House continuously ever since.

Alex charted the fall of the United States into fascism and despotism by a series of political slogans and catch phrases that gradually replaced true information:

Utopia Through Isolation

America for Americans

Sanctify Our Borders

Decency / Morality / Obedience

Contain and Control.

After a couple of hours, Alex couldn't stomach any more, but he'd learned enough.

There was no question that the assassination of Theodore Roosevelt in 1902 was the pivotal event that had set the United States on its nightmare course. He also had no doubt that Thad Casterson and Thomas Sedley had been the architects of that assassination.

Roosevelt should have died peacefully at Sagamore Hill in 1919. Instead he'd perished in an act of brutal and unconscionable violence in the nation's capital seventeen years earlier.

Alex knew now that if he ever hoped to have his life back, somehow he had to restore Roosevelt's to him.

* * * * *

Lani Rudin was pleased, and vastly relieved, to find Jessie O'Neil sleeping on her living room couch. She kissed Paul and affectionately stroked a stray lock of unruly black hair from his brow.

"I told you not to worry," she said. "Our Jessie's a survivor."

He shrugged, smiled. "I know," he admitted. "It's me she's going to be the death of."

Lani gave him a searching look, immediately seeing the worry beneath the smile.

"What is it, darling?" she asked. "What's she done? I mean *besides* the infamous play."

Paul sighed. He took Lani's hand and idly laced his fingers with hers. "She wants to work in my section."

Lani considered this, nodded. "Then let her. She's all grown up, Paul. She's brave and smart. She could help us if you'd let her."

He studied Lani's hand, seemingly fascinated by her fingers intertwined with his. "Dammit, Lani," he said finally. "What am I supposed to do? You know I can't fight you both."

"You don't have to, darling. We can fight for ourselves."

She reached up to stroke his cheek. Short curls of fiery red hair tumbled over her forehead, framing brilliant green eyes. A sprinkling of freckles swept across her nose. To Paul, she looked no older than the sixteen she'd been when he'd fallen in love with her ten years earlier. It still amazed him that she loved him back.

"There's something else, isn't there?" Lani asked, her fingers tracing the line of his jaw. It was making him crazy. He loved it.

"Yeah," he answered huskily, "but she won't tell me. Maybe you can pry it out of her."

He bent his head to kiss her, but they were interrupted by a disapproving voice.

"The least you two can do if you're going to ravish each other on the living room floor," Jessie said prissily, sitting up on the couch, "is turn on more lights."

Lani laughed as Paul wrapped a possessive arm around her.

"Hey, Jessie," she grinned. "I hear you want to be a saboteur."

"Guerrilla, freedom fighter, or partisan would be okay, too," Jessie replied, only half-joking. "I'm open to suggestion."

Lani thought for a moment. When she spoke, all levity was gone. She was completely serious.

"How would you feel about being one of the voices of Radio Free America?"

CHAPTER 20

The little blond boy playing alone on the jungle gym stopped Alex cold in his tracks. His heart surged in his chest, rising clear to his throat. He moved closer, wary of frightening the child but urgently compelled to get a better look. As Alex crossed the nearly deserted playground with the quietest steps he could manage in jackboots, the boy suddenly turned to face him, and Alex froze where he stood.

Jack. Oh God, Jack!

Did he call the boy's name out loud? Alex's eyes filled with scalding tears, blurring the child's image. He blinked several times, hard, and the boy swam back into focus.

The child regarded him with wide, frightened blue eyes.

"It's okay, Buddy, it's okay," Alex rasped hastily, the hoarse endearment slipping out before he'd realized it. "I won't hurt you."

147

"I didn't do anything!" the child cried. "I was just playing! Honest I was!"

"It's okay," Alex repeated. "Don't be afraid, son. You're not in trouble. I just want to talk to you for a minute, okay?"

"Mommy says I'm not s'posed ... not s'posed to talk to strangers."

"I know. She's right. I tell that to my little boy, too."

The child's alarm eased a bit as curiosity crept in. "You got a little boy like me?"

Alex nodded, the lump in his throat so constricting he could scarcely speak. "Yeah," he said finally, his voice no more than a croak. "Yeah, just like you."

He moved slowly toward the jungle gym. The boy watched, shifting position on the jungle gym until he'd draped himself over one of the top rungs, dangling his arms like a little monkey.

"What's your little boy's name?"

"Jack," Alex said softly. How could it hurt so much just to say a name? After a moment, he cleared his throat and asked, "What's yours?"

Again the child contemplated him silently, and in those few moments Alex saw the subtle differences between this little boy and his son. Still, the resemblance was remarkable.

"*Alex!*"

Alex started so violently at the achingly familiar voice that had he been an older or weaker man, his heart would have stopped.

He knew whom he would see before he turned, yet for some reason he was terrified of facing her. Would she be *not-Casey* in the same way that this beautiful child was *not-Jack*? He didn't think he could stand that, thought it just might tear the last of his sanity to shreds.

But he did turn around, finally, and her name escaped his lips as a whispered prayer.

"*Casey.*"

She rushed past him with a look of stark terror. Racing to the jungle gym she reached up, pulled her son down to her with an urgency born of desperation.

"Get down, Alex! Get down now! What did I tell you about running ahead without me?"

"But Mommy, I...."

She crushed the protesting boy to her, holding him fast in her arms. She took a few defensive steps backwards, glaring in fright and suspicion at the man who had been, in another life, her husband and lover.

"Leave us alone!" she hissed. "We haven't done anything. Please, he's just a baby!"

"Case-," Alex began, then caught himself. It would frighten her more if she thought he knew her name. He began again.

"Ma'am," he said gently, "I don't mean you or your boy any harm. I just need to talk to you."

At Casey's stricken look, Alex's throat closed in an aching spasm of grief. Unlike the child, there was absolutely no doubt that she *was* Casey. The green eyes in which he had so often, and with such happiness, lost himself, now stared at him with fearful suspicion. He knew how intimidating his appearance must be. He extended his hands to her, palms turned out as though in surrender.

"Please, ma'am," he said again, the lump in his throat seeming to grow even bigger. "It's very important."

Confused, she stared at him speechlessly. He looked every inch the Guardsman – tall, intimidating, dangerous. Yet there was something in his eyes that drew her. She knew it was crazy, but she found herself listening to him with something approaching trust. Patrick would never believe this. He'd think she'd lost her mind.

But he would be home in a few minutes. With Patrick there, she'd be safe. After all, he held a responsible position at the Inquisition Bureau and had some significant clout with the authorities. Maybe it was better to do as this trooper asked, at least until her husband got home. He'd know what to do.

"Ma'am?" the trooper repeated. Incredibly, he was almost pleading.

Finally, Casey nodded. "All right," she said uneasily, "but not here. I live just across the street. I'll talk to you there, but only for a minute." She shifted her son higher in her arms. "My husband is on his way home right now. He works at the FBI, and he'll be here any minute."

Alex nearly sagged with relief. She was willing to talk to him.

"Thank you, ma'am," he said with heartfelt gratitude, and Casey looked at him in bewilderment.

"Come on," she said warily. "It's this way."

* * * * *

150

Alex sat at Casey's kitchen table nursing a glass of lemonade and admiring little Alex's collection of toy cars. The boy seemed to have taken a shine to him, and Alex felt an almost unbearable tug at his heart. Unable to stop himself, he reached out and gently ruffled the child's downy blond hair.

Casey tensed as the trooper touched her son.

"So ... what is it you want of me, Trooper...." She glanced at the name stitched on his shirt. "...Brewster?"

Alex looked blank at the name. It took him several seconds to remember it was supposed to be his.

"I, uh," he stammered, realizing that he hadn't actually thought about what he was going to say to Casey if he found her. He figured he'd just know when the time came, but here it was, and in fact he was at a complete loss.

She looked at him questioningly. Alex took a breath and plunged in blindly.

"I'm a friend of your brother's, of Terry's," he blurted out, then almost winced at the crazy chance he'd taken.

Please, God, he prayed urgently, *let her have a brother named Terry in this life.*

Casey gave him an astonished look. Terry friends with a trooper? Well, she wouldn't have guessed that in a million years.

"Where exactly did you meet my brother?" she asked suspiciously.

There must be a faster way to dig my grave, Alex thought, *but I can't think what it would be.*

"Uh, at school," he answered lamely.

Casey's eyebrows shot up. "You're kidding, right?" she asked incredulously. Then she snorted. "That's pretty hard to believe. I thought all you guys ever did was shut schools down, not attend them."

Alex looked up at her in surprise, then, incredibly, he grinned. This was Casey, all right. Four years older than she would ever be in Alex's real life, mother of a son he hadn't fathered, but even sassier and prettier than he'd remembered.

He was sitting here with a loaded gun and a killer's reputation, and she was telling him off.

"Yes ma'am," he said with real pleasure, "I guess you're Terry's sister, all right."

Casey looked suddenly alarmed. "Is Terry in some kind of trouble?"

Alex shook his head, anxious to reassure her.

"Oh, no. No, ma'am. Terry's fine. He just ... well, when he found out I was patrolling this area, he said I should look in on you for him. Just make sure everything was okay."

Casey relaxed a bit. She allowed herself to sit down opposite him at the table. Even though he was a Guardsman, she found him strangely sympathetic. His eyes, a dark, midnight blue, unusually melancholy and kind, drew her. Strangely, they were very much like her son's. She was completely bewildered by this unlikely soldier.

What in the world was this man doing in the Guard?

Alex couldn't tear his eyes away from her. She was so unchanged, and yet there were subtle differences that four years of age and a harsher life had brought about. He found himself studying every line of her face, every stray wisp of her hair. He clasped his hands together to keep from reaching out to touch her. A tense muscle kicked along the line of his jaw.

Little Alex played happily at his feet, running the cars in and out around the legs of the chairs and table. Alex tore his gaze from Casey to smile down at the boy.

"You have a fine boy, Mrs. Malloy," he said hoarsely, her new name absurd on his tongue. "How did you come to name him Alex?"

Casey looked startled at the question. What a strange thing for him to ask! Taken aback, she wasn't sure how to answer.

"I ... well, I don't know, really."

She shrugged her shoulders. The grace and familiarity of that simple, offhand gesture trapped Alex's breath in his chest.

Unaware of his reaction, she continued musingly, "I've just always liked the name, I guess. Actually, we kind of argued about it, Patrick and I."

Patrick and I. She smiled sheepishly, and Alex nearly choked from the pain.

"My husband wanted to name the baby George Lee, but I insisted on Alexander James. It was silly, really, and I can't explain it even now. As far as I remember, I've never even known anybody named Alexander, but for some reason, I just knew that had to be my son's name. Patrick teased me that *Alexander Malloy* would a mouthful for such a little guy, but he went along with it anyway."

"It's a good name," Alex said gruffly. "Besides, no sane man bucks a mother's intuition."

She smiled, catching the Guardsman's gaze. There was something there, deep and unreadable. She flushed, and quickly he dropped his eyes. An awkward silence filled the kitchen, punctuated only by the rumbling car noises little Alex made.

Casey reached for the trooper's empty glass.

"Um ... would you like some more lemonade?"

Alex's gaze snapped back to hers. He didn't care about the drink, but a refill would buy more time with her.

"Yes, ma'am," he nodded. "Thanks."

As she rose and went to refill his glass, he was struck by a terrible thought that froze his heart, stabbed it with shards of ice. If he ever regained his real life, Casey would lose hers.

Abruptly he remembered a line from *Casablanca*: Bogart bravely reminding Bergman that the lives of two little people didn't amount to a hill of beans.

Easy for you, Bogey, he thought in acute, weary anguish. *Hell for me.*

Behind them, a key turned in a lock and the front door swung open. Patrick Malloy stepped inside his house and strode across the entryway, then froze in shock and alarm at the sight of an armed Guardsman camped in the kitchen with his wife and son.

Alex turned at the sound of his approaching footsteps and froze as well. Then he almost burst out laughing.

Well, I'll be damned, he thought with wild, bitter irony, eying the tall, handsome, rangy, bronze-haired young man.

He's me.

CHAPTER 21

Alex took leave of the rather bewildered Malloy family with a deep and abiding sadness, but with no regret. Somehow, during the past hour, he'd realized that his Casey was truly gone forever. Patrick's wife had gazed at him in confusion, and perhaps there'd been some faint echo of connection buried in the depths of her eyes, but she wasn't, and never would be, *his*.

The little boy was beautiful and achingly familiar, but he wasn't Jack. Not *his* Jack. Alex desperately needed his son, missed him with an agonizing grief so wrenching that he had to force it to the farthest recesses of his mind to keep his sanity.

God, but he needed his real life back. *His* reality.

As twilight deepened into darkness it occurred to Alex that not only was he stranded, he was also, once again, nearly starving. The lemonade sloshed acidly in his empty stomach.

He climbed onto the motorcycle and pulled on his helmet. Absently, as he had done from time to time during the day, he switched on the police scanner mounted at the base of the handlebars. The voice that came suddenly from the speaker nearly jolted him off his seat.

"...of Radio Free America. We have a right to know the truth! The government has deprived us of the rights guaranteed by the Constitution. Tonight we will remind everyone of those rights!

"Are you listening, America?

"*Congress shall make no law respecting an establishment of religion, or prohibiting the free exercise thereof; or abridging the freedom of speech, or of the press; or the right of the people peaceably to assemble, and to petition the government for a redress of grievances ...*"

As Alex listened, thunderstruck, to Jessie's defiant voice clearly speaking those great and noble words, all at once he knew to whom his heart now truly belonged.

* * * * *

Before Jessie and Lani had left that evening to do the broadcast from a pirate station the Brigade had spent weeks setting up, Jessie'd taken Paul aside, telling him they needed to talk.

"I have a big favor to ask of you, Paul. It's really important."

"Well, what's one more?" Paul sighed. "What do you need, Jessie?"

Her cheeks flamed in embarrassment, but she pressed on anyway.

"Paul, there's ... this man ... a friend of mine...."

"I might have known!" he broke in. "So that's it! Doggone it, Jess, what'd this guy do to you? I swear, if he so much as touched you or hurt you one little bit, I'll...!"

"No, Paul!" Jessie protested, though her heart ached with the truth. "That's not it at all."

"Uh huh," he muttered.

She slapped his arm lightly.

"I mean it, Paul! Would you cut it out and listen?"

"I hang on your every word, Jess."

Jessie sighed. Just thinking of Alex hurt her almost beyond endurance, but she had to make sure Paul knew what to do, just in case.

She gave herself a brisk mental shake and tried to sound casual, but emotion leaked steadily into her voice.

"His name is Alex Morgan. Remember that, Paul, please. If he ever comes to you, you've got to help him, no matter how crazy he sounds. Will you do that? For my sake?"

Paul looked at her skeptically, scowling at her anxiety.

"Well, Jessie," he said sternly. "How crazy is he going to sound?"

She shrugged, wincing. "Maybe not at all, but probably, well, a lot. But it's not what you think. It's kind of complicated. I need you to trust me, Paul. Will you promise? Please, it's really important to me."

"Alex Morgan," Paul repeated dutifully, shaking his head in resignation. "Might need me. Might be crazy. Well, what the hell, Jess. Sure, I'll watch out for him."

"Oh, thank you, Paul! I'll never forget this! I love you!"

Jessie rewarded him with a glorious smile and a hug so fervent it nearly squeezed the remaining breath from his body.

Lani appeared from the bedroom, toweling dry a crown of damp, fiery curls. She stopped at the sight of a blushing, flustered Paul literally squirming in Jessie's embrace.

"If you're finished twisting my husband around your little finger, Jess," she smiled, "it's showtime."

* * * * *

Alex rode deep into Rock Creek Park, which was now not so much a park as a vast strip of forested wilderness north of the city. The road became a lane and the lane a trail, and when the trail disappeared, Alex followed the creek bed. When he was deep enough into the woodlands to feel reasonably secure, he stopped and turned the radio back on.

Jessie had finished reading the Bill of Rights and was working on the Declaration of Independence. Her voice, tired, hoarse, but as fervent as ever, sounded so near that Alex almost imagined he could close his eyes and touch her.

He hoped they could start over together, but even if that proved impossible, he still desperately needed to see her one last time. She tugged at his heart and mind like an unfinished melody, maddening, arousing, haunting.

It was too late today to look for that guy she'd mentioned, Rudin. The Registry Office would have closed by five o'clock. Alex would be there first thing tomorrow. Rudin was the key to Jessie. He had to be.

Although uncertain exactly what he would do when he found the guy, Alex knew this much. He would do whatever he needed to do, whatever it took to find Jessie, to save Jack, to save the whole damn world if need be, or he would die trying.

In the waning light, Alex listened to Jessie's passionate voice speak the words he'd memorized as a grade-school child but had never really thought about all that much. Now they spoke to his heart.

"...We hold these truths to be self-evident, that all men are created equal, that they are endowed by their Creator with certain unalienable Rights, that among these are Life, Liberty and the pursuit of Happiness. That to secure these rights, Governments are instituted among Men, deriving their just powers from the consent of the governed. That whenever any Form of Government becomes destructive of these ends, it is the Right of the People to alter or abolish it...."

Alex listened until she finished, hoarse with exhaustion, and another speaker took over. He switched off the radio, but despite his loneliness, despite missing her so badly, he felt closer to Jessie now than ever. No matter what, he would find her and stand by her. He knew his purpose now, but to achieve it he would have to fight time itself.

So by the light of the cycle's headlamp, Alex set to work on the clever little device, so deceptively like a cell phone, that had destroyed the world.

CHAPTER 22

Casterson's device dutifully informed Alex that it was eight o'clock a.m., but otherwise nothing had changed. He'd given up working on it in frustration the night before, worried that he would run down the motorcycle's battery if he kept the headlamp on any longer.

With the small kit of supplies he'd taken from the van and packed on the cycle, he cleaned up and shaved down at the creek. Within fifteen minutes he'd done a credible job of reassembling Trooper Brewster.

He climbed on the motorcycle and out of curiosity tried the radio again. There was nothing but static, and disappointed, he shut it off. Ten minutes later, as he picked up the trail he followed into the park the day before, he gave the radio another try.

This time Jessie was there. His heart wrenched with both relief and anguish to hear her again, doggedly reading the Gettysburg Address. She sounded exhausted.

Though her voice transfixed him and he yearned for it to continue, Alex knew she was in danger. The longer she stayed on the air, the better chance she gave the authorities to track her down. He had to find Rudin at once. He was Alex's best hope of tracing Jessie.

When the trail finally became Rock Creek Drive again, Alex followed the narrow, winding road south. A hunch bordering on certainty told him where he'd find the Registry Office. He stayed with Rock Creek until it led back into Foggy Bottom, back to the site of Capitol University, back to the beginning of his nightmare.

* * * * *

In a soundproofed basement room beneath a run-down Y.M.C.A. on 17th Street, Jessie spoke steadily into the transmitter. They had sent her home the night before, but she'd been back on the air at 8:30 that morning.

As soon as Paul and Lani had left the apartment for work, she'd caught a bus and returned to the Brigade's temporary communications room. She wasn't going to argue with Paul again, so it was better that he didn't know. She'd have confided her plan to Lani, but there'd been no opportunity to tell her with Paul there.

Lani had told her they shifted locations, frequencies, and announcers constantly due to the extreme risk of exposure and arrest, but Jessie was hooked the minute she'd started reading the powerful words. She knew the transmission frequencies would be relentlessly traced, but whatever time they had, she would use.

In a dingy room less than a mile and a half from Judiciary Square, Jessie O'Neil took a deep breath and began reading the Bill of Rights all over again.

* * * * *

Smoke still rose in faint, trailing clouds from the smoldering shell of a building that had, in another lifetime, housed Alex's faculty office. He ignored the burned-out ruin and searched the other buildings along H Street until he found the Registry. Passing the main entrance, he turned down a driveway that led to a service entrance in the back.

Several government vehicles were already parked in the small service lot. Alex left the motorcycle in their midst.

He tensed, nerves taut, sweat trickling down his back, as a jeep pulled into the lot and parked barely fifteen feet away. Four troopers got out and headed toward him, and Alex busied himself with a reluctant strap on his helmet as they passed. A minute later, he followed them cautiously into the building.

Paul Rudin sensed the four Guardsmen bearing down on him well before he actually saw them. Without being obvious, he carefully studied their approach. Glancing through the grimy glass of the *Travel Permits* window, where his chief function for the last eight years had been to deny anyone permission to go anywhere, he counted the troopers and rapidly, instinctively assessed his chances and opportunities for escape.

"Close your window, Mr. Rudin."

The quiet, ice-cold voice behind him took him completely by surprise.

Bitterly Paul cursed himself for his carelessness. He couldn't believe he'd fallen for the old distraction routine. *Damn, but he was slipping!* His hand eased into the jacket of his business suit.

"Don't be stupid," the voice warned gruffly. "Close your window and put both hands on the counter. I wouldn't hesitate to kill you where you stand. Got it?"

Paul's nod was only the slightest of movements. He felt the muzzle of the revolver pressed against his back.

"Yes," he answered calmly, but his mind raced, gauging his chances. He'd been arrested once before and had barely survived his escape. He wouldn't be taken again, not ever.

With deliberate care he closed the window and turned around to face the Guardsman. The trooper's size advantage – he had at least four inches and forty pounds on Paul, the grim determination of his expression, the confined space, and most certainly the drawn service revolver convinced Paul the situation was not to his advantage. He would wait.

There would be an opportunity. There always was.

The trooper eased Paul's jacket open and removed the small, concealed pistol. His eyes glittered sardonically as he slipped it into his own belt.

"I'm sure you have a permit for this, right?" The service revolver never wavered from its bead on Paul's heart.

He looked the trooper in the eye. "Of course I do," he replied with acid calm. "Want to see it?"

The trooper shook his head. Paul thought he saw the ghost of a smile, and it chilled him.

"Look," Paul said, sweating now, his voice tight with anger and tension. "Am I under arrest? At least tell me whatever the trumped-up charge is this time."

The Guardsman ignored the question and made a slight sideways motion with the revolver. "There's a supply room in the back. Move."

Paul understood now. This wasn't to be an arrest, but an execution. He swallowed hard and walked slowly past the trooper, an escape plan already forming in his mind. He was stunned when the officer spoke quietly again, almost in his ear.

"I'm a friend, Rudin. Make it look good. The troopers who came in with me are the real thing."

Paul was so startled that he glanced back at the man, but he recovered quickly, kept walking, and began to plead.

"Please, sir, for the love of God!" he begged. "Don't hurt me! I'm disabled. I didn't do anything wrong, I'm a good worker. Please, I'll cooperate, just don't hurt me!"

Alex stole a look over his shoulder at the four Guardsmen clustered at the *Directory* window, harassing a beleaguered clerk, laughing at his feeble protests.

Alex shoved his revolver into Paul's back, urging him to move along faster. They entered the supply room, and Alex closed the door behind him and engaged the deadbolt. There was another door across the room, leading to the parking area.

"Lock it," Alex commanded, gesturing again with the gun. "And please don't try to make a run for it."

As he obeyed, his back to Alex, Paul said grimly, "What is it you want, Morgan?"

Alex's eyebrows lifted in surprise. "You know who I am?"

"You're too polite for a trooper, and you've already let me live five minutes too long. Actually, I was told to expect you to be crazy." He turned then and studied Alex carefully for a moment. "I can't say, however, that I've gotten that impression so far."

Alex snorted, a humorless bark of derisive laughter. He still held the gun leveled at Paul.

"Wait'll you get to know me."

"What do you want?" Paul repeated tersely.

The thin line of Alex's mouth tightened. "I need to find Jessie. I figure it's a good bet you know where she is."

Paul shook his head. "She's safe. You can wave the damn gun around all you want, but that's as much as I'll tell you."

Alex's smile was cold. "You're a fool, Rudin." He holstered the gun, his eyes drilling Paul's. "Tell me where she is."

A different anger, jealously protective, flared in Paul's dark eyes.

"I told you. She's safe."

Alex walked past him. He pulled the small pistol from his belt and handed it to Paul as he passed. The man was almost too startled to take it. Alex opened the rear door, then paused in the exit, looking back over his shoulder.

"Well, don't just freakin' stand there," he said impatiently. "Come on."

Paul had no idea why he followed.

* * * * *

"*...From the prodigious hilltops of New Hampshire, let freedom ring. From the heightening Alleghenies of Pennsylvania, let freedom ring. But not only that; let freedom ring from Stone Mountain of Georgia. Let freedom ring from every hill and molehill of Mississippi. And when this happens, when we let it ring, we will speed the day when all of God's children, black men and white men, Jews and Gentiles, Protestants and Catholics, will be able to join hands and sing in the words of the old Negro spiritual: Free at last, free at last, Thank God Almighty, we're free....*"

Paul's face paled with horror as he stood in the back parking lot, leaning close to Alex's police radio, listening to Jessie's voice, strained but charged with energy.

Alex's pulse hammered at the sound of her voice. He almost forgot where he was as the impact of the words she read swept over him. He was profoundly surprised and relieved that those words had survived, that they had ever been uttered in the first place in this nightmarish world.

It occurred to him then that if great evil often survived, even flourished, so too did great good.

Paul's anguished groan snapped him back.

"Oh God, Jessie, no! Not from the same place twice!"

Alex seized Paul's shoulder.

"It won't take them much longer to trace the broadcast," he ground out. "Where is she?"

Aghast, Paul shook his head, muttering to himself.

"I don't believe it! This can't be! I-I left her sleeping...."

Alex exploded in jealous fury. He seized the front of Paul's jacket in his fists and lifted him nearly off his feet.

"Tell me, damn you!"

All at once, the transmission sputtered into static. Jessie's voice was cut off. The radio went completely dead.

Both men froze. Then, with a wordless roar of desperation, Alex gave Paul a ferocious shake.

"*Where?*" he demanded desperately. "*Where is she?*"

Paul choked hard, tears of horror and self-recrimination stinging his eyes. Reflexively he reached up and clutched Alex's arm, easing the pressure on his aching chest.

"Why...," he gasped, pulling for air, "...why ... should I ... tell you?"

"*Because I love her!*"

Shaking with rage and fear, Alex felt Rudin's fingers dig into his arm in a spasm of pain. The man's face was gray and beaded with sweat, but oddly, some of the terrible dismay eased in his eyes.

"The old ... the old Y," Paul wheezed. "17th and Rhode Island."

Alex released him with a rough shove and mounted the cycle. He pulled on the helmet and gunned the motor into life.

Paul stood swaying in front of him, blocking his way.

"I'm going with you!" he gasped.

Alex shook his head. "Like hell you are!"

Paul reached out and grasped the handlebars with all the strength he could muster, his grip hard enough to blanch his knuckles. His words broke with every ragged breath.

"Dammit, Morgan, think! Where ... where're you going to take her that's safe? You ... need me, for Jessie's sake!"

Distraught and desperate, Alex weighed Paul's demand. Abruptly he breathed a savage curse and nodded.

Shakily Paul climbed on behind him and was nearly flung off backwards as Alex cranked the throttle wide open.

CHAPTER 23

Ashton Harwood, a small, wiry black man, had been dismantling the transmitter. He couldn't have been more surprised to see the kid show up again.

Actually, he knew very well the kid was a girl, but the dingy work pants, faded, shapeless, plaid shirt and battered cap turned her into a fairly credible boy. Ash found himself thinking of her as just *the kid*.

He'd told her he was packing up. Twenty-four hours was all they could risk at one site. She'd begged for a little more time. Ash had broken into highly secure National Guard frequency bands, as well as the public broadcasting channel. It was an almost unheard-of opportunity.

Against his better judgment, Ash agreed to stay on the air. A couple more hours only, he warned her. That was all. His thin, ebony face was stony with warning, even though he had to admit it had been a pleasure listening to her the previous day.

The kid agreed to his conditions, and Ash set to work reassembling the equipment. He couldn't shake his apprehension, however, and he was grateful for the automatic pistol tucked into his belt.

Freedom was a dangerous concept for a white man, but for a black man, the consequences of capture would be unspeakable. If they ever came for him, Ash would shoot as many as he could, and then, if there were no escape, he'd shoot the kid and himself.

He thought he was prepared, but in the end, the raid came with no warning. He had no chance.

* * * * *

When they were close enough to see the massed military vehicles, Paul tapped Alex's shoulder, signaling to him to pull over.

"Drop me here," he shouted over the roar of the cycle. "I'll find you. Go do what you can for Jessie!"

He leapt from the motorcycle before it stopped. Grunting a little from exertion, Paul watched as Alex veered back out into the street.

Alex parked the bike toward the edge of the tangle of vehicles, close enough to look inconspicuously part of the group, but clear enough for a hasty escape if need be. Troopers milled around the entrance to the dilapidated

Y.M.C.A. building, but there was no sense of urgency.

Whatever had happened there was over.

He moved carefully through the milling confusion. If Paul was nearby, Alex couldn't see him. As he turned the corner onto 17th, he came to an abrupt halt. An orderly was loading a gurney bearing a closed, black canvas body bag into a coroner's van. The shrouded body was a slight, pitifully spare form.

Swallowing hard, steeling himself for the worst, Alex moved toward the orderly.

"Hold it a minute," he demanded. It took all he had to keep his voice steady and authoritative.

The man stopped what he was doing, then spat in disgust.

"What now?" he groused irritably. "Dude, it's hot out here."

"Official business," Alex snarled, his hand dropping to the revolver. "Back off."

The orderly's eyes widened and he took a step away.

"Yeah, sure, okay, okay," he said hastily, raising his hands defensively, palms out. "Whatever ya say. Take all freakin' day with the stiff if ya want."

Sick at heart, with a fervent silent prayer, Alex reached down and slowly unzipped the bag. He stared in silence at the dead man's slack, bloodied face, the deep brown of the skin blanched to a pale, ghastly gray.

Not Jessie! Thank God, thank God!

His stomach churning with both horror and relief, Alex zipped up the bag. He had to wait a few moments to find his voice, to be certain it wouldn't betray him.

"He the only one?" he asked the orderly hoarsely, his back still to him.

"Yeah. Well, he's the only one that bought it. They hauled off some kid the black dude here was trying to shield."

Alex swallowed hard, his throat aching. He laid his palm reverently on the body bag, over the dead man's chest, in wordless thanks.

"What kid?" His voice was a harsh rasp.

The orderly shrugged.

"Hey man, who knows? Some Freebie I guess. Heard this dude here mighta been the one messing up radio transmissions the last couple a days."

He laughed, a mirthless, unpleasant snort, then became downright chatty as he relaxed his guard.

"Don't know why they bothered hauling the kid off, though. Might as well've shot her right here. Still, ya know, a kinda pretty kid like that – never mind she was dressed up like a boy – they make good examples, ya know? Gets people's attention. That one'll make a real good show, see if she don't."

Alex barely nodded, black nausea rising in his throat. He fought to steady his voice.

"Where'd they take her?"

"I dunno. Federal Pen?" The orderly shrugged again, shifting impatiently, his fingers drumming absently against his leg. "Look," he blurted, "are ya done with this guy? Ya mind if I get going? It's hot as the backass side of Hades out here, man."

Alex nodded. "Yeah," he grunted. "Get outa here."

The orderly grabbed the gurney roughly and with a careless shove pushed it into the rear of the van. He was starting to close the doors when Alex's grip dug into his arm with a pressure so fierce that the man's knees nearly buckled.

"Ow!" he yelped. "Hey, c'mon, man!"

Alex voice was low and deadly in his ear. "That body's valuable evidence, you miserable son of a bitch. Treat it with respect, like he was your own brother."

"Yeah, sure, sure. Ahh! C'mon, man, lemme go!"

* * * * *

Paul walked quickly across the street, sprinting breathlessly the last few steps to let the Guard vehicles pass. In the congestion of military traffic at Scott Circle, one motorcycle trooper peeled off and turned back toward Massachusetts Avenue. He stopped briefly at the curb and Paul climbed aboard. A few moments later, they vanished from sight.

* * * * *

Jessie emerged from oblivion into another, far more painful darkness, one so unspeakably foul that each breath left her gagging and gasping for air.

The so-called Federal Penitentiary was actually little more than the ancient, patched-up old stone-and-brick D.C. jail. Jessie, like its dozens of other inmates, was crammed in a tiny, airless, stone cell, barred by the impregnable slab of a solid oak and steel door.

The cell was lit solely by a narrow slit in the stone masonry high on the wall, a hole perhaps four by twelve inches in dimension. So little light entered that the near-darkness was perpetual and maddening.

The cell door had a scarred wooden ledge beneath a small, covered slot, which opened only from the outside. Stale water and a noxious slop that passed for food were occasionally shoved through it.

The cell stank of despair, sewage, and death. For those lucky enough to still be alive in the Federal Pen, it gave new and graphic meaning to the phrase *rotting in prison*.

Though depending on how you looked at it, fortunately or unfortunately, hardly anyone here actually stayed alive long enough to either rot or go mad.

The throbbing in Jessie's head was one of the more pleasant sensations telegraphed by her body. She raised a trembling hand and felt the painful swelling at the back of her skull. Ash had tried to protect her, but when the bullets hit him, he'd slammed into her, knocking her to the concrete floor. Shouts, gunshots, terror, and an explosion of splintered light were all she remembered of the raid.

Her head ached viciously, but she felt no blood, so she thought she would probably live. Given the circumstances, however, it didn't seem like a long-term prospect. Overwhelmed suddenly by fear, horror, and nausea, Jessie curled up into a miserable ball and wept.

Some time later – she had no idea how long – the slot in the door opened and a small metal bowl and cup were shoved in. The cover slammed shut over the hole and a latch clanked into place. Jessie lay huddled in misery, breathing around small, hitching sobs. Finally, driven by thirst, she staggered to her feet and stumbled the few steps to the door.

The battered bowl and cup sat on the ledge.

She wiped her eyes with her filthy sleeve and inspected the food. The dish contained some kind of noisome, indescribable glop. In the dim shadows, Jessie thought she saw it move with a squirming life of its own. She shuddered and gagged convulsively. It took a while before she had the courage or stomach to inspect the contents of the cup.

Miraculously, the liquid appeared to be water. She lifted the cup and sniffed. There was a faint, stagnant odor, barely discernible in the wretched air of the cell. Tentatively, she stirred the water with her finger, then placed her finger in her mouth and sucked hesitantly. The water tasted flat and stale, but it was cool, wet, and marginally palatable.

Desperately thirsty, Jessie drained the cup in two long, greedy gulps. She stood there trembling, cradling the cup in her hands. She realized it was small enough to fit snugly into her palm, her fingers fitted through the handle. It was all she had, so somehow she'd use it.

She moved to the hard concrete slab along the cell wall that served as a bunk. Lying on her right side, facing the wall, she drew her knees up until she was in almost fetal position.

Flexing her right arm, she held the cup tucked tightly into her palm. Despite her small size, if she leapt up quickly, one haymaker swing of her arm would put a good deal of leverage behind the metal cup, giving her a chance for one surprise attack.

Clutching her meager weapon, curled into the darkness, Jessie lay trembling. She wept, silently prayed, and waited.

* * * * *

Paul and Alex wasted precious time they couldn't afford going for each other's throats. Paul insisted on raising a team of Brigade commandos to penetrate the prison and rescue Jessie. He was certain the operation could be put together within three days' time. When Alex shouted that Jessie didn't have three days, Paul hollered back that, without a carefully orchestrated plan, she'd be damn well dead anyway.

Furious and distraught, they each knew the other was right.

Alex finally broke the deadlock, frantic in his desperation.

"For God's sake, Rudin, listen to reason! We have no time! Who has a better chance to get in and get her out than I do? You got another friendly trooper handy?"

Too angry and upset to admit the insane idea had any chance at all, Paul shook his head miserably. Sending Alex in alone was hopeless lunacy. It was little more than suicide. One slip and he'd have no backup. He and Jessie would be shot on the spot.

"It's too risky," Paul insisted. "You'd never make it, and Jessie wouldn't have a prayer."

"You're telling me they're planning on letting her live?"

Brought up short, Paul replied in a voice that was grim, sullen, barely audible.

"No."

"That's it, then. Dammit, Paul, we've got no choice. Can you get me papers? Some sort of transfer order for her?"

Paul sighed, raking a hand through his hair in frustration.

"That wouldn't work. Don't you get it, Morgan? They'd never transfer her away from the Federal Pen compound. Except to put her to death."

Alex swallowed hard, his breathing tight. If he got Jessie out, it wouldn't make one damn bit of difference what the papers said. He scarcely recognized the grating sound that came from his throat as his own voice.

"Then that's what it will have to be. Can you get an execution order for her?"

After a long moment, Paul gave a brief, jerky nod.

"How long?"

"Four hours."

And then Paul turned away and was gone.

CHAPTER 24

It was a place of indescribable horror, thick with the sounds and stench of misery, hopelessness, pain. Alex prowled the dismal, bloodstained corridors, shutting his ears to the pleas, moans, and cries from the cells.

He didn't allow himself to think he might not find Jessie, that she might not still be alive, that they might not get out of this place. Such thoughts would break him.

He did not hesitate, but strode purposefully through the cellblock, the *Transport for Execution* order in his hand.

Ain't we having some fun now, he thought, and despite his outer calm, an icy fist clamped around his heart and his stomach churned with dread.

Getting inside the prison had been preposterously easy, as Paul had promised it would be. After receiving a discreet bribe, the duty officer, a pompous, self-important blowhard, had been grudgingly helpful, directing Alex through the maze of interior compounds to Jessie's cellblock.

The first real challenge came from the lone sentry patrolling the corridor outside her cell door.

* * * * *

Officer Roy Seddich was an eighteen-year veteran Corrections officer. He'd found his niche in the Federal Prison Service. He had the taste and temperament for the work – in other words, he was a conscienceless bully – but he hadn't advanced as he felt he deserved.

This oversight, along with many other slights he carefully counted, left Seddich habitually ticked off and disgruntled. He saw no wrong in taking his just rewards wherever and whenever he wanted. Those arrogant sons of bitches running the show owed it to him for doing their scut work.

He'd seen the dark-haired girl brought in just as he'd been coming on duty that afternoon. Despite her ratty, unfeminine clothing, she was a real looker, and Seddich had been itchy with lust and frustration ever since.

He wanted the little bitch all to himself, and by the time the other guards had finally made themselves scarce, he'd nearly worked up the steam to disobey orders, bust into her cell, and do her rough and mean, the way he liked it. He'd show her who was boss around here.

Seddich had just about talked himself into risking it when a friggin' Guardsman showed up with transfer and execution orders. Goddam spoiled everything!

Seddich read the paperwork with sullen annoyance.

"Why'd they gotta do this now? Usually they wait 'til morning," he grumbled, one blunt, grubby hand adjusting the uncomfortably tight fit of his trousers.

Alex sized up the situation instantly. He shrugged, leering wolfishly.

"Well, hell," he grinned. "Reckon the Captain won't notice if it takes a little extra time to haul her down to the yard." He produced a twenty and shoved it into the sentry's grimy hand. "Twenty bucks says I go first. Deal?"

Seddich's astonishment turned cunning. He glanced at the watch strapped to his beefy wrist and calculated as quickly as the lumbering wheels of his mind allowed.

He figured thirty, maybe forty minutes until the orderly reappeared to retrieve the prisoners' bowls and cups.

He grinned, an ugly leer of sly, lecherous glee. *Time to par-tay!*

"Yeah, okay. Deal," he agreed. "But ya get ten minutes, that's it. Then I'm comin' in, and I'm gonna show that little bitch how things really work around here, ya get my drift? Hey, ya wanna learn a thing or two, you can stay and watch."

Seddich made an obscene gesture, then bellowed with laughter.

Alex's breathing was growing ragged with rage. He marshaled every ounce of will to keep himself from blowing out the sentry's brains and taking the risk of alerting the whole damned compound.

He considered his chances of simply overpowering the man, but he was as tall as Alex and, though much of his bulk was fat, easily fifty or sixty pounds heavier. Moreover, despite his crudity, the sentry was alert.

As much as it angered Alex to acknowledge it, the timing wasn't right. Not yet.

He held out his hand for the keys, and Seddich, who mistook the fierce glint in Alex's eyes and his harsh breathing as signs of bloodthirsty lust, grudgingly obliged.

"Just one thing, man," Alex said in a low voice, wrapping his arm around the man's shoulders, leaning in, swallowing his revulsion. "I like my privacy, ya know what I mean? Don't even want to see no eyeball peeking through that slot there."

Seddich looked sorely disappointed, but finally he shrugged and nodded, giving in.

"Yeah," he reluctantly agreed. "I guess you paid for it, huh?"

Alex clapped him on the back.

"Dude, there you go," he said. "Now don't you worry, I'll make real sure you get to be in there alone, too."

* * * * *

Jessie heard men's voices, but they were too muffled by the heavy door for her to make out what was being said, or to tell how many men there were. She tensed on her concrete-slab bunk and swallowed a choking sob.

She knew she wouldn't be released, so they were here for only two possible reasons: to rape her or to kill her. She trembled with the terrible suspicion that it was both.

Her hand tightened around the metal cup as she curled up into a defensive position. With her back to the doorway, she looked as though she were asleep.

In fact, she was coiled tighter than a steel spring.

She heard the scraping release of the heavy bolt on the cell door and the protesting groan as it swung open. For a moment dim light from the corridor slanted in. Jessie kept her eyes closed, straining to listen. Through her eyelids she sensed the change in the light.

The door closed with a solid thud and the cell was plunged into deep shadow once more.

Straining to listen, she thought perhaps only one of the guards had come in, although it was difficult to tell. Others could be standing behind the man she sensed moving toward her. She could hear his ragged breathing and the sound of his heavy boots thumping on the stone floor.

Jessie had no choice now. She would have to take the chance he was alone.

He loomed threateningly over her, and when his hand came down onto her shoulder, Jessie exploded into action.

With the force of furious desperation she sprang up, twisting, flinging her right hand hard toward the guard's unprotected face. The metal cup, clenched in her fist and impelled by the force of her wild swing, smashed hard into his jaw.

She felt a satisfying crunch, and the man staggered backwards with a rough grunt of pain. Adrenaline pumping through her veins, Jessie flew at him in a clawing frenzy, grappling for the revolver at his belt.

He grabbed her, his arms wrapping around her, lifting her off the floor. She fought, struggled, kicked, nearly got free. She heard a grunt of pain when she landed a hard kick on his shin. Nevertheless, by sheer, overpowering strength he subdued her, hauled her against him. He pinned her arms, all but squeezing the breath from her lungs.

At first she barely registered the raw whisper in her ear.

"Jessie! Stop, baby, stop! It's me! It's Alex! Jessie, it's me!"

CHAPTER 25

He rattled off the words in a frantic chant as she sobbed and slammed her fists against him. She was small, but he struggled to restrain her. It was like trying to hold a bag full of furious, spitting bobcats.

When Alex began to fear her mind had snapped and she would never recognize him, Jessie suddenly stopped fighting. She stood rigid and frozen against him, her fists clenched, her heartbeat racing like that of a captured wild creature.

"It's me," he whispered again, his hand reaching up to stroke her tangled hair. "It's Alex. Jessie, it's Alex. I'm here, sweetheart. It's okay. I'm right here. I've come to get you out."

"Al-Alex? How...? N-no, I ... you...." She choked on a sob, then her body shook violently and she flung her arms around his neck with a keening wail. "Ohhh, Alex!"

He held her as if he would never let go, kissed her like a starving man.

"Jessie," Alex groaned. "Jessie, thank God!"

She took his face in her hands and covered it with kisses. She laughed, tears pouring down her face, and she felt his cheeks wet as well.

She thrust her fingers into his hair, realized how short it was.

"What ... what h-happened to your h-hair?" she hiccupped.

Given his trooper's uniform and their dire circumstances, it was the most absurd question he'd ever heard. He laughed and kissed her again.

"Tell you later," he grinned against her mouth, then winced as a streak of pain shot along his jaw.

Seeing him flinch, Jessie gasped in dismay.

"Oh n-no!" she cried shakily. "I whacked you again, d-didn't I?"

Gently she explored the angle of his jaw just below his left ear, not far from the bruise she'd inflicted earlier. She felt him wince again as her fingers found a swelling lump the size of a golf ball.

He covered her hand with his and drew it to his lips.

"Sweetheart, I'd appreciate it if you'd go for the other side once in a while, okay?"

Jessie swallowed raggedly and managed a wobbly, sheepish smile.

"Okay."

She searched his eyes, hardly able to believe he was really there.

"Alex," she whispered. "You came for me."

He found her mouth once more, unable to get enough of touching her, of kissing her, of affirming she was really there and alive and whole.

She framed his face with eager hands, kissing him just as eagerly in return.

"Oh, love," she breathed. "How did you ever find me?"

He kissed her again. "Rudin," he said. He tried to scowl sternly at her. "Don't you ever leave me again, you hear? And if you ever try another hare-brained, stupid stunt like that last one, Jessie, I swear I'll...."

"Uh-huh." Closing her eyes and smiling, Jessie wrapped her arms around Alex and pressed herself against him. Effectively silenced, he hugged her back, bending to rest his cheek against her hair. It was with great effort of will that he finally pulled back.

Tenderly Alex lifted Jessie's chin, searching her eyes. Then he took her hand in his.

"We're out of time, honey," he told her. "Are you ready to do this? Getting in here was easy. Getting out, not so much."

"I know," Jessie nodded. She began to follow him to the cell door, then suddenly stopped.

"Wait, Alex, wait a minute!" she whispered anxiously. "There's still another guard out there, isn't there?"

"Yeah, but you leave him to me." He hoped he sounded more confident than he felt. The son of a bitch was built like a bull.

"No, listen, I've got an idea. It'll distract him, give us an advantage."

She paused, took a deep breath.

"Hit me."

"What?"

"Hit me, Alex! I mean it! He's going to see that I hurt you. You think a trooper would take a punch from a prisoner and do nothing?"

Alex's fingers tightened around her hand. His expression grim and mulish, he shook his head.

"No way, Jessie, not a chance. Come on!" He tugged her toward the door.

"Wait, Alex! Listen to me! Don't you get it? You can't be squeamish about this. If we're going to have any chance at all to get out of here, you have to convince them you're really a guard and I'm really your prisoner."

Alex paled, anguish in his eyes. His jaw clenched and a muscle kicked furiously in his cheek.

"Alex, you have trust me on this! We don't have time to.... Ow!"

Jessie yelped as Alex suddenly backhanded her across the face. He caught her as she stumbled backwards and crushed her against him with fierce protectiveness, stroking her hair and murmuring remorsefully into her ear.

"I'm sorry, Jessie. I'm sorry, baby, I'm so sorry."

She trembled, unable to hold back tears of pain and shock. Alex held her, soothing her, until the trembling stopped.

Jessie took a deep, shuddering breath and swiped at her eyes with the heel of her palm. The sharp sting of the blow was already fading to a dull throb.

She looked up reassuringly into his eyes and took a long breath. Then, without warning, Jessie screamed with rage, nearly stopping Alex's heart.

Shrieking like a banshee, she called him every vile name she could think of. She even made up a few that vividly described the circumstances of his birth and his attraction to sheep.

Awestruck, Alex simply stared at her, but when Jessie started swinging at him again, he ducked reflexively and grabbed her arm. He dragged her to the cell door and heaved it open with impressive drama.

"Crazy little bitch!" he hollered, hauling her out into the corridor. She kicked wildly at him with remarkably bad aim.

Seddich approached, leering, already fumbling at the buttons of his fly. Alex shouted, "Here, your turn!" and shoved Jessie hard into the guard's arms.

Alex fumbled his revolver free from its holster and slammed it into the startled man's skull with such force that he heard bone crack. Seddich dropped like a stone, dragging Jessie down with him.

Alex reached down and tugged her to her feet. She hugged him hard, her cheek pressed against his chest, about an inch from the name stitched above his shirt pocket.

"Thank you, Trooper Brewster," she murmured, clinging to him as long as she dared.

Alex held her close, burying his face in her hair. Even in her filthy shirt and ragged trousers she was beautiful.

"Any time, kid," he smiled, then took a deep breath. "Ready?"

* * * * *

Alex dragged the unconscious guard through the door and dumped him on the filthy floor. As an afterthought, he quickly searched Seddich's pockets and retrieved his twenty-dollar bill.

After all, the fellow was now going to enjoy a longer stay in the cell than Alex had.

It took a good deal of courage for Jessie to set foot back into her cell. It made her feel sick, but she dreaded staying alone in the corridor.

"Alex, we've got to hurry," she said urgently. "Someone's bound to come any minute."

"I know." He turned to her. "Give me your hands, Jessie."

She looked down and saw he held an open pair of handcuffs. She raised her eyes to his, and he saw the effort she made to remain calm. She offered him a small, shaky smile and held out her wrists.

"I'm sorry, sweetheart," he said. "It's just 'til we get you out of here."

"I-I know. I'm not afraid," Jessie whispered, but he had to take hold of her hands to stop their trembling.

Alex should have been prepared for the sight of her abraded wrists – he'd seen them the morning of the riot, after all – but the raw bruises shocked him all over again. He wanted to scoop Jessie into his arms and carry her like a child.

Instead he locked the handcuffs on her wrists as gently as he could. When she bit her lip to keep from wincing, he took both her hands in his and raised them tenderly to his lips.

"You okay?"

Jessie nodded. "I'm all right," she assured him. "Let's do this."

He nodded, gave her a hard kiss, and released her hands.

They moved into the corridor and Alex locked the cell where Seddich lay sprawled. It would buy them some time.

At the end of the cellblock corridor, before they turned the corner and ran into another sentry, Alex pocketed the key ring and took hold of Jessie's upper arm. His grip appeared rough, as though he were dragging her along, but in fact he supported her protectively against his side.

"Go as limp as you can without falling down," he murmured. "And when I give the word, run like ... Well, just run, okay?"

"I don't know about you," Jessie whispered, "but I plan to run like hell!"

Alex needed a moment to wipe the smile off his face before anyone saw them. Pride in her surged in his chest.

"Damn, but I love you, Jessie," he said in a low growl, bending his head to her.

Her gray eyes were shining. "I love you, too," she whispered.

They were out of time. Alex straightened, stiffened his shoulders, tightening his grip on Jessie's arm. She let her eyes half-close and her head loll weakly against his shoulder.

He stepped around the corner into the next corridor, taking long, measured strides. She stumbled to keep up, feebly resisting him, dragging her feet as though dazed with pain, exhaustion, and confusion.

A couple of sentries hooted and catcalled as they passed. Alex strode on in the same steady, determined pace. One of them, a rawboned fellow with a ragged scar across his neck and jaw, fell in beside them, cackling as he jabbed the end of his rifle bayonet at Jessie's back.

She bit her lip to keep from flinching, determined to maintain a limp, half-fainting stagger. Subtly shifting his hold, Alex pulled her closer and moved slightly to the side, shielding her from the bayonet with his body. The guard sidestepped a little, muttering under his breath, trying to outmaneuver Alex. He made a few experimental, thrusting jabs around Alex's arm, always keeping pace.

"Back off, man," Alex growled. "Captain'll have your ass if you mess with his fun."

"Aw, piss on 'im," the guard sneered. Then his tone turned wheedling.

"Hell, you know they're gonna waste her anyway. C'mon, man, let's you and me share." He feinted again with the bayonet and laughed, a high, gibbering sound.

On the pretext of jerking Jessie upright, Alex bent his head and caught her eye. She frowned imperceptibly, cautioning him not to react. They'd passed most of the detention blocks and were nearing the induction checkpoint where the duty officer was stationed. The corridors were far from deserted now. They had to find a way to quickly get rid of the guard.

Alex gave Jessie's arm a reassuring squeeze, then shot a scornful look over his shoulder.

"You wanna tag along and ask Captain Hayes can you do her, be my guest, pal," he snarled, never slowing his stride. "But he sent me to bring her down, and I ain't doing time in the brig for screwing up, ya got that?"

The scarred man blinked in surprise, decided the girl was too wrung out to be much fun anyway, and dropped back, grumbling.

Alex kept on walking, steadily dragging a groaning, incoherent Jessie.

He was forced to stop at the Duty Officer's desk for dismissal. Jessie sagged limply against Alex, moaning low in her throat, as the officer peered first at the papers, then at the prisoner.

"You Jessica Jordana O'Neil?" the officer demanded, raising his voice as though she were deaf. Jessie didn't respond. She let her eyes roll up and her head loll drunkenly backwards.

Alex swallowed, set his jaw, and gave her a hard shake.

"Stand up straight and answer when you're spoken to!" he snarled.

Jessie's head snapped forward and her eyes half-opened. She struggled to focus. "Huh?" she mumbled.

The officer barked his question again, his disgust evident.

"I said, are you O'Neil?"

She licked her cracked lips and struggled to speak. "Yeah," she finally croaked, sagging again.

The ghost of a cruel smile flickered across the officer's thin lips. He studied Jessie's bruised face, then turned his gaze back to her guard. He didn't miss the large, discolored swelling along Alex's jaw.

"Gave you some trouble, did she?" he asked dryly, the tight smile twitching.

Alex smirked.

"Not any more, sir," he replied.

"By your leave, sir," Alex continued. "My Captain don't much like being kept waiting to do his ... duty." This time Alex allowed a crafty smile to tug at the corner of his mouth.

The officer eyed him sharply, then nodded knowingly, and signed the release.

Alex nodded and received the orders back.

"Carry on, soldier," the officer said briskly. He gave one more disgusted glance at Jessie, then shook his head. "As far as I'm concerned, your Captain's welcome to every filthy Freebie I've got."

"Yes sir," Alex agreed. "I know just what you mean, sir."

He saluted, then turned on his heel and dragged Jessie toward the steel gates that secured the reception compound.

By the time they had passed through three more checkpoints, each time having their orders scrutinized by yet another series of mistrustful guards, Alex and Jessie were both soaked in sweat and raw with tension.

When the last gate closed behind them, Alex expelled a deep breath he'd had no idea he'd been holding. He could feel Jessie tremble against him, but her stride was rapidly steadying.

He'd stashed the motorcycle in a maintenance yard with street access, out of sight of the main guard tower. As they neared the yard, blaring sirens suddenly shrieked an alarm. Gathering darkness burst into blinding light. Dozens of floodlights flashed on.

They froze, met each other's eyes.

"Now?" Jessie gasped.

"Now!" Alex yelled, and they ran for their lives.

All hell broke loose behind them. Automatic weapons fire blasted over the scream of the alarms as bullets tore up the ground in every direction. Chunks of asphalt shrapnel flew into the air.

"Over here!" Alex shouted, grabbing Jessie's arm, steering her. They sprinted, weaving and dodging, toward the parked cycle.

When they reached the motorcycle he flung her into the saddle and leapt on in front of her, gunning the ignition into life. Fingers slippery with sweat and blood, her wrists still manacled together, Jessie grabbed hold of his belt with both hands. Alex threw open the throttle and the cycle roared out into the street in a hail of gunfire.

CHAPTER 26

An All Points Bulletin blared out over every military frequency less than five minutes later. Paul, restlessly pacing the confines of his apartment, heard it over the broadband receiver he'd had on for hours.

His face drained of color. Dark eyes hard, his mouth pressed into a grim, resolute line, he turned and strode back into the bedroom. Kneeling stiffly on the floor near the wall, he pulled up a corner of the carpet. A heavy steel safe was sunk into the concrete subfloor.

Paul lifted the circular metal cover and quickly dialed the combination. The lock opened, and he began methodically to remove the contents. Five minutes later, a 9mm pistol and two automatic assault rifles lay assembled on the bed. From a thick manila envelope he extracted five thousand dollars. It would be more than enough for the necessary bribes. He tossed the empty envelope back in the safe and secured the lock.

Resealing the metal cover and replacing the carpet, Paul straightened up painfully. His ruined chest ached and his breathing was tight and strained. Realistically, he knew his chances of being able to carry out his rescue plan weren't good, but he had to try. It was clear from the APB that Morgan and Jessie were in desperate trouble.

There was little time. He had to move.

Then he heard the deadbolt on the reinforced-steel front door turn.

"Paul? Paul! Honey, are you here?" Lani's voice was fraught with anxiety.

Paul closed his eyes and breathed a bitter oath. He didn't want to fight Lani on this. When she called again he answered, "In here," but he turned his back to the bedroom door and began with steady deliberation to pack the weapons into a duffel bag.

Lani burst into the room.

"Oh God, I just heard! Paul, there's an all-call out on Jessie! She's...."

She stopped in her tracks, eyes narrowing at the sight of the rifles.

"Paul, my God," she hissed. "What are you thinking? You can't...."

He turned to face her, his expression distraught. Anger, fear, and determination played across his gaunt features.

"What else can I do, Lani?" he said. "They have no more time."

With a cry Lani crossed the room and went into his arms. As Paul clung to her with a desperation that squeezed her heart, she reached up and framed his beloved face in her hands.

"There's still a chance, Paul! They haven't been caught yet. It's going to be hard, but we've got to wait. Don't you see? You nearly died once, and I couldn't stand it. Not again."

He shook his head. "But maybe I could ... "

She stopped his words with her fingertips, her eyes filling with tears.

"No, love, please. Please wait a little longer. Give them a chance. And I promise, if we hear that they've been captured, I won't ask you not to go."

With a shuddering sigh, Paul nodded and buried his face in Lani's hair.

Her hands lay against his chest, and as she felt the ropy ridge of scar tissue beneath her palms, she wondered if she could ever find the strength to keep that promise. As though it were yesterday Lani could see that terrible night that had nearly ended Paul's life. How could he ever survive such an ordeal again? How could she?

* * * * *

The January evening long ago was bitterly cold. Sixteen-year-old Alana Clifford stood shivering at the back door, impatiently calling the dog for the fifth time. Of all the times for Rufus to decide to wander away!

Lani knew she shouldn't have let him out in the first place. They'd all heard the spurts of gunfire from Bethesda High School half an hour earlier. Her father had been beside himself with rage and despair.

199

"Stupidity! It's criminal stupidity!" he'd shouted. "Why doesn't anybody listen to reason?"

Despite the warnings of the teachers and many parents, the rally had taken place. Now they could hear the result.

Lani never told her father that she'd almost gone to the rally herself. During her three years at Bethesda High, she'd occasionally heard rumors of Resistance groups organizing on campus. In fact, just before Christmas, she'd made friends with a boy in her math class who'd bragged of being in the newly formed Freedom Brigade.

She doubted he was – it was too dangerous a thing to talk about freely – but she was impressed and intrigued nonetheless. Their friendship had grown, and for the last week he'd tried to persuade her to go to the demonstration with him. She wanted to, but she was afraid.

Her dad got so completely ripped on the subject of demonstrations and protesters that it gave her pause. He growled that he was sick and tired of patching up idiotic agitators just so they could be taken out and hanged, or shot all over again.

"Alana, leave the dog and get in here! Shut the door, for goodness sake! It's freezing, and it's not safe out there!" Her mother's frightened voice reached her from the living room.

"I'm coming, Mom. And I'm okay. It's quiet out here now."

But she wasn't so sure it was okay. Lani pulled the door in a fraction more and stood half-sheltered behind it. She hated to give up on her pet. What if something had happened to him?

"Rufus," she called again softly. "Come on, boy! Good boy! Here, Rufus!"

She was rewarded by a sharp bark, then an agitated whine.

"Come, Rufus!" She called him now with real urgency.

Rufus whined again. Lani squinted her eyes in the falling darkness and could just make out the dog's shaggy form. He was digging and pawing at the edge of the frozen garden near the backyard fence, under the old apple tree.

Shivering, Lani stepped out onto the slush-covered porch and made her way across the muddy, icy yard. She stopped in horror when she saw the object of Rufus' intense interest.

A dead man lay in the garden.

After the initial shock, Lani's curiosity took over and she inched closer to inspect the body.

He wasn't a man, just a boy, really, lying in a mess of snow, dirt, and dark, pooled blood. His entire chest seemed to be one gaping hole, and Lani quickly averted her eyes from the gruesome wound. She looked at his face, and was stunned to realize she knew him.

He wasn't really a friend, just a kid she recognized from school. He'd graduated the year before, but even before that they hadn't hung out in the same circles. Vaguely she thought his name might be Paul.

Lani crouched beside the boy's body and gently touched his cheek, cold and white as marble in the faint moonlight. Suddenly he stirred beneath her hand, a gurgling moan rasping in his throat. Lani leapt to her feet with a choked cry.

Her father came running, and she would never forget what he did that night. Something hard and determined came into his ruddy face as he examined the dying boy lying under the bare branches of the apple tree. He said only three words: "Lani, quit crying." Then he lifted the boy in his arms, ignoring the blood that soaked his own clothes, and carried him into the house.

Paul's agonizing recovery was not rapid. For months he lay in the small, hidden room behind the kitchen in the Cliffords' house, hovering between life and death.

Of course, his last name had not been Rudin then, but a change of identity had been necessary once they'd been sure he would live. Otherwise he'd never have been able to find housing or employment, certainly not in a government office, nor would he ever have been free from persecution and the threat of recapture and execution.

From the hospital where he was Chief of Surgery, Dr. Clifford had stolen the pitifully inadequate drugs and medical supplies that – thanks to his patience and extraordinary skill – had saved Paul's life. He had also secretly procured the papers that turned Paul O'Neil into Paul Rudin.

Gradually, the doctor's daughter came not only to admire but to love the wounded boy, a youth bold in heart and gentle in spirit. And so it was to the bed of a barely-recovered Paul Rudin that Lani had first gone one early summer night so many years ago, in the hidden room behind the kitchen door.

* * * * *

"Please, Paul," Lani whispered now. "Will you wait for more word of Jessie? Just a little longer?"

There was a long and aching silence, and then, against her hair where his cheek was pressed, Lani felt him nod.

CHAPTER 27

Alex and Jessie led a wild and deadly parade. Racing recklessly toward the Potomac bridges, they were cut off by the National Guard at every turn. Alex managed to evade the vehicles and gunfire that relentlessly dogged them by plowing straight across West Potomac Park and the Ellipse, but they were intercepted again along the north side of the White House. The troops apparently had no qualms whatsoever about opening fire in the President's front yard.

Executing a tire-shredding turn, terrified that Jessie's back was unprotected as she clung like a cocklebur behind him on the bike, Alex sped up Pennsylvania Avenue, wildly dodging the mass of military traffic that bore down on them all at once, from every direction.

He drove in the street, on the curb, over plazas and dividers, and even on the sidewalk, sending pedestrians leaping frantically out of the way. Alex hoped that if they could just make it to the thick wilderness of Rock Creek Park, they might lose the Guard long enough to ditch the cycle and escape on foot.

Slim-to-none chance, he feared, but better than the odds they faced on the bike.

As if in answer to a prayer, he saw the gorge of Rock Creek open up below the roadway just ahead and to the right. Alex gunned the motorcycle and leaned hard into a nearly one-eighty turn, skidding toward a dirt access road that plummeted down the slope of the canyon from the opposite side of the overpass.

All at once the explosive stutter of a machine gun erupted ahead of them. A gun-mounted jeep bore down on them at high speed from the far end of the overpass, strafing the roadway with a deadly hail of fire.

A ferocious blow like the kick of a mule stunned Alex, sending hot pain shooting through his left arm and shoulder. The force of the impact slammed him backward against Jessie's chest, and for a few horrifying seconds he lost control of the bike. It canted and spun into a long, harrowing skid, sparks flying from the ground where metal scraped concrete.

Jessie screamed his name and shoved her left foot to the ground. Instinctively Alex slammed his booted leg down beside hers. Miraculously, they righted the bike, but it continued skidding directly into the path of the jeep.

As the motorcycle and its riders careened toward him in a cloud of dust and sparks, the jeep driver screamed and swerved hard, his foot stomping accidentally on the accelerator. In a blur of speed that strangely mimicked slow motion, the jeep smashed through the overpass barrier and soared into an arcing descent to the gorge below. Impact sent a blazing fireball fifty feet into the air.

Struggling to gain control, half-blinded by dust and sweat, his left arm now nearly useless, Alex wrenched the bike off the roadway. For fifty yards it bounced and skidded on and off the dirt access trail. When, with Jessie's help, the cycle finally stabilized, he accelerated quickly, pushing it hard down the side of the canyon, past the burning wreck of the jeep.

Following the creek bed, the motorcycle bucking and swerving over the rocky ground, they sped toward the forest where Alex had found sanctuary the night before. Jessie clutched his belt with white-knuckled fists as she held on for dear life, adrenaline flooding her trembling body.

Behind and above them, sirens wailed.

* * * * *

When the radio in the living room announced that the escaped prisoner O'Neil and rogue trooper Brewster had been killed in an explosion at the Pennsylvania Avenue overpass at Rock Creek, a wrenching cry of such grief and despair tore from Paul's throat that, for one terrifying moment, Lani feared he'd lost his mind.

Tears streaming down her cheeks, she wrapped her arms around her husband, but he pulled away and stumbled into the bedroom, slamming the door behind him. From behind the door came another howl of desolation and rage that turned her blood to ice.

"Paul!" she cried. "Oh, God, Paul, I'm so sorry!"

She pulled open the door and flung herself into his arms, frantic to ease his grief and guilt. But the moment she saw his ravaged eyes, she knew she could only hold him.

* * * * *

There could be no sleep for them that night. Paul lay in rigid exhaustion, holding Lani to him with fierce protectiveness. For the first time in his life, he was unable to find comfort in her words or her touch. He lay staring at the ceiling, eyes red and raw, cursing himself for letting Jessie go.

Why had she had to grow up? If only he'd been able to keep her safe from harm a few more years. His youth had perished, torn from him in pain and blood. Why couldn't hers have been spared?

God, how much did he have to sacrifice? Jessie's loss was more painful to him than any wound he'd ever suffered. He'd known the risks, but somehow he'd never really believed anything terrible could happen to either Jessie or Lani.

The thought that his wife might one day be taken from him as Jessie had nearly unhinged Paul with agony. With a ragged groan he pulled

Lani as close as he could against his chest, his arms tightening about her until they ached.

* * * * *

When it came, the rapid pounding on the front door startled, but didn't surprise them. The authorities had traced Jessie back to Paul. He and Lani had known it would only be a matter of time.

Lani slipped her husband's small .22 automatic from beneath her pillow. Paul rose quickly from bed, dragged on a rumpled pair of khakis, and retrieved the 9-millimeter from the dresser where he'd placed it earlier.

Leaving Lani barricaded in the bedroom, Paul padded through the darkness to the front door. The pounding grew more insistent.

"Dammit, Paul! You open this door right now! Please, Paul! It's me!"

Through the door, Jessie's hoarse, urgent voice flooded Paul with overwhelming relief.

He shoved the gun into his waistband and flung open the door, hauling her into his arms with nearly delirious joy.

"Jessie! You're alive! Thank God! Thank God!"

Paul hugged her and spun her around dizzily. "I can't believe it! Oh, God, Jessie, we thought you were dead!"

Lani ran up to them, laughing and crying all at once. She threw her arms around both of them and they clung together almost giddily, until all at once Paul stiffened and held Jessie away from him, his dark eyes swiftly scanning her head to toe.

He'd realized with sudden, sick horror that the stains smearing her filthy shirt were blood.

"You're bleeding! Oh God, Jessie, where are you hurt?" He turned desperately to his wife. "Lani, quick, get the med kit!" Even as he spoke he was shoving Jessie's sleeves up high on her arms, searching for any sign of injury.

Lani started toward the bathroom at once, but Jessie's hand darted out to grab her arm.

"No, Lani, wait! Paul, it isn't me. I'm okay." When Paul tugged her back and gripped her face in his hands, Jessie shook her head and insisted, "I'm not hurt. But Alex is! He needs help. You've got to come with me! I'll show you where."

She took their hands, dragging Paul and Lani from the apartment and up the small flight of cement steps that led to an exterior walkway.

"Come on!" Jessie whispered anxiously. "It's this way. We have to hurry! He's lost a lot of blood."

She led them to a weedy vacant lot next to the apartment building. In a corner, hidden in deep night shadows and screened by a row of thorny, untended hedges, Alex sat slumped against a low stone wall.

When he heard them approach, Alex lurched drunkenly to his feet, cradling his left arm against his side. His head spun, vision blurring. Jessie's anxious face was visible in the moonlight, and he tried to focus on it.

Pain throbbed along his entire left side from neck to hip. He gasped and bit back a groan as his knees nearly buckled again.

His sleeve was soaked with blood.

Jessie ran to his side, slipping her arms around his waist, bracing him as he swayed against her.

"It's all right, Alex," she whispered. "Hold on, we're home now. You'll be all right."

He stared at her blankly. Desperately Jessie turned to Paul.

"You'll have to help him, Paul. He can't walk any more. It took us hours to get here."

"Morgan ... Good God," Paul said, appalled. He took a step toward Alex, reaching out to help support him. Alex gestured dismissively with his good hand.

"'S all right," he muttered, his words slurring. "Jus' looks messy. Hurts, but I c'n walk okay."

He took a step forward and his face drained of all color, turning chalk white. Eyes widening with a stricken expression, Alex shook his head as though puzzled.

"Well, maybe ... not," he mumbled, and slumped to the ground before Paul could catch him.

CHAPTER 28

By the time the three of them half-carried, half-dragged Alex into the hidden basement rooms concealed behind a floor-to-ceiling bookcase in the Rudins' apartment, he was beginning to come around. He slumped heavily in an old kitchen chair, folded his arms wearily on the scarred wooden dining table and lay down his head. He took deep, shuddering breaths, and slowly his dizziness passed, but he hardly had the strength to raise his head.

"Just rest now, Mr. Morgan," Lani said, giving a gentle, reassuring squeeze to his uninjured shoulder. "Jessie will help you get cleaned up, and I'll send Paul down with some food and medicine."

Instinctively Alex trusted the calm, whiskey-voiced redhead who offered sanctuary, even though he had no idea who she was. He mumbled thanks, closed his eyes again.

Jessie stepped into the small utility room that served as bathroom in the basement. A minute or two later she reappeared carrying a bowl of warm water and several towels. She set them down on the old table, pulled a chair up beside Alex on his left side, touched his cheek with her fingertips.

The cold pallor of his skin worried her, and she prayed his injury wasn't too serious.

"Alex," she said firmly, hiding her distress. "Sit up now. I need to clean the wound. Can you help me get your shirt off?"

"Inna minute," he muttered, and Jessie saw him slipping away again.

"No," she told him sternly. "Not in a minute. Now."

She helped him sit up straight. He winced but didn't protest. Vaguely, with one hand, he began to fumble unsuccessfully with the buttons of his shirt.

Jessie gently pushed Alex's hand away, unbuttoned his shirt for him, and tugged it from his waistband. Wringing out a clean cloth, she gingerly soaked the material around his shoulder until the fabric came free from the wound.

Alex flinched, pulling in a hissing breath. His body quivered, but Jessie bit her lip and pressed on.

The wound wasn't as bad as it might have been, but it was bad enough. She knew it would bother him for days to come. The bullet had grazed his upper arm two or three inches below the shoulder, leaving a raw, jagged gash.

The gash was bloody and painful, but not too deep. Cleaned up, rested and fed, he would be on his feet again before long.

Paul came down the stairs a few minutes later carrying a tray containing a medical kit and a large covered plate. He set it down on the table.

"My wife's fixing more food," he said to Alex, "but you and Jessie can start on this. And there's water and juice in the little fridge." He pointed to a minuscule refrigerator in the corner. "We keep survival rations in here."

"Where's here?" Alex asked groggily, still trying to focus.

Paul shrugged. "Our humble hideaway," he smiled. "Under Georgia Avenue."

Disoriented, Alex blinked and turned stiffly in his chair to look around.

Paul said, "There're some clothes in the supply closet that ought to fit you both well enough. Oh, and due to his unfortunate recent demise," he added dryly, "I think it's time to lose Trooper Brewster."

With a murmur of gratitude, Jessie stood up and went to Paul, wrapping her arms around his waist. He enfolded her in a hug, and for a long moment they held each other without speaking.

Embarrassed by his feelings, Paul exhaled in a huff, brusquely swiping a knuckle across suddenly moist eyes.

"You ever scare me like that again, Jess," he warned, his voice husky with emotion, "and I swear I'll shoot you myself."

"Don't worry, Paul," Jessie agreed, "I promise we'll be the very model of law-abiding citizens. For a while, anyway." She stretched on her toes to kiss Paul's cheek, and again he hugged her fiercely.

At the sight of Jessie in Paul Rudin's embrace, Alex's fuzzy vision abruptly cleared. He stiffened, jealousy hot in his chest. He knew he owed Paul his life, but at the moment he felt like taking him apart, piece by piece.

His eyes narrowed and his mouth drew into a taut, angry line.

"Paul?" Lani called from the upstairs apartment. "Could you come here a second?"

"Coming, honey." Paul grinned and reluctantly released Jessie, placing a last, fond kiss on her forehead. "The boss calls," he said with cheerfully, still buoyantly relieved that Jessie was alive and safe and where she belonged. "I'll be right back."

When he left, Jessie sighed and sat back down beside Alex. She soaked the washcloth again. "Here now, let me see your arm," she said, but he jerked away.

"No. Leave it be. I just wanna rest."

Taken aback, Jessie stared at him, misunderstanding his abrupt refusal to cooperate.

"Oh, come on, Alex. I know it hurts, but we can't just leave it alone. If that wound becomes infected, you could lose your arm, or even your life."

"Yeah, some life," he muttered, dropping his head to his folded arms again. "Hell with it."

Bewildered, Jessie reached out to stroke his hair. He shrugged off her hand with a muffled snarl. She realized then that he was not so much in pain as he was angry. Seething, nail-spitting angry.

"What in the world are you so mad about all of a sudden?" she asked in a tone so genuinely puzzled that it made his teeth ache.

"For God's sake, Jessie," Alex grumbled, glaring at her now with hot, dark eyes. "He's a married man!"

Jessie stared at him dumbly, the wet washrag she still held dripping onto the concrete floor. Her eyes narrowed, her head cocked. Then she suddenly burst out laughing.

"You think that Paul and I are...? Oh for Pete's sake, Alex, he's my *cousin!* We grew up together. He and Lani are all the family I have."

With a groan, Alex buried his face deeper in his arms, but he felt the suffocating pressure in his chest dissolve.

Jessie slapped him gently with the washrag.

"I can't believe it!" she yelped. "You were *jealous!*"

Alex straightened wearily, a sheepish expression on his face. "Yeah, I ... well, hell, I'm sorry, Jessie. I guess I wasn't thinking straight." He slumped with relief.

Thank you, God, he thought.

"It's all right, Alex," she said softly. "I, um, I guess I was jealous, too, for awhile, you know." When he looked at her, Jessie paused and nibbled hesitantly on her lower lip. "Well, I mean, I've been kind of wondering ... did you ever ... you know, did you ever find your...."

"Wife?" he finished for her.

Despite his gentle tone, Jessie stiffened, gave a small, jerky nod. Unable to meet Alex's gaze, she turned her attention back to his wounded arm. She kept her eyes lowered, knowing if he saw her expression, he would know the hope – and dread – she felt.

Alex studied her downcast eyes. "Yes," he said, but with no trace of either excitement or disappointment that she could discern. "I found her."

Jessie worried her lower lip. Oh, this was hard.

"And?" she said carefully. She held her breath.

Alex shook his head. "What I told you before was true, honey. My wife died four years ago. The Casey I found here is a stranger."

He struggled to find the right words. "See, you can't love someone who looks back at you with just ... nothing ... in her eyes. I've been grieving for Casey a long time, Jessie, maybe too long. I think I'd already let her go without realizing it. You get in the habit of grieving, and it gets familiar, it gets almost ... comfortable."

Alex took a deep breath, wincing at the pain in his shoulder. Jessie stopped, fearing she'd hurt him, her eyes filled with worry.

"I'm sorry," she whispered.

He shook his head, one corner of his mouth tugging into a crooked smile.

"It's all right, Jessie," Alex said. "I'm okay. I know where my heart is now." He reached over and gently tipped up her chin. "It's all yours, sweetheart."

Jessie's heart soared. She flung an arm around his neck and pulled him into a long, happy kiss that was filled with promise.

From behind them came the sound of someone awkwardly clearing his throat. "Uh, I hate to interrupt you two, but Lani's up there in the kitchen whipping up enough food to feed an army. Okay if I come in?"

Paul stood in the doorway at the top of the short flight of stairs, holding another tray. A mix of amusement and embarrassment colored his cheeks and curved his mouth. Reluctantly Jessie slipped from Alex's embrace.

"Oh, I ... well, of course, Paul," she stammered, her cheeks blazing. "We were just...."

Both Paul and Alex raised arched eyebrows in anticipation of her next words. Jessie looked from one to the other, made a helpless gesture.

"...just," she went on, groping for words, "saying how hungry we were."

Now it was Alex's turn to blush, despite the pallor of his skin. Paul made a small, choked sound that might have been either surprise or laughter. Without comment he set the second tray on the table. Whatever was in the covered dish smelled wonderful. Alex's stomach growled, and he blushed again.

Paul straightened up. "Okay," he said. "If you two think you can stay out of trouble for awhile and ... manage ... all right by yourselves, Lani and I'd like to get a little sleep. It's been one hell of a day, to say the least."

Jessie rose and went to him, laying her palm on his chest and kissing his cheek.

"We'll be fine," she assured him. "Thank you, Paul. For everything. Lani, too."

"Yeah, that goes for me, too," Alex said gruffly. "Thanks, Rudin. I owe you." He looked up into Paul's keen brown eyes.

Jessie's cousin smiled wryly and clapped a hand on Alex's uninjured shoulder. "Morgan," he replied dryly, "it's good to see you're gonna live." Then he turned and climbed the stairs, closing the door behind him. The bookshelf slid into place with barely a sound, leaving Alex and Jessie alone.

The hush that fell over the little annex was deafening. Jessie thought Alex must be able to hear her heartbeat. She sat back down, her emotions confused, her body weary as adrenaline drained away.

What had happened to that rush of hope and happiness she'd felt just moments before? Intensely aware of Alex's searching gaze following her every move, she wrung out the washrag in the warm water, thinking how easily he was able to wring her heart in much the same way.

She had no defenses where he was concerned. He'd told her he was over Casey and she wanted so badly to believe him. But what if he changed his mind? She didn't think she could stand being pushed aside again. His abrupt withdrawal from their lovemaking in the van had hurt more than she wanted to admit.

Not wanting to think about that night, Jessie concentrated on washing Alex's wounded arm. She used the damp cloth to wipe away the smears of blood on his chest and side. The tip of her tongue appeared just above her lower lip as she focused on the work.

Alex drew in a sharp breath, hot arousal taking him by surprise. Jessie's vulnerability and her sweet, maddening touch brought him the most acute combination of pleasure and pain he'd ever known. His muscles quivered in reaction and he squirmed uncomfortably on the chair.

Lost in her thoughts, Jessie set the bowl and washcloth aside. She opened the medical kit and took out some gauze pads and a small bottle of dark, evil-looking yellow liquid. She frowned, and Alex uneasily guessed the direction of her thoughts.

She was remembering.

He cleared his throat. "Jessie, look, honey, maybe we should talk about, um, you know, the other night...."

She shook her head. "You don't have to say anything, Alex. I understand. You didn't know what would happen with Casey."

"No, honey," he said carefully. "I don't think you understand quite how I felt. How could you, when I didn't either?"

Jessie shrugged. Busying herself, she uncapped the bottle and poured some of the medicine onto a wad of gauze. Firmly she took hold of Alex's arm, turning him slightly away from her.

"Hang on," she said. "This stuff stings like the devil."

Alex shrugged. "It's okay. I don't ... Jeez!" He choked and came straight up off the chair, gasping as the caustic liquid bit into the wound. Jessie held on, tugged him back down.

His eyes watered, sweat poured from his ashen face. He croaked, "God Almighty, what *is* that stuff?"

"Iodine," she said apologetically. "I know it stings, Alex, but it really is good for preventing infection. And I think, just to be safe, we'd better put some sulfa powder on the wound as well." When he eyed her warily, cradling his arm protectively against his chest, she said, "Don't be a big baby. The sulfa won't hurt, I promise."

He watched her every move suspiciously as she tore open a small paper packet and began to sprinkle a talc-like powder onto his arm. He remained tense and ready to bolt.

Gradually, as the pain of the wound dulled to a low throb, Alex began to relax. Jessie wrapped his arm in gauze.

"You see?" she said with an overbright smile. "Just like I said. That wasn't so bad now, was it?"

"Are you kidding?" Alex gritted, glaring at the iodine bottle. "You could use that stuff to etch steel."

Jessie's smile faded. She began straightening the medical kit.

"We're lucky to have iodine, Alex," she said defensively. "And even luckier to have the sulfa. Don't you know how hard it is to get? Even the military hospitals don't always have a decent supply. Things were supposed to get better now that the government's eased up on trade restrictions with Nazi Britain, but Paul still has a tough time getting hold of drugs, especially controlled ones like sulfa."

Alex stared at her, drop-jawed. "Nazi ... *Britain?*" he repeated, staggered.

Jessie sighed in exasperation. "Oh, come on, Alex, this is really getting old. Shouldn't a history teacher know this stuff?"

Alex closed his eyes and shook his head miserably.

"The Nazis won the Second World War?" he asked in a strangled voice.

Now Jessie looked shocked. "World *war?*" she repeated incredulously. "What world war? What are you talking about?"

Alex's brain felt muddled. He struggled to think clearly.

"How ... how did Great Britain end up under the control of the Nazis?" he asked carefully.

Jessie said, "I don't know, they came to some kind of agreement. We studied it a little in school. Appeasement, I think they called it. We just stayed out of it." She shrugged. "Look, Alex, it's been that way for ages, and we've got enough problems of our own. What good does it do to worry about something you can't do anything about?"

"I don't know," Alex said wearily. "I don't know anything anymore."

"You're tired," she said. "We both are. We need to eat and get some rest. Okay?"

As she took his hand, her gray eyes imploring, Alex tried hard to get a grip. Shoving aside dark thoughts of a vast Nazi regime in Europe – and God knew where else – he took a deep breath and tried to focus on the here and now. If they were to survive and stay free, he and Jessie had to trust each other implicitly. He knew he still had to put things right with her.

Alex nodded. "Okay." He paused, chewing his lip. "Look, Jessie, I still need to talk to you about what happened between us the other night, when we ... well, when we started to make love."

Cheeks flushed, she looked down to her clenched hands in her lap, her back stiffening. She started to protest, then thought better of it. After a moment, she looked up again and nodded warily.

Alex drew in a steadying breath.

"To begin with, I want to say straight out that there's no excuse for what I did, starting up and then leaving you like that. I know now that I hurt you, but honest to God, honey, I thought at the time I was doing the right thing. I thought I was sparing you."

Jessie's eyes widened. "Sparing me?" she echoed in complete astonishment. "Sparing me from what?"

"From the very hurt I seem to have ended up causing you."

She frowned. "Alex, I just don't get it. Didn't you know I wanted you to make love to me? I was so grateful to you, so glad to be alive! Why did you stop? What did I do to make you so disappointed and mad?"

Blowing out a breath, he took her hand, laced his fingers with hers. As much as he regretted leaving her, he knew it would have been worse if he'd stayed and taken her for all the wrong reasons.

"You didn't make me angry, sweetheart, and you sure didn't disappoint me. I just couldn't stand ... I didn't want it to be that way."

She searched his eyes, trying to understand. "What way? Alex, I wanted you. And I-I thought ... you wanted me, too."

"Of course I did, baby." The words came in a rush now. "I wanted you so much it made me crazy. It still does! But I couldn't take you on the floor of that damned prison van. And even more than that, I wasn't sure of my own heart, so...." He shook his head in frustration. "I'm sorry. None of this is coming out right."

Alex lurched to his feet, took Jessie's hand and hauled her up against him. Her eyes seemed to fill her whole face as she looked up into his. He could see confusion and hope and raw desire.

Though he swayed slightly on his feet, Alex's battered, weary body leapt to life. He wanted Jessie with a hunger that staggered him. But this was exactly how he'd hurt her before. He had to get it right this time.

"Sweetheart, don't you get it?" he said. "The first time ... no, *any* time ... it shouldn't be like that ... not desperate or selfish, or something done out of gratitude. You deserve so much more than that. So much more." He began to gently to stroke her hair. "I don't know what else to say, honey. Will you try to forgive me?"

A long moment passed in which he searched her eyes. When he saw her confusion turn to joy, he nearly went to his knees in relief. He bent his head to kiss her, and she was right there to meet him.

CHAPTER 29

Alex had expected to find little more than a basic washtub and faucet in the utility room. He was happily surprised – and very grateful – to discover a tiled shower installed next to a steel double sink that was large enough to wash clothes in. A commode stood in a small, partitioned niche.

Ignoring Jessie's warning to keep his bandage dry, Alex turned on the shower and stepped directly under the full force of the steaming water. The feeling of relief was so incredibly pleasurable that he groaned aloud.

At that moment, with hot water sluicing over him in a shower stall so narrow his shoulders all but touched the opposite walls, Alex couldn't have enjoyed it more had he been at the Ritz-Carlton.

While he showered, Jessie ate like a stevedore. By the time he emerged from the utility room twenty minutes later she was seated at the old table, the last scraps of her hearty meal shoved aside, fiddling with Casterson's cell phone.

Automatically he reached out to take it from her, then thought better of it. After all, no matter what he'd tried, nothing had happened. He might as well let Jessie have a shot at it.

He moved toward her, clad in clean, worn workpants and shrugging on a shirt. She turned to him and looked up, her frankly appreciative smile fading to a worried frown.

"Oh, Alex, look what you did! The bandage is soaked! You were supposed to keep it dry."

Shirt half on, he scowled at the useless, sodden gauze clinging to his upper arm, then sheepishly shrugged his good shoulder.

"Sorry," he replied without remorse, his smile charmingly lopsided, "but short of taking my arm off and leaving it outside the shower, there wasn't much I could do about it. I don't suppose I could find someone around here willing to do a little more tender ministering?"

"Hmmm." Jessie pursed her lips. She stood and took firm hold of his uninjured arm, hauling him down into the chair she'd just vacated. "Sit," she ordered sternly.

She rummaged once again through the medical kit and found the dreaded bottle of iodine. She held it up with a smirk.

"I'm afraid all the Sisters of Mercy were suddenly called away to an emergency meeting of the Tender Ministrations Society," she said with honeyed sarcasm. "Will I do?"

Alex groaned and closed his eyes.

* * * * *

Jessie was merciful after all, allowing him to rest and eat before she went to work again on his shoulder. Alex devoured Lani's stew as though he'd eaten nothing in a week. Meanwhile Jessie investigated the contents of the tiny refrigerator and triumphantly came up with a gallon jug of reconstituted grape juice. With a raging thirst caused by exertion and loss of blood, Alex nearly drained it.

The result was dramatic. Alex's head cleared and he seemed to come fully back to life. No longer faint and woozy, he sat at the table while Jessie went to clean up, busying himself tinkering with the cell phone, trying not to imagine her body clothed in nothing but water.

He had more success with the device – which was none whatsoever – than he did with his unruly imagination. He swore again and shifted into an even more uncomfortable position. She was everything he craved, and she was absolute hell on all his good intentions.

When Jessie emerged from her own shower, fetchingly clad in nothing but a man's soft, blue cotton shirt that hung nearly to her knees, her cap of tousled mahogany curls shining and damp, Alex swallowed a groan.

He stood up and crossed the room in two long strides, ready to take her in his arms. Jessie frowned and shook her head, placing her palms on his chest. Oh dear, *that* was a mistake. The moment she touched him, it was all she could do not to climb all over him.

"You ... your shoulder," she reminded him in a husky stammer. Heaving a put-upon sigh, he released her and sat back down, shrugged the shirt off his shoulder, grudgingly allowed her to rebandage his arm.

Although she didn't douse him with the iodine again, redressing his wound was still a grueling process that taxed them both. Jessie noticed that Alex picked up the cell phone again and studied it with great concentration as she worked. When he flinched, biting back a curse, she tried to think way to distract him from pain while she worked.

"Alex," she said finally, "tell me some more about Jack. I was wondering ... do you think he'd like me?"

For a long moment, he didn't respond, didn't even look at her, and Jessie wondered if she'd made a terrible mistake reminding him of his lost child. *As though he could ever forget,* she thought. She waited, hoping he wouldn't be angry with her again.

Alex wasn't angry, but for a while he couldn't speak past the terrible constriction of his throat. Thinking of his son knocked all sense of peace from his mind and filled him with such desperation and urgency that he literally couldn't sit still.

He lurched to his feet, pulling away from Jessie, yanking the shirt back onto his shoulder. He paced the small room like a caged panther, raking a shaky hand through his short, tawny hair.

"I'm sorry, Alex," Jessie said, re-rolling the bandage to stop the trembling of her hands. "I shouldn't have asked that. I-I always seem to say the wrong thing." She stopped, mortified, and looked away from him.

Alex sighed. He walked back to her and took her hand in his. Sitting down beside her, he gave her a grim, shaky smile.

"No," he said gently, his voice unsteady. "I'm glad you asked, honey, I really am. I think ... I think I'd like to talk about him."

He met her gaze, and she was surprised to see tenderness, pride, and even a little amusement in his eyes.

"Do you know he could read when he was three?" Alex asked without preamble. "Blew my socks off. Ah, God, sweetheart, he's such a great kid. He's nuts about dinosaurs and Legos. And Thomas, too, of course, not to mention all eight thousand of Thomas's friends."

Jessie nodded, looking completely puzzled. "Well," she said, shrugging, "I guess at least I know what dinosaurs are."

He took her hand, caressing it gently.

"Don't worry, sweetheart. Jack'll tell you all about it. Actually, he'll bug the heck out of you." He swallowed hard against the hitch in his voice, and his words softened to a caress. "He'll love you, Jess. Like father, like son, you know?"

Heat spread through Jessie at Alex's touch. With difficulty she withdrew her trembling hand from his and reached across the table to retrieve the cell phone he'd set down. She fumbled with it a bit, then dropped it into his shirt pocket, patting it gently. When she spoke, her voice trembled as much as her hand.

"This ... this device might give you a chance, Alex. A chance to have your life and your son back." Her eyes brimmed with tears as they locked again with his. She swiped them away with the back of one hand. "But if – no, I mean *when* you figure out how to put things right, how much will everything be different? I mean, what if I can't...."

She swallowed, gathered the courage to say it as hot tears stung her eyes.

"What if ... what if I can't ... find you?"

Alex swallowed hard. With a rough tenderness he took hold of her arms and stood, raising her up with him, hauling her into his embrace.

"I swear to you, honey," he vowed, holding her against his chest and stroking her hair, "no matter what ever happens, I'll find you. Do you trust me?"

Jessie reached up to touch his face, her eyes searching his. Yes, she trusted him. And yes, she believed him. She drew in a shaky breath and nodded.

"Yes," she whispered. "Of course I trust you. I love you, Alex."

He closed her hand in his, drawing it to his lips. "I love you, too, Jessie," he said against her fingers, kissing them one by one. "You're mine."

He tipped her chin up, kissed her with infinite care, keeping rein on the excitement that shot through him as his lips grazed hers. She sighed, a small breath of delight, and opened to him. Her lashes fluttered closed and she leaned into him.

229

They explored, teased, tasted. With a great force of will that left him shaking with need, Alex finally tore his mouth from Jessie's and drew back, setting her gently away from him, framing her face in his hands. Jessie opened her eyes slowly and regarded him with dazed bewilderment, her pulse racing.

"Don't stop," she whispered. "Don't ever stop."

Alex pulled her close again and nuzzled her hair, inhaling the sweet, intoxicating scent of her.

"Sweetheart," he rasped, hardly able to untangle his tongue. "The other night, I didn't even think ... Ah, baby, I can't believe I'm gonna be this stupid again. I don't have anything. Um, maybe I could ask Paul ... Oh, yeah, right, *that's* a good idea ..."

He winced, hearing himself ramble idiotically. His whole body was taut and trembling, his cheeks flaming. Mortified, he buried his face in Jessie's tumbled curls.

Miraculously, she rescued him. Unwrapping her arms from around his waist and ducking out from under his chin, she pushed up the sleeve of her shirt. As he looked at her in bewilderment, she pointed to a small raised scar inside her upper arm, just above the elbow.

"It's all right, Alex. You see?" she said, her love for him shining in her eyes, all shyness gone. "I've had the Sterinol implants since I was eleven. All girls have to get them." She paused again and licked her lips, an unconsciously erotic gesture that nearly tore the last of Alex's control to shreds. "Is that what you were worried about?"

Dumbly, Alex nodded.

He should have been relieved. Hell, he *was* relieved. Unrestrained lust roared through him and he pulled her tightly against him. Ah, she felt so damn good ...

Petition to Bear Child. The words flashed through his mind, suddenly chilling him.

No antibiotics, he thought bitterly, *but children are routinely sterilized. Ain't it a wonderful world.* He swallowed against that now-familiar anger and his eyes clouded with pain.

Jessie knew at once she was losing him. She placed her palms against his face, soothing the tense muscles, forcing him to meet her eyes. She felt his breathing quicken as her fingers tenderly stroked his stubble-roughened jaw.

"Please love me, Alex," she murmured. "Come back from wherever you are and love me. Don't make me wait any longer. Please, I can't wait any more."

He looked deeply into her eyes and was lost. All at once, Alex no longer cared what miseries existed outside that room. Jessie loved him, and for now, that was enough to make him grateful to be alive. It was more than enough. It was everything.

With a low growl of need and hunger, Alex lifted her off her feet and into his arms, cradling her against his chest. He ignored the protesting lance of pain in his shoulder, but Jessie gasped.

"Oh no, Alex, your arm!"

His head dipped as he claimed her mouth, stopping her words, quieting all but her moan of pleasure. He carried her to the bed and laid her down gently, his body hovering over hers as he stretched out with her. She reached up and wrapped her arms around his neck, hungrily pulling him to her.

"Easy," he murmured. "We'll go slow, sweetheart, I promise."

"I don't want slow, Alex. I want you."

So he gave her all he had, body and soul.

* * * * *

Later, in the deep quiet of the night, Jessie lay across Alex's chest, listening to the gallop of his heartbeat, Gradually, their breathing was slowing.

Alex stroked her back gently. She could feel a fine tremor in his fingers.

"Are you sure you're all right?" he asked anxiously. "Did I hurt you, baby?"

He felt her shiver slightly, her skin warm and moist against him. She toyed with the buttons of his open shirt, which he'd been way too busy to bother shedding.

"Of course you didn't hurt me, she smiled "You were ... amazing. I had no idea." She raised her head, looking at him searchingly. "Are you ... Alex, you're not disappointed, are you?"

"What?" Was he *disappointed*? Was she crazy?

"It's just ... I wasn't sure...."

"Lord have mercy, sweetheart," he rumbled, embracing her, grinning with pure satisfaction. "If you'd disappointed me any more, I'd be a dead man."

Cheeks flushed, Jessie smiled with a secret, perfect happiness. She nuzzled him again, this time teasing the crisp, damp hair of his chest with her lips. He sucked in a sharp breath and she smiled all the more.

Jessie said, "Lani told me about making love, you know. She said if I was with the right man, it would be the most brilliant joy imaginable." She paused, as though reflecting on it.

Alex raised his head from the pillow. "Well?" he prodded.

"Welllll," Jessie purred, drawing the word out maddeningly, "I think Lani has a terrible habit of understating things."

Alex dropped his head back with a laughing snort of relief. Jessie inched higher on his body, drawing another shuddering gasp from him, then kissed the hollow of his throat. She was serious now, almost solemn.

"I never would've believed anything could be so incredible, Alex. So wonderful. I've never felt like that in my life."

Amazingly, neither had he, and he told her so.

He'd been devoted to Casey, there was never any question of that. Making love with her had been sweet and satisfying, and when she'd conceived Jack, Alex had thought his heart would burst with pride.

But nothing had ever rocked him like this, left him so deeply moved that he truly hadn't known where he ended and Jessie began.

Maybe he and Casey had just been too young, too untested to find that deep a connection, or maybe ... maybe....

Maybe Jessie was, and was always meant to be, the other half of his soul.

He drew in a deep breath and exhaled, his fingers tangling in her hair.

"Jessie, you're so beautiful, so fine. You feel so good to me."

Her eyes shone with happiness. Her lips parted slightly and she whispered his name. Incredibly, Alex felt himself leap to life. His hands strayed down her back to her hips, caressing her. She moaned and wiggled sinuously, drawing her knees up to straddle him. He felt her heat pour over him, and then thinking at all was impossible.

In one swift, smooth motion Alex rolled over, carrying Jessie with him, losing himself in her.

* * * * *

Forgotten in his shirt pocket, the little cell phone hummed. With a ping, *SYNC ON* winked out.

They would never know which one of them, in fiddling with the various keys, had initiated the sequence of commands that opened the microchip circuits and activated the preset program. For ten seconds the device was completely blank, all activity apparently extinguished. Then a flashing red *FIND* command blinked on.

As Alex and Jessie soared together in wild release, arms and legs entangled and hearts racing, the device's intricate program sped flawlessly through its commands.

* * * * *

Alex gathered Jessie beside him in an achingly tender embrace, tucking her against him. She sighed and snuggled against him, slipping her hand under his shirt, marveling at how perfectly they fit together.

Ninety seconds after the *FIND* command was activated, it winked out as well. Immediately *AUTORET* appeared onscreen, its green command light blinking steadily. Casterson's cell phone was now busily engaged in running its intricate – and quite extraordinary – *Automatic Retrieval* function.

Alex and Jessie fell asleep in each other's arms, sated, exhausted, intimately entangled. They could have slept through an eight-point earthquake.

CHAPTER 30

Jessie swam up drowsily from a deep, dreamless sleep, a relaxed, satisfied smile still curving the corners of her mouth. She purred, stretched luxuriously, and reached for Alex.

Eyes still closed, she frowned drowsily at the rough feel of a heavy wool blanket next to her skin. What did she need a blanket for? It was summertime, and the room was already warm. She stirred, and instead of Alex's arms cradling her, she felt the coarse, lumpy cushion of a pile of burlap flour sacks. Jessie opened her eyes, decided reasonably that she was still dreaming, and closed them again.

A moment later she came wide-awake with a jolt of full-blown panic.

As though still trapped in sleep, she tried to scream, but her throat closed and she couldn't make a sound. She thrashed against the blanket that tangled around her and gave in to hysteria.

Then, mercifully, the screams came.

"Alex! *Alex! ALEX!*"

He seemed to materialize out of nowhere in the dim light, wrapping her struggling body in his arms, pulling her protectively against him. Her cheek rubbed against coarse, starched fabric, her hands caught in straps that seemed to run vertically up his chest. The strange sensations increased her confusion and she struggled to escape. Alex tightened his hold, letting her flail against him. Just as he had in the prison cell, he murmured soothing reassurances into her ear, his voice hoarse and strained.

"Jessie, it's all right, it's me! I'm here! You're all right, sweetheart, you're okay. Listen, Jessie, listen to me. Settle down, it's all right, it's all right."

Finally his words got through to her. She sank down against him, her heart racing like that of a wild creature. Alex sat on the pile of burlap sacks, leaned back against the rough stone wall in the corner of the storage cellar, rocked her gently. He continued to murmur soothing words to her, and when she had calmed enough to listen, he tried to explain the unexplainable.

"It brought us both, Jessie," he said, a sort of giddy wonder in his voice. He still could not really believe it. "One of us must have stumbled on the program. No matter, it brought us both."

"What ... brought us?" She had no idea what he was talking about.

He risked easing his hold on her enough to tug the cell phone from a pocket and place it in her hands. She stared at it without comprehension. Then, as realization dawned, she regarded it with an awestruck horror.

"But it ... Alex, you ... It was with *you*. How could it...?"

He took her face in his hands and kissed her with a tenderness and relief that took her breath away. When he'd awakened after the convulsion in time and had discovered, after a moment of sheer panic, that she hadn't been taken from him, his relief was so profound that it had brought him to tears.

"I think," he said, scrubbing a hand across his face, "its sensors – or whatever it's got – couldn't determine where you ended and I began, so it brought us both."

Jessie gripped his arm with one hand, clutching the cell phone with the other.

"But *where*, Alex? *Where* did it bring us?" She looked around again, but the cellar receded into shadows. She could see only stacks of crates, barrels, and lumpy sacks. A small, grill-covered window high on one wall admitted just the faintest gray shaft of early-morning light.

Alex shook his head and gently opened her fist.

"Not where, Jessie. *When*. Look at it."

His gaze dropped to the device and hers followed. Once again, SYNC ON glowed green. The time and date displays flashed: *5:13 A, 07-03-1902.*

"We're still in Paul and Lani's basement, sweetheart. It's just that...." Alex looked around, captivated. "... they don't seem to have moved in yet."

Jessie looked up at him in stark disbelief. "This thing says it's over *a hundred years ago*?" When he nodded, she gasped, "But that's crazy! It's impossible!"

Alex grinned. "Apparently not."

She shook her head. "This is insane! Things like this just can't happen!" She looked at him, saw the delight and wonder in his face. "Oh my God, you're enjoying this, aren't you?" Punching his chest, she demanded again, "Aren't you?"

Alex laughed, took the device back from her, released her. "Wait here a second, you've got to see this," he said, getting to his feet. She scrambled up with him.

"No," he said, putting a firm, gentle hand on her shoulder to hold her in place. "Stay here, honey. I'll be right back."

Shivering in spite of the stuffy warmth of the basement, Jessie pulled the blanket around her and squirmed backward into the shelter of the corner. She squinted to make out Alex's shadowy form as he moved across the dark, dusty cellar.

There was the swift sound of a match striking, a scraping of metal and glass, then the room was bathed in a flickering, smoky yellow light. The acrid odor of phosphorus and kerosene rose to Jessie's nostrils, making her eyes water. She blinked, rubbed her eyes, and stared.

Alex stood in the center of the cellar, next to a wooden support pillar. An old-fashioned kerosene lantern hung on it from a large spike.

He was dressed in a starched, white linen collarless shirt with blue and black pinstripes, the sleeves rolled back nearly to his elbows, the thick bulge of bandage apparent on his upper arm. A tie hung loosely around his neck. Suspenders held up dark, rather baggy, light woolen trousers. His legs were a little too long for the trousers, his leather boots visible well above the ankle.

Jessie took in enough of the room around them as she gaped at Alex to realize they were in the storage cellar of some type of general mercantile store. The barrels and crates were everywhere, all stenciled with their contents and manufacturer's name.

She asked, a little dazedly, "Where did you get those clothes?"

"There's a dry goods store upstairs," he replied happily. "I got things for you, too." He turned and picked up an enormous pile of clothing that had been neatly stacked on a nearby barrel. He walked to Jessie and held the clothes out to her.

"Here," he said. "I hope you like these. I had to guess at the sizes, but I'll go upstairs again and change them for you if they're not right."

Jessie stared at the yards of lace, cotton, linen, light wool, ribbons and flounces. It seemed enough to clothe an entire family, and she was hot now in just the blanket.

"I'm supposed to wear all that?" she asked, aghast.

Alex nodded. "You'll have to, honey, if you want to go outside."

She looked incredulously again at the huge pile of material.

He grinned devilishly. "I did skip the corset. I figured you didn't have much need for it, and I can't say I'm crazy about the thought of holding all that whalebone and steel." His eyes swept her with admiration and no little heat.

"Thanks," she muttered, but the corner of her mouth kicked into a tiny smile at his obvious approval. She clutched the clothes to her breast, and her small chin tipped up. "Turn your back," she ordered.

Laughing in surprise at her endearing, if somewhat after-the-fact modesty, Alex shook his head and turned around. He walked back to the barrel that had held Jessie's clothes and picked up the thin, curved, stiff piece of white material that remained. Awkwardly he wrestled the stubborn collar into place at the neck of his shirt, loathing it instantly. He knotted the tie, deciding that – should he ever return home – he would never again complain about having to get dressed up. He rubbed his wounded arm, which ached from the effort of fastening the collar.

"All right, you can look now," Jessie said hesitantly.

Alex turned, his right hand frozen in the act of massaging his painful shoulder, and his breath soughed out in a low, admiring whistle.

"Wow."

"Thanks, but I'm not sure if everything's on right." She tugged at the long skirt.

"Trust me, honey, I think you got it better than right. You look amazing." He chuckled. "On the other hand, how you look without it's even better."

Jessie blushed and shook her head. "Am I supposed to be able to move in all this?" Then, unable to resist, she grinned and pirouetted in a small circle.

The high-necked, shirred white blouse ended in large, puffed sleeves at her elbows. Pleats of eyelet lace decorated the bodice. The skirt, a pale dove gray like her eyes in sunlight, fell nearly to the floor above several layers of petticoats. Jessie's stockinged feet were just visible beneath the hem. Soft gloves covered her hands, concealing her raw, abraded wrists.

"I have no idea how to work these," she said, holding a pair of high-buttoned shoes out to him.

Alex crossed to her and took the shoes.

"Here, sit down, sweetheart."

He took her hand and led her to one of the slightly less dusty crates, where she perched tentatively, as though suspecting the wooden box might suddenly explode beneath her. Alex reached into his pocket and extracted a thin, looped tool with a long handle.

"Button hook," he explained, and kneeling before her, he lifted her feet one at a time and slipped on the soft boots. Supporting her trim, booted ankle in his hand and working the buttons was a remarkably erotic experience, and Alex felt himself harden. Sweat dampened his neck and forehead, his cheeks burned, and he cleared his throat restlessly. Only the thought of how long it would take to put all the damned stuff back on again kept him from tearing off all their clothes right then and there.

When he finally had the shoes fastened, he helped her to her feet. "There's just one more thing," he said huskily.

Jessie rolled her eyes. "Oh, no, Alex, please. If I have to put on one more stitch of clothing...."

He raised his fingertips to her lips to gently shush her.

"You'll like this, sweetheart, I hope." He looked suddenly nervous as he reached into his pocket once more, taking out a small gold ring.

Jessie stared at it in astonishment. Alex took her left hand in his and carefully removed her glove. He slipped the wedding band onto her ring finger. His eyes locked with hers and held.

"I, James Alexander," he said solemnly in a deep, low voice, rough with emotion, "take you, Jessica Jordana, to be my wedded wife...."

When he finished what he had to say, he drew her into his arms. The taste of tears on her cheeks and the sound of the reciprocated vows she murmured into his ear made his heart and soul come completely undone.

It was over an hour before they got all the clothes back on again.

CHAPTER 31

"We should go, honey," Alex said gently, taking her arm. "Somebody's bound to be here soon to open the store."

"I know," she said, still gazing about in wonder. "But, oh, Alex, isn't it absolutely wonderful?"

He had to agree that it was, and in fact Alex was just as charmed and fascinated by the general store as Jessie was. Never had he seen such a thoroughly modern, enchanting antique.

Laden with all manner of fabric, clothing, furnishings, and accessories – from men's silk hats and cravats to matchboxes, shaving mugs, and morbidly fanciful, guillotine-shaped cigar-cutters – enormous shelves and tables stretched in long, straight aisles to the far end of the polished wood floor.

Ladies' millinery occupied an entire wall. Jessie gaped at the colors, frills, and small luxuries that had all but disappeared from the world she knew. She had no idea what half of the items for sale were used for, but she delighted in examining them, in touching them. It seemed impossible that such pretty things were real.

The prices left them both shaking their heads in amused amazement. Men's suits cost ten dollars, wool overcoats sixteen, shoes a dollar. An exquisite Limoges china dinner service for twelve, including ornate, hand-decorated serving pieces and platters, was less than thirty dollars.

"Want to stock up on your trousseau?" Alex teased, holding up a sheer, hand-stitched silk nightgown priced at fifty cents. Jessie gasped in delight, then quickly caught herself and tried to frown sternly at him.

"Alex, shame on you! You already stole a wedding ring!"

He shrugged and smiled sheepishly. "Don't worry, honey. I didn't exactly steal it. Actually I sort of ... bartered ... for it."

Jessie raised her eyebrows skeptically. "Uh-huh. And may I ask, my darling, with what? I assume you arrived here as unadorned as I did. No, wait, I take that back. You *were* wearing your shirt."

Her eyes shone with affection and amusement.

Grinning, Alex laced his fingers with hers and led her behind one of the huge oblong counters that ran the center length of the store.

He opened the drawer of a brand-new antique cash register and removed a slip of paper, handing it to her to read.

"Never fear, Mrs. Morgan," he said with a gallant sweep of his hand. "You have married an honorable man."

Jessie read the note, frowned, looked at him in confusion. "I don't get it. What does it mean?" she asked, bewildered.

He smiled and took it from her, laying it back in the drawer. "If they take my advice, it will not only pay for the clothes, the ring, and the cash I took, but there'll be enough left over to buy a small – or maybe even a middle-sized – nation."

Perplexed, Jessie looked again at the words Alex had printed carefully on the paper:

Buy General Electric, IBM, Standard Oil, Apple, Microsoft, and Disney. PS: Tell the kids and grandkids.

* * * * *

Stepping out into the morning light of the summer of 1902 was, to Alex, the delight of exploring the dry goods store many times over. He stood for a moment on the wooden boardwalk of Georgia Avenue, watching the street come to life in the morning sunshine. Milk and ice wagons were already jouncing along up and down the road.

With a musical clang and rattle, a trolley wobbled along its tracks down the muddy center of the street, *Columbia Heights & Soldiers Home* emblazoned on its bright red sides in gold script.

Were it not for the mud and the unmistakable odors of swamp, horses, and primitive sanitation, Alex might have believed he'd died and gone to Disneyland.

Everywhere the street was festooned with red, white and blue bunting and flags for the Fourth of July. Almost reeling in delight from the colorful assault to his senses, Alex grinned and offered his arm to Jessie. She looked astonished and stepped back in instinctive caution.

He reached out and took her hand, wrapping it around the crook of his arm. He held it firmly in place with his hand.

"It's all right, sweetheart," he said. "Here it's all right."

Encouraged, Jessie smiled, and she walked close to his side as they began to stroll down the street. Alex walked protectively on the outside, realizing that the gentlemanly habit his mother had insisted on had actually once had a purpose. The street was filthy from mud and horse traffic. Jessie watched in speechless amazement as Alex cheerfully tipped his hat to the people already out and about, passing them by on the boardwalk.

At the sound of gunshots behind them Jessie cried out in alarm and Alex nearly jumped out of his skin, whirling to face the danger and shoving Jessie roughly behind him. All at once three small boys darted by, laughing uproariously and clutching fistfuls of firecrackers. A scruffy, taffy-colored mongrel dog yapped at their heels in an excited frenzy. The boys and dog disappeared down a nearby alley, and more explosions quickly followed.

"Oh my God, Alex," Jessie breathed, "I-I thought...."

He blew out a breath, patted her hand. "I know, sweetheart. Me, too. I guess this is all going to take some getting used to." He paused to let the pounding of his heart ease, then asked hopefully, "Listen, honey, are you hungry?"

She smiled in vast relief. "Starved!"

"Well then, Mrs. Morgan, my dear, may I have the great honor of escorting you to breakfast?"

She nodded, mimicking his florid tone. "Yes, Professor Morgan, you most certainly may. I should be ever so delighted to have the pleasure of your company."

As they walked on, Jessie suddenly said, in a small tone that wrenched Alex's heart, "Is all this real, Alex? Was the world really like this once?"

He looked down and met her eyes, misty and so full of yearning. Unable to trust his voice, he could only nod.

"Whatever happened?" she whispered, and a tear spilled down her cheek.

* * * * *

They'd been disappointed to pass two dining establishments and find them closed. Too early, Alex surmised, but it perplexed him. Eight o'clock shouldn't have been too early to expect breakfast. Finally they noticed the more frequent appearance in the street of hansom cabs, and it was not long then before they came to a row of respectable-looking, even elegant, hotels. All were decked out in flags and bunting. Both pedestrian and street traffic had picked up even more, and the avenue bustled with activity as Alex steered Jessie through the ornate doors of the Warren House hotel.

Later, in the elegantly over-decorated dining room, revived by an enormous breakfast of omelets, steak, biscuits, grits, gravy, and fruit, Alex grinned as he counted out seventy cents to cover both meals, plus a generous tip for the waiter.

"Thank you, sir," the waiter smiled, bowing graciously. "Would you care for a cigar?"

Alex glanced at Jessie and saw her wrinkle her nose in disgust, but he couldn't resist. "Yes, indeed," he said expansively, tossing another dime on the waiter's tray. The man inclined his head again.

"Very good, sir. I'll return with it directly."

After the waiter was out of earshot, Jessie hissed, "Alexander Morgan, don't you dare smoke that thing around me!"

Alex reached across the table and took her hand, entwining their fingers. "Don't worry," he laughed. "The only time I ever tried to smoke I turned six shades of green." As he gently caressed her palm with his thumb, his expression grew serious.

"Look, Jessie, we have to come up with some kind of plan. There isn't much time. Roosevelt will be hit tomorrow when he makes his Fourth of July speech at the Capitol. We've got to try to find Casterson, and we've got to inform the police."

Jessie's face paled with alarm. "The police? No way! That's suicide, Alex!"

He shook his head. "It's different now, sweetheart, it really is. I think we can trust them here."

"No! It's too dangerous. How can we risk it?" she insisted. "You can hardly just walk up and announce that the President is going to be...."

Jessie clamped her mouth shut as the waiter reappeared at Alex's side bearing an elegant wooden cigar box. He offered the open box and Alex stared distractedly at the cigars for a moment, as though unsure what they were, then he cautiously selected one.

"Thank you," he said, handing the waiter another nickel, and the man smiled broadly.

"Thank *you*, sir. And happy Independence Day!"

Alex's gaze shot to the man.

"What?" he demanded, aghast, uncomprehending.

The waiter's face clouded in bewilderment.

"I-I merely wished you a happy Independence Day, sir," he stammered, regarding Alex with some alarm. "It's the Fourth of July."

"But that can't be! Isn't this the third?" Alex had already half-risen from his chair.

The waiter's faced blanched as though he feared Alex might be dangerously unstable. "No sir," he assured him hastily. "I'm sorry, but it's quite definitely the Fourth."

"The President is speaking *today?*" Alex asked, all color draining from his face.

"Yes, sir," the waiter responded uneasily, more disturbed than ever by Alex's distress. "This very morning. At eleven o'clock."

Alex dropped the cigar on the table and reached his hand out to Jessie, who took it and stood at once, her face pale.

"Uh, well, my dear," he stammered, "we must be off." He turned again to the waiter. "Thank you," Alex said curtly, and they all but ran from the room.

"Sir, your hat!" the waiter called after him, seeing it was still on the table. But they were already gone. He debated following them out to the street, but he was leery of the unpredictably volatile gentleman. After a moment's hesitation, he popped the brand-new hat on his own head with a satisfied air.

It was a damned fine hat.

* * * * *

On the street, running to keep up with Alex's long stride, Jessie panted, "How could it be the wrong date? What happened? Alex ... please, wait! Slow down! I can't keep up with you!"

Realizing she was half-running, half-stumbling in the long skirt and high-buttoned shoes, Alex stopped and turned around. His expression was raw and anguished.

"I don't *know* what happened! Maybe it's inaccurate over such a long period of time. Maybe we hit some control that changed the date. Who the hell knows?" From habit he raked a hand through his hair, though there wasn't much length to rake. Jessie reached up to lay a hand on his chest. Her eyes were distraught.

"How much time now, Alex? How much time do we have?"

He plucked the cell phone from a pocket, held it between them to shield it from view of any passerby. They both stared at it.

10:07 A, flashed on the small screen.

CHAPTER 32

This trip was actually Thad Casterson's fourth to 1902, and for the first time in his life, he was being taken seriously.

As he strode now through the hallway of the Senate Office Building, heading for his father-in-law's office, his chest swelled with pride and purpose. So many years of planning, so much risk, so much perseverance in the face of obstacles and derision, and now he'd show them all. Now his life's greatest challenge was met and his greatest goal was about to be achieved.

Thanks to Thaddeus Isaac Casterson, visionary computer genius and humanitarian, America was about to be set on the road to Utopia.

Thad had made all four trips in the space of a week, although he had spent nearly six months' time in 1902. He had long since ceased being amused or amazed by the paradoxes of time travel and took them quite for granted, as though he were doing nothing more than taking a commuter train to Baltimore.

During his first trip, he had gotten the lay of the land, so to speak. Capitol University, barely hatched from parent Capitol College up in Columbia Heights, had yet to occupy its present site in Foggy Bottom. In 1902 those familiar streets were the location of the Camp Fry cavalry depot. Thad needed to establish two secure bases of operations at the military camp, bases that would correspond to the present-day sites of his campus office and nearby apartment. It would be too risky to come and go from anywhere else.

On his second trip, two days later, Thad had equipped himself with elaborately Photoshopped documents that not only gave him orders to requisition laboratory and office space at Camp Fry's military hospital, but also secured an appointment to Georgetown University. He gained an introduction to the charismatic Senator Thomas Sedley of Maryland.

During this trip, Thad stayed in 1902 four months, strengthening his courtship of both the Senator and his only daughter, Agnes, a rather plain, melancholy spinster given to periodic fits of the vapors and to writing extravagantly maudlin poetry. He returned home to the present ten minutes after he'd left.

The third trip was a giant step forward in Thad's plan of action. Agnes, sickly and prim, considered pitifully passed-by at age twenty-five, couldn't believe her good fortune when he proposed marriage, and she eagerly accepted.

Thad already had the Senator's ear; having his daughter cemented the relationship.

Their mutual vision of a United States insulated and isolated from the tragedies and follies of the world at large progressed from a dream to an obsession. Sedley was convinced only Roosevelt stood between him and the realization of his life's political ambition. He would be President, and with an iron hand he would steer America away from the disastrous course of international involvement Roosevelt so recklessly pursued.

By the end of that third trip, Thad had already discreetly hired an assassin.

One glitch came completely unexpectedly. Thad had constructed two identical devices, which he fondly christened *Timelapse Alpha* and *Timelapse Beta*.

In the temporary, but nevertheless powerful disorientation and shock that always accompanied the first few moments of time travel, he had somehow misplaced the *Beta* device. When a frantic search for it at home and at his office – now taken over by that history teacher, Morgan – failed to locate it, Thad was forced to leave it behind.

Still, the *Alpha* device was enough for his purposes, and after the GREAT EVENT took place (Thad always thought of it in capital letters), he had all the time in the world to go back and retrieve the *Beta*. The thought tickled him: *All the time in the world.*

Besides, he couldn't wait to see Utopia.

* * * * *

"You shall have to move faster than that, gentlemen, to keep up with me! Why, if we were back in the Badlands of Dakota, the bears would have had you for breakfast by now!"

President Theodore Roosevelt laughed heartily at his own jest and bounded through the corridors of the Capitol Building with his usual inexhaustible, youthful energy. The aides panting in his wake grinned weakly and doubled their efforts to keep pace with him.

"Yes ... sir ... Mr. President," conceded one, gasping for air. "I suppose ... they ... would have."

As he rounded a corner, Roosevelt heard someone call his name. He stopped and turned toward the familiar, if not entirely welcome, voice. His aides wheezed gratefully to a halt and, half-doubled-over, tried desperately to catch their breath.

"Mr. President! Sir!" Thomas Sedley called again, hurrying toward Roosevelt. Thad Casterson strode just behind him, swaggering with self-importance.

"Mr. President, I feared we'd missed you!"

Roosevelt eyed him steadily, with wary good humor.

"Senator Sedley! Why, you are the very man I wished to see! As a matter of fact, I wrote a good portion of my Independence Day speech with you in mind."

Sedley blanched, almost squirming. He knew Roosevelt was no fool. "Sir," he stammered, "surely you flatter me."

The President's mouth quirked at the corner, his eyes keen and amused. "I doubt you will think so, Thomas," he replied dryly, "when I've done with the speech." He paused a moment more, gauging Sedley's nonplused reaction, then he set off abruptly again. "I am a bit pressed for time, gentlemen. Will you walk with me?"

Sedley fell in beside him. He gestured toward Thad.

"Sir, you remember my son-in-law, Professor Thaddeus Casterson?"

"Of course I do," the President beamed. "You are at Georgetown, are you not, Professor?"

Thad cleared his throat. Roosevelt's encompassing charisma and powerful personality had left him nervous and stammering on the one other occasion they had met – his marriage to Agnes. It took him a moment to speak, and even then his voice quavered, leaving him flushed with anger and resentment.

"Yes sir, Mr. President," he replied, concealing the sullen fury that burned in his chest. "I'm honored that you would remember."

"Oh, I'd be hard-pressed to forget," Roosevelt smiled, not without humor. "As I recall, you share Senator Sedley's conviction that I am a capricious, diabolical tyrant hell-bent on the ruination of this country."

Thad nearly choked. "No, sir, not at all," he stammered. "It's just ... I mean, I believe...." He stopped and gathered his wits, fusing his anger into courage. "It's just that I believe America's future lies in isolation from the sordid and ruinous affairs of other, less enlightened nations.

The energy and prosperity that abounds in this country could be turned to create a Utopian society, free from hunger, crime, and want!"

Surprised at the young man's vehemence, Roosevelt eyed him more carefully.

"Utopia, is it then? Well, that is certainly a noble goal, Professor Casterson."

He smiled wryly and turned his gaze to Sedley.

"Thomas, I see you have quite an ally in this passionate young man. I shall have to aim my speech at both of you!"

Sedley smiled tightly. With a hearty laugh, Roosevelt threw a companionable arm over Thad Casterson's stiff shoulders as they continued down the corridor toward the East Portico platform.

* * * * *

A large crowd had already formed on the lawn below the speaker's platform, which was draped with the Stars and Stripes and the Presidential Seal. With McKinley's assassination still fresh and bitter in the public consciousness, Marines had been stationed at regular and visible intervals across the Capitol grounds, as well as on the roof. The hard-eyed men scanned the crowd with implacable thoroughness, never flinching at the frequent explosions of firecrackers amid the crowd noises, band music, and laughter.

Theodore Roosevelt emerged onto the platform to greet his wife and children, already seated there, just as Alex and Jessie leapt from a hansom cab at the curb of Constitution Avenue. Alex threw the cab fare at the startled driver and grabbed Jessie's hand. She hitched up her skirt and they ran toward the lawn.

Alex pulled her forward through the crowd, pausing only a moment when she got hung up and was nearly jerked from his grasp.

"Come on, sweetheart," he rasped. "We have no time!"

Finally, they made enough headway to see the platform clearly. Alex jerked to a halt as Thad Casterson followed Roosevelt into view.

"There!" he exclaimed, pointing at the platform. "That's him! The thin fellow with the curly dark hair. Standing behind Roosevelt. That's Casterson."

Although the President Casterson of her world was heavy-set and fuller in the face, Jessie could immediately see his resemblance to this young man. A chill ran down her spine. She grasped Alex's arm.

"Surely he's not going to try to hurt him up there, in front of everybody!" she whispered.

Alex shook his head in frustration and dread. He looked frantically about the crowd, but he could see no clear direction from which the threat might come. And Jessie was right. Unless Casterson was a suicidal fool – and his descendants' ascent to the Presidency made that highly unlikely – he wasn't about to haul off and shoot Roosevelt from the platform. Alex felt his panic and helplessness spiral out of control. *How?* his mind screamed. *Where?*

* * * * *

On the platform, Thad Casterson approached the President and his family with respectful deference. "Sir," he said, raising the volume of his voice to be heard above the band and the crowd. "It's very warm this morning. Might I hold your coat?"

Surprised again, pleased at the young man's civility, Roosevelt nodded. "Why, thank you, Professor. Indeed you may." He shucked off the heavy woolen suit coat and smiled broadly, handing the garment to Thad. "I intend to do a good deal of sweating today!"

Thad laughed politely, but it was a strange, constricted sound.

* * * * *

Alex watched, mesmerized with fascination at the sight of a living, breathing Teddy Roosevelt, as the President removed his coat and handed it to Casterson. Something about so simple an action bothered him, gnawed at the edges of his memory, but he couldn't....

"Oh my God!" Alex hissed. Suddenly, he knew. Oh sweet God in heaven, he knew! He pulled Jessie close to him and whispered frantically in her ear. Her eyes grew large with horror.

"In the history of my world," Alex explained in a tumbling rush of frenzied words, "there was an assassination attempt against Roosevelt in 1912. He was wounded, but the force of the bullet was stopped by the eyeglasses case and rolled-up copy of his speech that he was carrying in his coat pocket. Wearing his coat saved his life."

Both of them looked up again to the platform and saw the innocent, deadly sight of Casterson holding the President's coat.

"There's a shooter here, Jessie. I've got to find him. You go get help. Get a cop – a policeman – or one of the Marines. Get somebody!"

When she stood frozen to the spot, Alex pulled her roughly against him and kissed her swiftly and hard. "Do it, Jess!" he ordered. "They're on our side! Do it now!"

"Yes, all right," she whispered, and she turned to push away from him through the crowd. Alex plowed away in the other direction, shoving people aside like a deranged offensive lineman, ignoring their angry curses. His eyes searched their faces desperately.

The President stepped up to the podium as the band broke into *Hail to the Chief.* Slowly the crowd fell silent.

"Friends, I shall keep my remarks brief today," he began, "as I know I compete with fried chicken, potato salad, and fireworks."

The crowd chuckled. Roosevelt continued in a booming voice, yet there was no sense that he was shouting.

"My fellow citizens, today I seek to address your minds and hearts. We are a great nation, and by the fact of that greatness we are brought into relations with the other nations of the earth. We must not fear the future, nor our part in it as a leader of the civilized world. We must face that future seriously, and with energy, resolving to approach problems with an unbending, unflinching purpose, and to solve them aright. This is our duty to a civilization far greater and more important than any other."

He paused, warming to his subject. "Nations that expand and nations that do not expand may both ultimately go down, but the first leaves heirs and a glorious memory. The other leaves neither. It is the great and fundamental purpose of this nation, and my sworn duty, to champion the cause of human rights on all the earth, for human rights reign supreme over all other rights.

"There are those who would argue the expansion of this nation. They have become a powerful opposing force in our government, and I have been asked how I shall deal with that opposition. To that I say, if you have a high-spirited horse that bolts from you, there are two remedies. You can put him on a curb bit and hold him back, or you can take an axe and knock him on the head and kill him. Either way, he won't bolt again.

"I am inclined to favor the bit over the axe."

He paused again as a wave of laughter rolled over the crowd.

"It is in the interest of the community of civilized men that we dedicate ourselves and the future course of this nation to ... to...."

Stunned, Roosevelt trailed off into silence. The crowd shifted in bewilderment, but they did not see what he saw. At 11:13 a.m. on the Fourth of July, 1902, President Theodore Roosevelt stared into the barrel of a gun aimed directly at his heart by a man whose eyes burned with a cold and intense purpose.

Roosevelt honestly felt no fear for himself, but Edith and the children sat directly behind him on the dais. Twelve-year-old Kermit Roosevelt jumped to his feet in alarm as he saw his father, gone suddenly and uncharacteristically quiet, instinctively shift position to shield his family.

The seconds seemed to blur into an eternity. Behind Roosevelt, Thad Casterson unconsciously dropped the President's coat and strained forward to see.

Kermit, his mother reaching her hand out behind him in surprise and confusion, blurted out, "Father, what...?" and took a step toward the President.

Suddenly, there was a shout from the crowd below, and – with a blindside tackle – Alex launched himself into the shooter.

The gun fired straight up into the air with an explosive blast that sent the crowd on the lawn, as well as the one on the platform, into pandemonium.

Roosevelt came instantly to life, lurching back to protect his family. Secret Service officers swarmed over them.

Below him on the lawn there ensued a wild melee, with no one quite certain who the villain was, nor how many villains there were.

When the Marines arrived moments later and waded into the chaos, Jessie tried to reach Alex, but she was pushed back by the sheer number of people. Throwing all caution to the wind, she hurled herself into every minute opening she could find and pressed her way forward through the crowd.

The Marines took over, and not gently. In less than two minutes they hauled two dazed, bleeding men to their feet and shackled their hands roughly behind their backs.

Thad Casterson stared in gaping disbelief at the ruination of his flawless plan. He was stunned not only that the assassination had failed, but that he recognized *both* of the men being hauled away by the Marines. One was Amos Ketchin, the fiery-eyed zealot Thad had hired as the shooter. The other was – Goddammit, he was sure of it! – Alexander Morgan.

After Morgan's hands were cuffed behind him, a big marine roughly shoved him forward. He stumbled, and Thad caught a horrified glimpse of the *Beta* device as it fell from Morgan's pocket to the ground. Within moments, it had been trampled.

* * * * *

Stunned and bleeding, Alex was hauled viciously to his feet, his arms wrenched backwards. He reeled with pain, the nerves of his wounded left arm shrieking in agony. He had taken the full impact of his collision with the shooter on his injured shoulder, and the brutal insult had torn the wound open. Blood soaked his shirtsleeve as his hands were roughly manacled behind him. As he looked around wildly for Jessie, someone shoved him, and he fell forward, barely keeping his balance.

A marine barked, "Get the damned sons of bitches out of here!"

Jessie saw Alex being dragged away. She fought her way through the crowd to follow, and managed to reach him just as he was being thrown into one of the waiting police wagons.

"No!" she yelled furiously at the soldiers. "He's not the one!"

One of the Marines pushed her aside.

"This ain't no place for ladies, ma'am," he growled. "Now everybody just get back!"

Jessie screamed Alex's name at the top of her lungs. Dazed, bleary, he saw her just as the wagon's steel doors began to close.

"Casterson!" he yelled. "Go, *go!*"

After a moment of agonizing indecision, Jessie gathered up her skirts and ran.

CHAPTER 33

Alex slumped in the corner of a tiny, airless, miserable cell, done in by exhaustion and the merciless midday heat. His hands were manacled in front of him with a pair of wrist irons held apart by a rigid, foot-long bar. A similar device shackled his ankles, and through both looped long lengths of heavy chain that encircled his waist and ran the length of his legs. *Like Marley's ghost*, he thought. *But without the fun.* Altogether he was wearing at least thirty pounds of chains.

The listlessness of his posture belied the frenzy of his mind. He knew the cell phone had fallen from his pocket; he'd heard the crunch of metal and plastic as it was crushed underfoot. It was certainly destroyed, but he supposed that was better than it having been found intact. How could he possibly have explained it?

When he'd been taken from the prison wagon, he'd struggled furiously, demanding a lawyer, demanding *anyone* in authority, insisting the threat to the President's life was still extreme. One of the Marine sentries had lost patience with him, decking Alex with an almost casual fist to the jaw.

When he came to his senses in his cell, Alex grimly detached himself from the aching miseries of his body – pounding head, wrenched and cramped muscles, throbbing shoulder and jaw, raging thirst. He had the sinking feeling they wouldn't trouble him much longer anyway.

The prison photographer had chatted cheerfully as he set a big camera on its tripod in Alex's cell and took his official picture. As he left, the fellow happily promised he'd be glad to do a gallows shot as well, if Alex wanted. For posterity, don't you know.

Alex gazed numbly down at the iron manacles and chains, tried not to think of what was in store for him.

His thoughts tumbled over one another. The worst was not knowing what had happened to Jessie. No matter what outcome he imagined, his stomach churned with anguish for her.

He regretted shouting to her to find Casterson; it was foolhardy and dangerous. Had he been thinking straight and not in the throes of panic, he never would have sent her alone in pursuit.

On the other hand, finding Casterson was their only chance to put things right and return to their own time. It panicked Alex almost as much to think Jessie might *not* have gone after

Thad as to think that she had. If Jessie abandoned the search and came to the prison instead to try to help him, they would surely be lost forever.

Casterson still must have one of the devices. All he needed to do was back up a few hours and try again. He had, after all, all the time in the world.

* * * * *

Jessie caught sight of Thad Casterson as he hurried toward a waiting hansom cab at the First Street curb. Frantically, she pushed through the milling, excited crowd clustering in the street. Thrusting a coin into the hand of a driver, she breathlessly instructed him to follow Casterson's cab, but not too closely. The driver's dark, sharp eyes took in her beauty and her furious, anguished expression.

Fury of a woman scorn'd, he thought, and grinned.

Aloud, he courteously replied, "Yes'm," and helped her up into the seat. In spite of the awful news he'd just heard about some no'count bastard trying to take a shot at Mr. Roosevelt, the driver couldn't help but chuckle as he looked back at the lady. He took up the reins and gave them a quick snap. The cab moved off with a lurch, jolting rapidly over the rutted road.

Jessie was surprised to see an army camp come into view about where she thought Paul's Registry building ought to be. Ahead of her, Casterson's cab stopped and he climbed out. Jessie could see him pay the driver and give some further instructions. The man nodded, then moved the carriage to the opposite side of the street, where he reined in the horse and settled in to wait, head already nodding in a quick nap.

Casterson continued on foot down 23rd Street, turning on a side path through the many barracks-like buildings. He passed out of sight.

"Stop, please! Stop here!" Jessie called to the driver. She was out of the cab before he had a chance to climb down to assist her.

"Ya want me to wait for ya, Miss?" he asked, his voice kind, his dark eyes concerned.

"No. No, thank you." Jessie quickly handed another dime up to him, then lifted her skirts and took off at a run after Casterson. The driver shook his head and clucked to his horse.

"Never no dull moment with women, huh, Horatio?" The horse snorted and tossed his head. "Yep," the driver smiled. "That's what I think, too."

* * * * *

Alex, his eyes closed and his body slouched wearily on the filthy bunk, scarcely reacted to the sound of his cell door opening. A shaft of light poured into the dim chamber.

"Mr. Morgan?"

Listlessly, Alex opened one eye at the unexpected tone of the man's voice. It was civil, almost apologetic. All at once the man thrust a canteen at him.

"Here. You need this. Take it."

Both eyes snapped open now, and without questioning the gift, Alex lifted his manacled hands and grasped the canteen greedily. He gulped the cool water so rapidly that his throat and stomach knotted in spasms.

The officer standing before him reached out in some alarm.

"Go easy, Mr. Morgan. You'll make yourself ill."

Alex choked and lowered the canteen. Wiping his mouth roughly with his filthy sleeve, he looked up at the uniformed officer and laughed with a bitter snort.

"Since they're likely going to hang me anyway, I doubt a stomach ache is much to worry about." His eyes darkened as he handed the canteen back, and when he spoke again, his voice cracked with strain. Alex hated the pleading tone of his words, but for once he didn't care how he sounded. He had to make somebody understand.

"You got a minute, Lieutenant?" he asked raggedly. "The President is still in real danger. Nobody will listen to me."

The young officer extended a hand to Alex and hauled him, astounded, to his feet. As Alex watched incredulously, the lieutenant took a set of heavy keys from his dark blue jacket pocket. He fitted one into the lock of the wrist irons and began to free the prisoner from his chains.

"I'm Lieutenant Mike Richards, Mr. Morgan. Secret Service. Nobody's going to hang you." He paused and met Alex's eyes as he removed the heavy shackles.

"And I most certainly *will* listen."

* * * * *

Fifteen minutes later Alex sat on a comfortable wing chair in the Commandant's office. A doctor had been summoned and was busily cleaning and stitching Alex's wounded arm. The Commandant offered him a glass of whiskey and he downed it gratefully, choking slightly on the sharp bite. He ached with weariness, but out of the sweltering cell, his head began to clear.

"Mr. Morgan," Lt. Richards said solemnly, "I fear we've treated you rather badly. When President Roosevelt heard you had been detained, he dispatched me at once to extend to you his most sincere apologies and enduring gratitude."

Richards held out his hand and Alex grasped it, his expression puzzled.

"But how...?" he began.

Richards shook his head, his mouth drawn in a tight, hard line. "He was looking down the barrel of that revolver, sir. He saw you save his life. I'm ashamed to say that you did my job, Mr. Morgan, but I'm damned grateful that you did."

Relieved, Alex nodded and shook the man's hand firmly.

Richards continued, his tone deadly serious.

"Sir, you have reason to believe the President is still in danger?"

Alex nodded. "The men who orchestrated this crime are still at large, and I believe one of them, Thaddeus Casterson, has the means to make another attempt soon on Mr. Roosevelt's life. We've got to find him, and find him fast. I think he may run to ground somewhere in Camp Fry because it's ... well, because he'd be familiar with the area."

The doctor finished his less than gentle work and stepped away. Alex let out a breath of relief. He hadn't realized how tensely he'd been holding himself against the pain. The Commandant picked up a bundle of clean, folded clothing from a small table by his desk and handed it to Alex.

"My quarters are at your disposal, Mr. Morgan, if you would like to refresh yourself. I wish I could offer you other compensation."

Alex stood stiffly, flexing his cramped, protesting muscles. "Thank you, sir. There is indeed something you can do."

Twenty minutes later, when Richards' detachment of mounted Marines rode out from the prison gates, Alex rode with them.

* * * * *

Jessie followed Thad Casterson to a small, deserted, lab/storage building adjacent to the Camp Fry military hospital. As she stepped through the door, he jerked his head around in surprise, dropped the device he'd been reprogramming, and grabbed for a pistol lying on the counter in front of him.

Whirling, he leveled it at her.

"No, Thad! Don't!" she cried, holding her hands palms out in a defensive gesture.

His eyes widened incredulously. "Who are you? What do you want? How do you know who I am?"

"I'm Alex Morgan's ... wife," she said slowly, trying out the word for the first time. "We came here together to find you. Please, Thad, you have to listen. You have to stop this terrible thing."

Thad shook his head and a cunning smile spread across his face. "I have to admit I was rather astonished to see him show up like that. *Auto-Retrieve* is the most sophisticated function of *Timelapse*."

The smile faltered momentarily as Thad's eyes narrowed. "How'd he figure it out? And how did it bring two of you?"

Though she'd paled at the sight of the gun trained on her heart, Jessie's cheeks colored now.

"We're not sure how the program was activated. Tripping it was mostly an accident. And as for it transporting us both, Alex was ... he was ... holding me."

Casterson smirked, and the gun wavered slightly. His insolent gaze swept Jessie from head to toe.

"I see. Well, I don't know Morgan well, but he did strike me as a fellow of good taste."

Jessie took a tentative step forward and Thad's expression immediately hardened. He raised the gun once more.

"Stay where you are, Mrs. Morgan. I've no desire to hurt you, but I'll not be deterred by you or your husband or anyone else. In any case, there's nothing you can do. I'm simply going to go back again and get the job done right."

He reached back and picked up the device. Keeping the gun trained carefully on her, he keyed in a sequence with one thumb that Jessie couldn't follow. Tears of desperation welled in her eyes.

"Please, Thad, you've got to listen. You've already hurt me. Me, and millions of other people."

Casterson snorted. "You misunderstand, Mrs. Morgan. I've seen the future, and it's glorious. My vision will bring Utopia. And the beautiful simplicity of it is, to set the plan in motion, all I have to do..." – his eyes glinted with madness – "...is hold a man's coat."

Jessie groaned. "Oh, please, don't!"

He looked at her in annoyance. "Of course, I'll have to change the plan a bit. Get there earlier, alert the Marines. Alex will be arrested before he ever sets foot on the Capitol lawn. You, too, I'm afraid. Sadly, I fear you two are doomed to suffer an early separation."

At the callousness of his words, Jessie's fear was replaced by a furious anger.

"I come from the horrible future you created, Casterson," Jessie snapped, her voice tightening, her chin rising.

The words tumbled out in a rush. "Do you know what your damned Utopia will really be like? People live in fear and oppression, wondering each day if they'll be shot down in the street. If you're accused of a crime – and maybe your crime was that you said or read or thought something that wasn't in line with official government propaganda – then you'd betray your own mother, your own child, to save your life! Your precious Utopia is the world I grew up in, Professor, and it's a world of hypocrisy and injustice and brutality and hate!"

For a moment, she saw shock and uncertainty in his eyes. Then, coldly, he snarled, "That's nonsense."

Jessie pulled off her gloves and held her scarred, raw wrists out to him. "Chains did this, Professor Casterson. Look at the mark of chains!"

Thad blanched and his jaw clenched. Jessie saw a small muscle ticking in his cheek. He began to sweat, and not simply from the heat of the day.

"Please, Thad, please listen. I'm telling you the truth," she said, taking a step toward him.

His eyes widened, their expression at once flustered and defiant. Jessie stopped. Thad began to wave the gun erratically.

"Stay back! Don't come any closer! I ... I made precise calculations, and the computer checked and rechecked them! I eliminated even the smallest degree of error!"

"But you can't eliminate chance, Thad. You can't eliminate greed and fanaticism and lust for power. Don't you see? You can't build a noble world on a horrible murder!"

Casterson shook his head. He indicated the far corner of the room, gesturing with the gun. He backed up against the counter. A large metal storage cabinet was just to his left. Heartsick, Jessie saw the inevitable in his eyes: a steely, shrewd madness.

"Get over there, Mrs. Morgan," he ordered coldly. "If you don't do as I say, I *will* kill you. Do you understand?"

She nodded, convinced by that baleful glare.

Thad watched her out of the corner of his eye. When she moved away from him toward the corner, he laid the gun on the counter and turned his attention back to reprogramming *Timelapse*. As the room had no windows, he turned up the light from the kerosene lamp on the counter to cast enough illumination to allow him to see the key pad.

"Thad?" Jessie said softly. He ignored her. She tried again. "Thad, do you know that Alex's little boy will never be born in the world you're creating?"

Watching him closely, she imagined she saw him flinch. She pressed on, grasping at the thinnest strand of hope.

"Jack is gone because Alex doesn't exist. His father was only seventeen when he was executed by a tyrannical government. So Alex was never even born."

Casterson gritted his teeth, concentrating fiercely on the device. "Shut up," he growled.

"That university you taught at doesn't exist, either. You know what's there? The Federal Bureau of Inquisition. Alex said there were art museums and libraries in your world. Well, we've got institutions that spread propaganda and detention compounds where innocent people are tortured and executed. Where's your Utopia in that, Thad? Where's your damned Utopia?"

With an inarticulate growl, Casterson grabbed blindly for the pistol. His hand hit the side of the lamp, toppling it. Kerosene poured out onto the counter and ignited in an instant blaze of heat. The flames raced toward a stack of lab notebooks and wooden boxes of chemicals at the end of the counter.

Jessica lunged for the *Timelapse* device in Casterson's hand. He cried out and struck her to the floor, but she clutched at his leg and he stumbled, falling heavily against the storage cabinet. Behind them the room exploded.

* * * * *

Alex rode hard with Lt. Richards' detail. Ignoring the street traffic that parted and scattered before them, they galloped down the wide, muddy expanse of Pennsylvania Avenue.

All at once, with a keening blare of its horn, a rickety motorcar, festooned in bunting and packed with over-stuffed dignitaries and their wives, turned the corner onto the avenue from Nineteenth Street, leading an Independence Day parade – pulling directly into the path of the horses. Both Alex's and Richards' mounts shied.

Amid the chaos that followed, both human and equine, Alex fought for control of his horse and gradually calmed him, but the street was a mess. The squadron of mounted Marines were mired in mud and snarled in the parade.

Alex pulled his mount's reins hard to the side and guided him clear of the confusion in the street. He pressed his heels into the horse's sides and the animal responded, bolting wild-eyed down the road toward Foggy Bottom and Camp Fry in the distance.

Alex heard the explosion from half a mile away, and he saw a dark plume of smoke rise in the sky directly ahead. The horse shied again, and only the desperate grip of Alex's hands on the reins steadied it. He urged the animal on.

By the time he reined up in front of the blazing laboratory building, a pump crew had arrived and the soldiers were already working with hoses and buckets to halt the spread of the escalating fire. In a controlled frenzy, other soldiers and Medical Corps personnel were evacuating patients from the adjacent infirmary.

Alex dismounted and sprinted to the soldier nearest the blaze.

"Is anyone in there?" he shouted.

The soldier nodded, his face smeared with soot, grime and sweat.

"One man for sure," he hollered back over the roar of the fire and wind. "Fire started in the lab, but we can't get to it!"

Alex broke and ran for the building.

"Hey!" the soldier cried after him. "You can't go in there! Hey, somebody stop that man!"

* * * * *

An inferno raged in the lab. Cinders and burning pieces of roof fell through the ceiling, igniting more sections of the floor. Jessica and Thad, shielded by the metal cabinet, had fallen in the only area of the room not yet consumed by the flames. Thad lay pinned under the cabinet, the scalding metal searing his skin. He moaned in torment.

Jessie scrambled across the floor to him, shoving away smoldering rubble with her bare hands. Jacking her arms under him, she tried to pull him from the debris, but the crushing weight was too great. She heard something snap sickeningly, and Casterson screamed in agony.

Frantically, Jessie tried to lift the cabinet, but it wouldn't budge. She was forced to pull her hands back from its scorching heat.

"Give me your hand, Thad!" she cried, blinding tears streaming down her face. Desperately she tried once more to pull him free, but all at once he hauled her back toward him with surprising strength. She fell beside him on the already smoking floor.

Casterson held her wrist in a tenacious grip with one hand. With the other, he picked up the cell phone from where it had fallen beside him and pressed it into her open palm.

"What are you doing?" she sobbed.

His words came in heaving gasps, but his streaming eyes were lucid, the glint of madness gone. His gaze was rational, sorrowful, even apologetic.

"I thought ... I thought I could make a perfect world. I don't know what went wrong...." His words slurred and faded, trailing off. She shook him.

"Oh, Thad, please, don't! Let me help you get out of here!"

He shook his head weakly.

"No ... time now. Funny ... never thought I wouldn't have ... enough time." His voice sharpened and he roused himself to meet her eyes. His gaze bored into hers.

"Get out of here," Thad gasped. "Find Morgan. And don't ... don't forget to ... hold him."

The ceiling collapsed with a roar and both Jessie and Thad screamed. As the burning debris rained down on them, Jessie scrabbled backwards, clutching the cell phone, searching blindly, frantically through the black wall of smoke and cinder for any path of escape.

She couldn't breathe, couldn't see. Her lungs felt as though they had been ripped from the inside out. Gagging, coughing, she felt her knees buckle, but she held onto the device with both hands.

Strong hands caught her before she hit the floor.

Alex hauled Jessie into his arms and carried her through smoking debris to the doorway. He staggered into the narrow hallway, but flames cut them off in every direction. A roaring, ripping sound shook the entire building, and Alex looked up in horror toward its source. His gut twisted in terror as the entire roof buckled and caved in. Just before he threw himself down protectively, hopelessly, over Jessie's body, Alex saw gaping daylight above, through the billowing smoke and flames.

CHAPTER 34

With a roar to rend the universe, the fabric of time warped and fractured, catapulting Alex once more through the end of the world. This time, for the first time, he actually saw the entire event, although his senses were overwhelmed by the shattering concussion and brilliant light. He was almost unable to comprehend what was happening.

He knew enough, though, to clutch Jessie tightly against him and wrap his arms and legs securely around her body. Letting her go would be a tragedy he would never survive, physically or emotionally.

When the storm around them abruptly ceased, Alex had no idea how much time had passed. He gasped for air like a drowning man; his stomach knotted and heaved. He struggled to release Jessie's limp body so she might breathe more easily with his weight off her.

Tears spilled down Alex's cheeks as he held Jessie in his lap and rocked her, murmuring her name. He had no idea where they were, other than in a windowless, empty room, weakly lit by a single, dim overhead light, furnished only with a large conference table and a few chairs. Miraculously, there was no sign of the fire.

But Jessie wasn't breathing.

With a cry, Alex shook her unresponsive body. Desperately he laid her on the floor and covered her mouth with his, blowing air into her choked lungs.

"C'mon, Jessie, please!" he gasped between frantic breaths. "Breathe, baby, breathe!"

He placed trembling fingers on her throat, under the point of her jaw, feeling for a pulse. Relief flooded him as he felt the faint but steady throb. Still, her lips were blue and he could see she wasn't breathing on her own. Unaware he was sobbing, Alex leaned over her again and blew repeatedly into her mouth. He was talking to God like crazy now, begging, pleading, bargaining.

Please oh please oh please God!

With a sudden, convulsive gasp, Jessie arched up and drew in a huge gulp of air. When she wheezed and began to choke, Alex turned her quickly to her side. Her body was racked with coughing.

It was the most beautiful sound he'd ever heard.

* * * * *

When Jessie's distress finally eased, they sat huddled together for a long time. Neither could muster the courage to let go of the other or to walk out the door and see what awaited them. For a long time, it was enough that they were alive and that they held each other.

Casterson's device lay on the floor. They regarded it warily. Jessie heaved a ragged sigh, whispered hoarsely, "I guess we should look."

"Yeah," Alex agreed, but it was some time before he could make himself pick it up.

He turned it so Jessie could see the screen. Nothing unusual was displayed, simply the proper, 21st century date and *3:46 P.*

"Well," he remarked dryly, "it's been a long day."

Jessie laughed and instantly began to cough again.

"Easy, baby," Alex murmured. "Easy, it's all right."

He patted her back gently until her breathing eased. She shuddered against him, burying her face in his shirt. He laid his cheek against her hair, which, like their clothing, was singed and reeked of smoke. Alex closed his eyes and thanked God again.

They were content to sit, but when the device's time-of-day readout blinked to *4:05 P,* Jessie asked shakily, her voice cracking, "What's outside that door, Alex? Your world or mine? Or something else altogether? Something ... *terrible?*"

He shook his head. "I don't know, sweetheart. You want to find out?"

She shivered, and he wrapped his arms tighter around her, sheltering her. "I'm afraid," she whispered.

"I know," he said. "I am, too. But no matter what is or isn't out there, Jessie, we're alive, and we're together." He tipped her head up and gazed into her eyes. "I will never leave you, honey. And I will love you as long as I live." He bent his head and kissed her tenderly, protectively, possessively.

A wild burst of heat and exhilaration flooded Jessie's body, a sudden desperate need to feel truly *alive*. She could hardly believe the whispered words that came to her lips.

"Love me, Alex," she pleaded. "Just once more, now, before we have to face whatever's out there."

He couldn't have said where the strength came from, but all at once it was there. Alex leaned down and kissed her like a starving man, embracing her as though he would never let her go.

After a long moment, breathing hard, he asked unsteadily, "Are you sure? Are you all right?"

When she nodded and touched his cheek, Alex kissed her again with infinite gentleness. When they parted, he stood, walked a little shakily to the door, and bolted it. When he returned, Jessie reached for him, and he gathered her into his arms.

She arched against him. Their kisses began as comfort, but soon heated into something much more urgent. All at once they were pulling frantically at each other's clothing. Alex lifted

Jessie to straddle his lap, and as they all but devoured each other, he sank into her.

There was no doubt they were alive.

The device blinked *4:26 P.*

* * * * *

When they cautiously emerged from the conference room, hand clutched in hand, Jessie hung back, unable to shake her nervousness. The unmistakable sounds of voices and bustling activity reached them from the far end of the corridor.

Alex shared her apprehension as he scouted the corridor. He noticed some restrooms and pointed her to them.

"Go in and wash up, honey," he said gently. "I'll do the same. There's not much we can do about the clothes, but the water'll make us feel and look better."

"How are we ever going to explain the clothes?" Jessie asked anxiously. "It's bad enough they're a hundred years old. People might notice that they're also still smoldering."

"That's okay," Alex said dryly. "So am I." He drew her to him and kissed her tenderly.

"Alex, be serious," she scolded, but she cracked a small smile.

His brow furrowed. "Well, I guess we could tell people we're in the cast of *Les Misérables*," he suggested dryly. "And we've just manned the barricades. You'd make a very fetching Eponine, by the way."

At her bewildered look he shook his head. "Sorry, sweetheart. I suppose Victor Hugo was banned, huh?"

"Hmmm." Jessie frowned, disengaging herself from Alex's embrace. He watched her carefully.

She walked to the restroom door, pulled it open and peeked cautiously inside. A moment later she exclaimed, "Oh, it's so nice!"

She looked back over her shoulder at her husband. And smiled.

"Paul had a way of ... finding ... banned books," she said. "I remember Cosette: *Her soul had been cold. Now it was warm.* Now I understand."

* * * * *

As he walked with Jessie into the familiar main lobby of the University Administration Building, Alex's heart hammered in his chest. He was almost afraid to believe what he was seeing.

Please, he pleaded silently, tears welling in his eyes. *Let everything be right again. Please let all this be real!*

Soap and water had actually worked wonders, and no one seemed to take much notice of their eccentric clothing or worse-for-wear appearance. *Thank God for unflappable students*, Alex thought.

He took Jessie's arm and tried to hustle her to the building's front exit, but she hung back, giddy with wonder at the sights that surrounded her: the cheerful, bustling people, the rainbow of colorful clothing, the pervasive sense of purpose and activity that had no undercurrent of fear or desperation.

Most people were holding, tapping on, listening to, or talking into little devices like Casterson's. Jessie was worried at first and nervously asked Alex about it. He reassured her that the little cell phones and palm-sized computers she was seeing were *nothing* like Casterson's. She breathed a great sigh of relief.

And then there were the *books*.

People carried them openly. Jessie saw stuffed backpacks and bags. She had just turned to ask Alex about this when she suddenly stopped, frozen in her tracks.

Her attention was riveted by a young man who stood behind the long Information counter in the center of the lobby. He was turned away from her, talking animatedly with a smiling older woman.

Alex followed the line of her gaze, and she heard his quick, startled intake of breath. Jessie stepped away from him, and he let her go.

She moved in amazement toward the young man, oblivious now to everything else around her. The woman behind the counter caught sight of Jessie first, her surprised expression getting the man's attention. When she told him to look behind him, he turned around.

"Paul!" Jessie cried, tears springing to her eyes. "Oh, Paul!"

She broke into a run, dodging around the end of the counter to launch herself into the startled man's arms. As she flung her arms around his neck, he laughed in astonishment and took a staggering step backward to keep his balance. After his initial shock, he cheerfully and gamely hugged her back.

"Well, hi there," he grinned, at a loss for what more to say. Over the top of Jessie's head he caught his co-worker's eye. She rolled her eyes and shrugged.

Paul inclined his head and spoke softly into Jessie's ear. "Um, do I know you?" he asked, his dark eyes puzzled, but bright with amusement.

Stunned, Jessie gasped and released him at once. Her hands slid down his chest and she could feel the solid muscles beneath his shirt. This man was whole. Unscarred.

Not Paul. Jessie made an inarticulate sound of embarrassment and disappointment. Her cheeks flamed.

Mortified, she stepped away from the man, cleared her throat, and found her voice.

"I'm so sorry!" she stammered. "I-I thought ... I was sure ... you look so much like someone I-I know."

"Hmmm. Lucky guy," the man smiled.

Despite her humiliation Jessie couldn't take her eyes off him. She tried not to stare, but his resemblance to Paul was absolutely amazing. She began to babble helplessly.

"It's just ... it's so uncanny ... honestly, you look just like...." Her voice trailed off.

"Like who?"

She shrugged sheepishly, stammering a little. "My ... my cousin, Paul Rudin."

The dark-eyed man grinned and shook his head. "Sorry. Close, but no cigar." He offered her his hand.

"I'm Paul O'Neil."

* * * * *

Paul politely refrained from asking about the strange, soiled clothes Jessie and Alex wore, or about the definite scent of smoke that wafted from them.

However, Alex apparently felt the need to explain – something about a colleague he owed a favor to in the Theatre Department who needed extra zombies for the debut production of his post-nihilist performance piece. It didn't surprise Paul. Just that morning, a couple of BFA acting students had shown up to meet with their faculty advisors costumed as bullfrogs. Happened all the time.

Despite the bizarre circumstances, Paul liked Jessie right away. He felt an inexplicable connection, a rightness and familiarity between them. He'd figure out later how to explain it all to Lani when he got home.

He also liked Jessie's husband, and he was surprised to discover that the Alex Morgan standing in front of him looking like overdone toast was actually Professor J. A. Morgan of the History Department. Lani was gonna love that bit of gossip.

"What do you do here, Paul?" Jessie asked. She was fascinated by the row of small, stand-alone screens along the counter that showed amazing graphics and films, as though there were tiny movie projectors inside them. And she was almost as intrigued by the stacks of colorful catalogs and brochures.

Paul patiently explained about registration, student aid and counseling, campus activities. Her eyes had grown so wide that he was puzzled. After all, how awesome could a registration packet be?

"Can anybody take classes? Could I?" she asked him. Whoa, was she actually holding her breath, waiting for him to answer?

Paul nodded, relieved when she exhaled.

"Well, spring semester's almost over. You can apply for the fall, though. If you're admitted, you can take any undergrad courses you want."

"Are there any history classes?" She was all but dancing with excitement.

"Well, sure." He picked up a new catalog for the coming fall semester and flipped it open, found the History Department's schedule of classes.

"Here," he said, running his finger down a page of courses in American History. "There're all kinds of classes, depends what you're interested in, how many units you want. This fall they're offering *America to 1850*, *The Progressive Era*, *Emergence of a Modern Nation* – that'll be your seminar, won't it, Dr. Morgan? – *A Social History of Immigration*, and *Women in Politics*."

He stopped as Jessie gaped at him, then he smiled. "Interested in any of that?"

"Yes," she said. "I'll take all of them."

Paul's eyebrows arched. "All of them?"

Jessie nodded. "To start with, anyway."

Paul shrugged, handed her the catalog, grinned. "There you go. Have fun."

Alex cleared his throat, gently took her arm. It was time to go.

"Thanks for your help, Paul," he said. "We'll come back tomorrow, after Jessie's seen her ... uh ... her advisor."

"Great. Well, I'll be here, you need more help," Paul smiled. On a sudden impulse, he blurted out, "Or just if you want to, you know, get together, talk, get some coffee, whatever. You guys want to come over sometime, my wife Lani makes a killer margarita."

Alex's eyes met Jessie's, saw her heart was as full as his.

He swallowed the lump in his throat, offered his hand to Paul. "We'd like that. It was good to meet you, Paul. Really good," he said, hoarse with emotion.

Paul took Alex's hand, surprised and a little confused at the inexplicable surge of affection he felt for the young professor.

Jessie leaned up and kissed his cheek lightly. "'Bye, Paul," she said softly, her eyes glowing. "Tell Lani I miss ... I-I mean, I can't wait to meet her. See you tomorrow."

As she and Alex turned away, Paul was seized by the powerful and completely baffling conviction that he had been waiting all his life for Jessie to come home.

* * * * *

As they stepped out into the late afternoon sunlight – at this time of year it wouldn't be twilight for at least another hour – Alex turned and looked back at the entrance to the

291

administration building. He tugged gently on Jessie's arm, stopping her.

"Look," he said quietly, not trusting his shaky voice to say more.

Over the entrance to the brownstone building with its ornate, arched windows was carved the legend *CASTERSON HALL*. A tarnished brass plaque was set into the portico. Alex and Jessie peered at the engraved inscription:

Thaddeus I. Casterson Hall. Founded 1924 in loving memory of Dr. T. I. Casterson, who died on this site 4 July 1902, by his beloved wife Agnes Sedley Casterson. Where Time and Eternity meet, there is our Journey's End.

Tears scalded Jessie's eyes. She could almost feel the desperate grip of Thad's fingers on her wrist as he pressed the *Timelapse* device into her hand, saving her life and Alex's when he could have saved his own. She reached blindly for her husband's hand and laced her fingers tightly with his.

"He could have saved himself, Alex," she whispered hoarsely. "He could have lived and let us die."

"I know, sweetheart," he answered gently. "I know."

* * * * *

"Daddy!"

The eager, excited young voice behind him froze Alex where he stood. He shook his head blindly and his eyes welled with tears. He clenched Jessie's hand so hard that his knuckles turned white and he felt the small bones of her hands compress. Instantly he lightened his grip, but he couldn't bear to look in the direction of the voice.

"Daddy!" the voice called again, laughing.

The child was closer now, his running footsteps thumping lightly on the concrete walkway. Jessie stole a quick look past Alex's shoulder. Then, nodding gently, she took his arm and turned him around.

Jack Morgan ran up the wide steps of the building and leapt into Alex's arms as his father dropped to one knee to embrace him.

Alex choked, sobbed, hugged the little boy to him as though his life depended on it. He buried his face in the child's sweet smelling, tousled hair. Jessie felt her own hot tears spill as Alex held his son close, his shoulders shaking.

Then, as though he couldn't bear another moment without seeing his child's face, Alex stood Jack up in front of him and smoothed back the little boy's ruffled hair.

"Hey, Buddy," he rasped, his voice thick with emotion.

The boy look puzzled and touched his father's cheek. He ran curious, exploring fingers across Alex's face.

"Grandma said we could come meet you at work. Hey, Daddy, you got a funny haircut. And you hurt your face. Is that why you're crying? Want a kiss to make it better?"

"Yeah." Alex's voice cracked and gave out. He gave Jack a crooked smile as tears streamed down his face.

Jack stood on tiptoe and kissed his father's cheek. He said, "There you go, Daddy. All better. You can stop crying now. If you want, when we get home, you can play with my Lego train."

Alex laughed and stood up, sweeping the boy up in his arms again, hugging him fiercely.

"Thank you, Jack. I would love to play with your Lego train. Buddy, I missed you so much and I'm so glad to see you!"

"Me, too," Jack said, snuggling in against the hollow of Alex's neck. From his vantage point on his father's shoulder, Jack stared straight at Jessie. She was wearing dirty, dress-up clothes, just like his dad was, but she was smiling at him in a kind of hopeful way, and she looked very friendly. She was pretty and she looked nice.

She seemed to be waiting for something. Maybe she wanted to play trains, too.

"Hi," Jack offered, opening and closing his fingers in a small wave.

"Hi yourself," Jessie smiled. Her lower lip quivered a little as she moved forward and took his small hand in hers.

Alex turned to her, but Jack continued to hold her hand.

"Jack," Alex said gently to his son. "This is Jessie. She's coming home with us, to love us and to be my wife and your new mom."

Jack looked at his father and Jessie in utter astonishment, eyes wide as saucers. "Really?" he asked. "How come I never seen her before?"

Alex grinned and kissed the child's cheek. "It's a long story, Buddy. I'll tell it to you later. But yes, she really is."

Curious, Jack reached out with his other hand to touch Jessie's face.

"Does Grandma know?"

His father shook his head. "No, not yet."

Jack's eyes lit up with excitement.

"Can I tell her? Can I?"

Alex looked to Jessie.

"Yes, sweetie," she answered. "It would make me very proud if you did."

Jack squirmed in his father's arms.

"Put me down, Daddy. Grandma's coming. She'll be here in a minute!" He turned to Jessie and explained earnestly, "She has to walk a lot slower than me." Jessie nodded solemnly as he repeated, "C'mon Daddy, let go! I gotta go tell her!"

He squirmed again and Alex reluctantly released him. Jack sprinted back down the path. Through the trees Alex could just make out his mother's approaching figure.

Frannie opened her arms to allow Jack to hurtle into them, then looked up and raised a hand to wave to her son. The hand faltered in mid-air as she froze, staring. Even at that distance, Alex and Jessie could see the stunned expression on her face as Jack jabbered excitedly to her.

Jessie moved to stand close beside Alex.

"You've thought of a way to explain all this to your mother, right?" There was humor in her voice, but also a good measure of anxiety. "How since you left for work this morning, you not only cut off your hair and changed into antique clothing − fried antique clothing, at that − but you also got beat up and shot, foiled an assassination attempt, led a jailbreak, walked through fire and, incidentally, acquired a wife?"

"Well, I'm working on it," Alex grinned. He was ridiculously happy, even though his astonished mother was bearing down on them at a determined pace, Jack skipping at her side.

He said, "You know what they say, Jessie. Actions speak louder than words."

With his heart so full of emotion that he thought it might explode in his chest, he turned and swept Jessie into his arms. He pulled her close and kissed her with all the passion and joy that surged in him.

Then he kissed her again, spinning her around dizzily, until she threw back her head and laughed, gasping for air.

But all at once, she froze. She'd forgotten they were right out in the open, in full view of everyone passing by.

"Alex!" she hissed, pushing against him. "Are you crazy? Put me down!"

He laughed and twirled her around again.

"Not a chance, Mrs. Morgan. This," he grinned, "is an absolutely whole-hearted, one hundred percent public display of affection!"

She looked at him in astonishment, then her stunned expression unfolded into a beam of pure joy. As he kissed her again, it would have been hard to say which one of them was the most enthusiastic.

CHAPTER 35

Despite the evidence of her own eyes, and despite the strange, intricate little cell phone thing Alex showed her before smashing it to pieces, Frannie doubted she would ever really believe the story.

Throughout that first evening she sat numbly, listening to Alex and Jessie, unable to stop staring. She took in every detail but could make no sense of the whole. She thought more than once that evening that either she or her son – or quite possibly both of them – had gone stark raving mad.

In spite of her confusion she could see that the pretty, gray-eyed young woman Alex kept so close to his side was pale with exhaustion, and when Frannie suggested they call it a night and talk again in the morning, Jessie was visibly relieved.

Halfway up the staircase she paused and faltered, unable to climb another step. Alex, mounting the stairs just behind his wife, caught her as she swayed. He lifted her into his arms as though she were no more than a child, and murmuring fond, tender endearments, carried her to his bed.

She was asleep before he'd even unwound her arms from around his neck.

Gently Alex undressed Jessie and covered her with the sheet, but even that small exertion left him lightheaded, sore, aching with fatigue. As he straightened up, stretched stiffly, and started toward the bathroom, his gaze fell on the opposite wall of the bedroom.

The room doubled as his study, and the entire wall was covered with floor-to-ceiling, overflowing bookshelves. A sudden bizarre notion occurred to him, and smiling wryly at absurdity of what he was about to do, Alex walked to the bookcase and began to search.

* * * * *

"Mom?" Alex said, making Frannie jump.

He'd come up behind her as she'd stood at the kitchen sink washing the last few dishes. She was tired, but she couldn't sleep, and she'd hoped a few tedious chores might calm her ragged nerves and churning thoughts.

She turned, her hand flying to her throat. She almost hadn't recognized the bruised, shorn, resolute man standing there as her shaggy-haired, bookish son. Then she sighed heavily.

"My goodness, Alex, you scared me! I didn't hear you come in."

"Sorry," he apologized. "But I thought you should see this."

Frannie realized then that he was holding out a large book to her. She took it in some bewilderment and read the title: *The Progressive Era 1900-1910: Glorious Years of Confidence.* It was a lavishly illustrated, coffee-table book, and she remembered buying it for Alex a Christmas or two ago.

She opened it to the page he had marked.

There were two grainy, vintage photographs on the page, both of men who appeared to be hardened criminals. They wore filthy, bloodstained clothing and were shackled in heavy iron chains. The photographs had obviously been taken in their prison cells.

The caption under the left-hand picture identified the tangle-haired, wild-eyed subject as Amos Ketchin, age 37. The text explained briefly that he had attempted to assassinate Theodore Roosevelt in the name of some lunatic cause and had been hanged in the fall of 1902. Neither the man's name nor the incident meant anything to Frannie.

Her gaze drifted to the second photograph.

In that moment, she finally *believed.*

Manacled, disheveled, battered and bloody, her son stared defiantly back at her from the page.

Frannie opened her mouth to speak, but then had no idea what she'd intended to say. Tears welled in her eyes and her hands shook uncontrollably. She held the book away from her body as though it might cast an evil spell on them all. Alex took it from her trembling hands.

Frannie found her voice. "Read it to me," she whispered.

"Sit down, Mom," he said steadily, taking her arm and guiding her to the kitchen table. "Sit down here."

She sat, and Alex began to read, his voice strong and deep in the quiet room.

MYSTERY MAN: Ketchin's violent attempt on the President's life was thwarted by James A. Morgan (above), who in the confusion was also briefly imprisoned by authorities who mistook him for a second assassin. Though a hero, he remains a man shrouded in mystery. No records of his life or photographs other than this one are known to exist. Although his body was never found, Morgan is said to have perished in a fire at Camp Fry Depot, today the site of Capitol University. Historians agree that James A. Morgan was undoubtedly a Secret Service agent operating under an assumed name, thus explaining the mystery of the man who never was.

It was a long time then before either of them spoke. Frannie's fingers repeatedly traced Alex's image in the book. Her son reached out and gently laid his hand over hers. Tears spilled down his mother's cheeks.

"It's true, isn't it," she said. "Everything you told me is true."

"Yes, Mom. Everything."

She looked up at him, and he was not surprised to see anger and confusion and resentment come into her eyes.

"Then why did you destroy the device, Alex?" Frannie cried, painfully clutching his hand. "You could've done such good! You could've saved Lincoln, or Kennedy, or King! You could've made sure those horrible terrorists got arrested before they ever got on those September 11th planes!"

She paused, breathing hard, and in her distress aimed directly for his heart. "You could've waited a few seconds longer at that stoplight so the truck wouldn't have hit you! And we could've gotten earlier treatment for your father, before ... before he...."

"Don't, Mom. C'mon, please, don't do this."

He stopped her, holding both her hands together as though in prayer and pressing them against his chest. "Don't you think I thought of all that? Over and over?"

It was an enormous understatement. In truth, the temptation to keep the *Timelapse* device to use again had been overpoweringly irresistible. He'd almost lacked the courage to destroy it; it had been a very near thing.

Frannie shook her head miserably. "You could have done so many things! So much good!"

Alex had no regrets to match his mother's. Once he'd made the decision to destroy the device, he'd known instinctively that it was right. An enormous weight had lifted from his shoulders.

He reached out and tipped his mother's chin up so that she met his eyes.

"Don't you understand, Mom? Nothing's ever that simple. After all, Thad Casterson thought he was doing good, too."

EPILOGUE

From the outset of her union with Alex, one thing troubled Jessie deeply. She confessed to him her regret that their marriage had been without benefit of clergy, and although Alex knew he would never take more sacred vows than those he had spoken to her in the basement of a dry goods store in 1902, he was only too happy to honor her wishes.

So on a beautiful June morning there was an intimate, heartfelt exchange of vows in West Potomac Park. Under blooming cherry trees, in a ceremony presided over by the university chaplain under the benevolent gaze of Lincoln and Jefferson in all their sculpted splendor, James Alexander Morgan and Jessica Jordana O'Neil again pledged their hearts, souls, and lives to one another for all time.

* * * * *

Even without the aid of *Timelapse*, four years passed in the blink of an eye. Jessie had indeed taken the history courses that so intrigued her, and a good deal more besides.

Alex urged her to apply to law school, and although she laughed and demurred, protesting that Jack, preschooler Lexie, and baby Jimmy needed a mother, not an attorney, he could see the flash of eager interest in her eyes.

Eventually, humoring her husband, but not really expecting anything to come of it, she sent in the forms.

At the end of one particularly uproarious evening, Alex groaned happily and pulled Jessie to him in their bed in the dark, and finally, blessedly quiet, bedroom. All three children were miraculously asleep at the same time, in their own beds and cribs. No one needed water, a new diaper, or one more story.

"How long do you think we've got?" Alex grinned. He could feel Jessie smile against his chest as he caressed her arm.

His fingers passed lightly over the small scar above the inside of her elbow, where the Sterinol implant had been removed in a storefront clinic where the on-call doctor had been too rushed and overworked to ask many questions.

Jessie snuggled against Alex, warm as a cat in the sun, listening to his heartbeat under her ear.

"Mmmm ... lots of time," she murmured. "Two or three seconds at least. And if Frannie holds down the fort, maybe...." – she dropped her voice to an inviting purr – "...five whole minutes." Then, after a small pause, she asked with sudden seriousness, "Will you do something for me, Alex?"

With a low growl, he pulled her up to lie atop him. He raised his head and kissed her. Against her mouth he murmured huskily, "I'd do anything for you, sweetheart."

She smiled and pulled back slightly, looking down through her dark lashes into the deep blue of his eyes. The delicious pressure of her breasts against his chest was rapidly making him crazy.

"Like what?" she teased, challenging him.

"What would you like?"

Jessie feigned petulant indecision. "Well," she said finally, "none of that old boring stuff, like you taking a bullet or walking through flames for me."

Alex shook his head in solemn agreement. "Been there. Done that."

"I know. I was thinking more along the line of babysitting."

He laughed and looked perplexed. "Honey, I'm always glad to watch the kids, you know that."

"Yes, I do, but it's just that I'm going to be asking you and Mom to do a lot more for a while." She paused, grinned, "I got accepted to Georgetown Law."

Alex whooped and sat bolt upright, flipping Jessie over in his arms. She laughed and wrapped her arms around his neck. He tucked her beneath him and moved his long body over hers, gazing deeply into her eyes. He couldn't stop smiling.

"Seems to me," he said, growly with emotion, looking down at her, "this is how we began. Who'd have ever thought that scruffy kid...."

"I wasn't scruffy," she protested, her mouth curving with pleasure.

"...would turn out to be Madame Counselor-at-Law."

Jessie plunged her fingers into his tousled, sun-bleached hair and pulled him to her. Against his mouth she whispered, "I like *Madame Chief Justice* better."

And that – Alex figured, losing himself delightedly in her – would just be a matter of time.

TIMELAPSE

Selected Orange Rose Finalist

Terms of Surrender

LORRIE FARRELLY

Captain Michael Cantrell has lost his home and everyone he loved. On the frontier, he finds himself in the middle of Annie Devlin's war. Standing with the stubborn young rancher will test the limits of his courage – and his passion.

AVAILABLE NOW AS PAPERBACK OR EBOOK!

The Much-Anticipated Sequel to
TERMS OF SURRENDER

Terms of
Engagement

LORRIE FARRELLY

When Tess Rutledge is at her most
desperate – hunted, on the run, and close
to death – only Dr. Robert Devlin's skill
and compassion can save her.
They have a chance for a future together.
If they survive.

AVAILABLE NOW AS PAPERBACK OR EBOOK!

Dangerous

LORRIE FARRELLY

**Burned-out, ex-LA cop Cam Starrett
is sick of urban trauma and warfare.
He longs to escape to a peaceful place
where life is calm and serene.**

Be careful what you wish for!

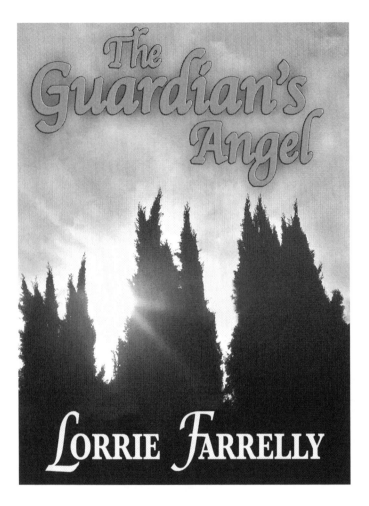

The Guardian's Angel

Lorrie Farrelly

Elizabeth Driscoll is running for her life, inextricably bound to a compelling man and a troubled young child who, only hours before, were strangers to her. Now the danger is not just to her safety, but also to her heart.

AVAILABLE NOW AS PAPERBACK OR EBOOK!

ABOUT THE AUTHOR

A Navy brat and graduate of the University of California, Santa Cruz, **LORRIE FARRELLY** *is proud to be a Fightin' Banana Slug (well, okay, they're really lovers, not fighters). Following graduate school at Northwestern University, she began a career in education that included teaching art to 4th graders, drama to 8th graders, and finally, math to high school students (if anybody loses asymptotes, she can probably find 'em...).*

She's a three-time winner on "Jeopardy!" (despite forgetting the chemical symbol for sulfuric acid ... oh, wait – she never knew that in the first place), has shepherded wide-eyed foreign exchange students along Hollywood Blvd. ("As many stars and lunatics as there are in the Heavens"), and happily curried and shoveled as a ranch hand at Disneyland's Circle D Ranch. And always, she writes.

Lorrie has won a Presidential Commendation for Excellence in Teaching Mathematics. She's been a Renaissance nominee for Teacher of the Year and a finalist for the Orange Rose Award in romantic fiction. She's never won the lottery, except where her family is concerned. For her, they're the ultimate prize.

25249577R00180

Made in the USA
Charleston, SC
19 December 2013